"Stanley West, an extraordinary novelist and storyteller who writes with searing beauty and truth, has written a lyrical and moving novel . . . a story that pierces to the core of life . . . compelling reading for people of all times and places . . ."
—*Richard Wheeler, Golden Spur Award author of some thirty novels*

"West has again captured an often untold yet important part of the human story . . . encouraging for all who may feel it's too late to make a change . . ."
—*Brad Walton, The Brad Walton Show, WCCO Radio*

"It's about people who are trapped . . . about heroism and losing something you cannot get back."
—*Don Boxmeyer,* Saint Paul Pioneer Press

Acclaim for Stanley Gordon West's
Finding Laura Buggs

"A story that reaffirms the miracle and wonder of life, and ultimately its preciousness . . . a terrific, uplifting read, written with great insight and compassion."
—*Harvey Mackay,* New York Times *best-selling author of* How To Swim With the Sharks

"Powerful storytelling . . . with a twist that Edgar Allan Poe would have enjoyed . . . one of those rare, haunting scenes that will stick in my mind for years. Stanley West is becoming one of my favorite writers . . . a man who looks back on his years in St. Paul with a lifetime of experience. I recommend him to everybody."
— *Steve Thayer, author of* Weatherman *and* Silent Snow

Acclaim for Stanley G. West's
Amos: To Ride a Dead Horse

"West's first novel is powerful and moving . . . a celebration of the human spirit . . . a heart-stopper, a strong, unblinking deeply human tale."
—*Publishers Weekly*

"West has penned an unusual, well-written novel . . . The book features some marvelous descriptive passages that will be remembered long after the last page has been turned. The skillful plotting and the warm human relationships make it exciting, first-rate reading."
—*Judy Schuster,* Minneapolis Star Tribune

"This is a remarkable story . . . West show himself to be a sea-soned storyteller, offering the reader a variety of emotions . . ."
—*Clark Morphew,* St. Paul Dispatch

"I have just finished *Amos*—an extraordinary book. I read it straight through—literally unable to put it down . . . it is a cel-ebration of the capacity of the human spirit for compassion and sacrifice and courage . . ."
—*Millicent Fenwick*

Acclaim for Stanley G. West's
Blind Your Ponies

"Stanley West writes novels that transform the world. In this tender story of love and courage and grit, he gives each read-er a vision and a dream. This is the best reading you will find."
—*Richard Wheeler, award wining author of* The Fields of Eden

"Stanley Gordon West, one of my favorite authors, has done it again. *Blind Your Ponies* is the kind of novel that takes years to write . . . but well worth the wait. A wonderfully haunting book . . . where every character has a ghost, and every ghost has a great story to tell."
—*Steve Thayer, author of The* Weatherman *and* Silent Snow

Wood Lake, Wisconsin

GROWING AN INCH

Stanley West was born in Saint Paul, and grew up during the Great Depression and the World War II years, attending the city's public schools and getting around riding the streetcars. He graduated from Central High School in 1950. He attended Macalester College and the University of Minnesota, earning a degree in history and geology in 1955. He moved from the Midwest to Montana in 1964 where he raised a large family and he has lived there ever since. His novel *Amos* was produced as a CBS Movie of the Week starring Kirk Douglas, Elizabeth Montgomery and Dorothy McGuire and was nominated for four Emmys.

Also By Stanley G. West

Amos: To Ride a Dead Horse

Until They Bring the Streetcars Back

Finding Laura Buggs

Blind Your Ponies

Sweet Shattered Dreams

GROWING
AN INCH

Stanley Gordon West

LEXINGTON-MARSHALL PUBLISHING
SHAKOPEE, MINNESOTA

Published in the United States by Lexington-Marshall Publishing
15085 Halsey Avenue, Carver, Minnesota 55315

The cover photo used with permission from BP America Inc.

Library of Congress Catalog Card Number: 2003092072

ISBN 0-9656247-1-4
ISBN 978-0-9656247-1-8

Book design by Richard Krogstad
Book production by Peregrine Graphics Services
Printed in the United States by McNaughton & Gunn, Inc.

Reprint: October 2019

With love for
Andrew and Stephen
and Susan

and for Patches

The Best Years of Our Lives

—written by Robert E. Sherwood

GROWING AN INCH

Chapter 1

I'm hiding in the old furnace. I'd been careless, walking out to the alley with the garbage. I'd started believing the killer wouldn't risk coming back. Low overcast clouds made it dark, but, luckily, I caught a glimpse. Something blurred in his hand. A gun? With only a second to spare, I darted through the back door and down the basement steps. He followed seconds behind me. I crawled headfirst into the old furnace, pulled my legs through, and slowly closed the oval door. Inside, pitch black. I huddle, afraid to move, afraid I'll bump something that will give me away.

I hear him on the stairs. He must have been desperate to come into the house like that, or he'd been watching and knew I was the only one home. He has come to kill me, the only one who can put him in the electric chair. I hear him ransacking the basement, things hitting the floor, glass breaking, furniture being dragged, uncovering every nook and corner that could hide me. It sounds like a tornado touched down in our basement.

Darn, I should've gone through the kitchen and out the front door. There's only one way in or out of the basement. The stairs. The basement windows are too small to crawl through even if I got the chance. I pray Irene doesn't come home, or Clark and Dad. The legbreaker would kill them. No witnesses this time. I have the crazy impulse to crawl out and run for the stairs, get it over with before any of them come home. Save their lives if not my own. I wonder what it feels like to be shot, to die. I hate that cold, hard face, that evil man. I want to kill him for what he's done. But he has me, there's nothing I can do.

Then I realize I can't hear him. The basement is deathly quiet. He hasn't climbed the stairs, I'd recognize their wooden creak. He is very close, sniffing like a rabid dog. I can't tell

1

if I'm hearing my breathing or his. My pounding heart echoes against the cast-iron sides of the furnace until I'm sure he can hear me. I try not to move a finger, an eyelash. Does he know I'm in here? I expect him to try the furnace door any second.

In the breathless darkness, I try to remember how in the heck I'd gotten into this awful mess.

The trouble began the day my mother died.

My name is Donny Cunningham and I was fourteen the day she died. I stood four foot eleven and weighed one hundred and thirteen pounds. When I was seventeen and a senior at Saint Paul Central High School, I stood four foot eleven and weighed one hundred and thirteen pounds. No one seemed to know why I quit growing. My dad didn't know why. My doctor didn't know why. My teachers didn't know. Our priest didn't know.

But I know.

Right off the bat I want to tell you I'm not stupid or in sight-saving class or anything like that. Shoot, I'm as smart as the next guy and half the time smarter. But sometimes things go bad even for smart people and your life swerves onto paths you never dreamed in your worst nightmare. It can happen in a blink, before you can catch your breath. Your whole life has changed from what it was and it can never go back.

We all lie. Sometimes we lie to save our own skins, sometimes to save someone else's skin. Sometimes we lie to cover what's bad or wrong, and sometimes we lie to do good, like telling someone who's ugly that they look nice or telling the Gestapo you don't have any Jews hiding in your attic when you do. I had to lie to save my family.

My mother always called me Donald. She was the only one. Everyone else called me Donny. I guess "Donald" died with my mother. She said one day I'd be a writer but not until I was a lot older, that I hadn't experienced enough of life when

I was so young. I was so small kids would always pat me on the top of my head like they would a puppy. It was bad enough when boys did it, but I really hated it when girls did.

I've had girlfriends, in grade school and high school. I like having a girlfriend, but they all outgrow me. I learned plenty fast that girls don't like a boyfriend who's shorter than they are. It got a lot worse the last two years when all the girls at Central seem to be growing like weeds and I'm stuck. I figured a guy is better off never falling in love 'cause they'd just break his heart when they find someone taller. Then he'll feel lousy about himself.

My dad had loved my mother awfully hard. He couldn't get along very well without her. That left me, the oldest of the kids, to help look after my sister Irene and my two brothers, Clark and Stewy. Stewy, the youngest, didn't seem to remember our mother much, and he didn't understand why my dad was so sad sometimes.

Far as I know, my dad never took a drink before my mother died. He'd never been drunk. He started drinking about a year after she died, just a little at first. It seemed to help him get along. We owned a Standard filling station over on Marshall and Wilder and he and Mom were real proud of it.

Mom would organize "Sparkle" parties and we'd all have something to do. Gosh, it was hard work, but she made us feel real important with the task she'd give us. We scrubbed together to make our Standard station sparkle. It was our family calling to be the brightest and cleanest gas station in the Twin Cities, with the best service, bar none.

Being the oldest, I'd graduated to using the ladder and scrubbing the red tile along the roof and polishing the shiny blue service shield above the doors. We scrubbed the white brick and polished the globes on the pumps and we'd hose and scrub down the driveway. Irene would do the windows, inside and out, and Dad would paint any woodwork that needed touching up. It would take all day, but Mom would bring apple turnovers and malts and egg salad sandwiches from the drugstore and from the bakery across the street. We each got a Coke out of our machine, one in the morning, one in the afternoon. Though we'd be worn to a frazzle when we finished, we felt proud of our station.

My dad was a darn good mechanic, kept a lot of cars running through the war years when you couldn't get parts or tires or stuff like that. In 1949 he still had the wartime posters on the inside walls of the station like an art museum. One said WHEN YOU RIDE ALONE YOU RIDE WITH HITLER, and it showed a guy driving alone in his car with the outline of Hitler riding beside him. At the bottom it said JOIN A CAR-SHARING CLUB TODAY! We used to laugh because Irene, in pigtails, would go up to the cars with only one person in them and ask if Hitler was riding with them. Dad would get after her but she'd sneak up and do it anyway. She felt it was her wartime duty.

When I was a senior at Central, my brother Clark was thirteen and in eighth grade, and my sister Irene was twelve. Stewy had turned five. Once I heard my mother say that he was an accident. I didn't know what she meant at the time, and I wondered how you could be an accident. My brother Clark started stuttering after my mother died.

A huge lady named Miss Boomray was what they called a "Friendly Visitor" for the Ramsey County Welfare Board. Friendly, shoot. She reminded a guy of a cranky hippopotamus. When she walked, she'd tip to the left, tip to the right. I always wondered: If she wasn't on level ground, would she tip over? A couple years after my mother died, when my dad got picked up by police for being drunk in public, Miss Boomray picked up our family's scent and started keeping notes on us. After spying on us for a while without our knowing, she made it her mission in life to break up our family, send us kids to different orphanages or foster homes. She said my dad wasn't a capable parent and us kids were being neglected. She said he drank too much and wasn't a fit father.

He was a fit father; he just missed my mother something

awful. So did I. He was never mean to us or hit us or anything like that. He was happy when he was drinking. Miss Boomray, we called her Miss "Doomsday," kept a beady eye on us and tried to nail my dad. Sometimes I had to cover for him. Sometimes I had to lie to her, but I wasn't going to let the Friendly Visitor send Stewy off to live with a bunch of snot-nosed strangers in some orphanage where they'd pick on him and steal his food. I made it *my* mission in life to keep our family together.

It helped when we could enroll Stewy in kindergarten. We enrolled him in two, at Longfellow Grade School in the morning and at Gordon Grade School in the afternoon. That way, even though little kids were only supposed to go to kindergarten a half day, he was looked after all day. The only problem was sometimes he'd forget where he was and call his morning teacher, Miss Sawyer, Miss Templeton, and his afternoon teacher, Miss Templeton, Miss Sawyer. And he'd forget which rug was his for rest period. His teachers figured he wasn't very bright.

Stewy was bright, sharp as a tack. He just didn't have a mother and that's hard on little kids. It didn't help that Miss Doomsday was always snooping around, scaring Stewy, and scaring Irene and Clark. Once, when things weren't working out, my dad said Stewy could go live with our Aunt Ruth in California. Stewy cried something awful and wouldn't eat until Dad promised that wouldn't happen. I wasn't going to let that happen either. When my dad had his bad times, I knew it was up to me to keep our family afloat.

Three days before my mother died she and Dad went downtown to see the movie *The Best Years of Our Lives* at the Orpheum. She said it was better than *Gone With the Wind*. When I think about it, she never said exactly what it was about the movie that she loved so much, but the next night she came into my room when I was getting ready for bed.

"Donny," she said, "you've got to see that movie. You're about to begin the best years of your life. Make every day special and wonderful." And she hugged me longer than usual.

A day after the funeral I snuck off and took the Selby-Lake streetcar over to Minneapolis and went to *The Best Years of Our Lives* at the Uptown Theater on Hennepin. I knew it would come to our neighborhood theaters after it showed downtown, but I wanted to see *what* my mother had seen in the story. I wanted to feel close to her, as if she were a part of the movie she loved so much. I wanted to feel her sitting there beside me, living it. I wanted to find out why she wanted me to see it.

I fought hard to keep from crying. I missed her so much I could hardly breathe. I was glad it was so dark in the theater. Virginia Mayo tells Dana Andrews she gave him the best years of her life. On the way home, riding across Minneapolis, I wondered if my mother could have known that the best years of her life were over.

She was wrong about me. She said I was about to live the best years of my life. She couldn't have known that I'd already lived the best years of my life, too.

Chapter 2

In September 1949 we were seniors at Saint Paul Central.
On the first Friday of the school year we had a football game.
I hoped I'd be able to go, if my dad got home in time. He
said he would but sometimes he'd forget and not show up
until late.

Before the fifth period bell rang, boys were passing out
marbles in front hall. They were telling kids to set their
marble on the floor when the clock hit 1:20. I think Jerry
Douglas was behind it, a senior jock. The large auditorium,
where we had study hall, had a slanted floor, and I didn't
believe anyone would dare do anything that crazy in Miss
Whalman's class. She was the scariest teacher in the school.
Shoot! She could pick me up by the shirt collar and throw
me through a plate-glass window. I didn't need a marble, I
always had a few in my pocket to play odd or even. I wanted
to be in on it but my assigned seat was in the front row, just
to the right of the little table Miss Whalman sat at during
the hour.

I tried to do my trigonometry, but I could feel that avalanche of marbles about to come roaring down. Would anyone dare do it? The clock worked its way around to 1:19 and
I held my breath. I'd been in on my share of pranks at Central but this was close to suicide. The big clock on the side
wall clicked to 1:20, and for a second the earth stood still.
Then, like someone opened a gate, they came rolling from
every corner of the auditorium, picking up speed and roaring
like a cattle stampede.

Criminy, Miss Whalman came out of her chair as if her gir-
dle was on fire. The first marbles hit the wall of the stage and
bounced in all directions like hail. The way she hopped,
you'd think someone gave her a hot foot. Then, when she figured out what was going on, she stopped and stared back at

the rampaging marbles. She stood solid in her long, black dress, smoldering like a tree trunk that had been hit by lightning. When the last marble settled along the stage, she spoke.

"It would appear that some of you have lost your marbles."

Everyone laughed as if they'd forgotten where they were, and then the auditorium fell deathly quiet, all the oxygen sucked out of it. I couldn't tell if she was trying to be funny. That would be something for Whalman. Kids held their breath and hid behind their books so she couldn't nail them with her daggerlike eyes. She pointed at me and Barton Burns and my throat went dry.

"Take the wastebasket and pick up the marbles."

She didn't say please, but she had to know Barton and I couldn't have rolled one, sitting in the front row. We collected the marbles quickly, there must have been a hundred, and I slipped a handful in my pocket.

"The entire study hall will spend seventh period here today, no excuses!" She perched on the edge of her chair as if she expected another avalanche of marbles or worse any second.

Holy cow, I had to pick up Stewy at Gordon right after school and now I'd be an hour late. Clark and Irene took him to Longfellow with them in the morning and brought him home for lunch. Longfellow was only a couple blocks from our house.

Clark would walk Stewy up to Gordon for the afternoon and hightail it back to Longfellow for his own classes. What would Stewy do when I didn't show up? I told him to always wait for me no matter what. It worried me that he was new at this, his first week at school, and he might get lost.

Shoot, I could see little Stewy, standing alone on the playground, crying and thinking I'd forgotten him. And if Stewy was lost, maybe someone would report it. I could see Miss Doomsday, stalking like a hungry hyena, licking her chops and writing in her notebook that the kid was deserted and wandering in the city without adult supervision.

Just before seventh period started, I stood in line behind Gretchen Luttermann at Miss Whalman's table. I figured Gretchen, a strange, timid girl, must have been studying to become a ghost the way she dressed and drifted down the halls. I noticed her when I was a sophomore and one look told me she was not happy.

"I didn't roll a marble; my father is waiting for me in the car," Gretchen said.

Whalman didn't even look at Gretchen and she spoke so loudly everyone in the auditorium could hear. "You should address your fellow students. Their childish behavior keeps you here, not I. Take your seat."

I knew my story would be treated the same way and I slunk back to my seat. The minutes crawled by and I could imagine Stewy trying to cross Marshall. I decided to tell Miss Whalman I had to pick up my little brother after kindergarten, that he might get run over if I didn't get there on time. I'd decided I'd walk out and take the punishment later. But before I could stand, she eyeballed us kids in the front row as she ran her finger down the seating chart.

"Janet Aker, Myrrhene Allen, Charlene Arntson, Karen Bell, Barton Burns, Thomas Coppe, Sue Cross, and Donald Cunningham. Obviously, none of you rolled a marble. You may be excused."

We glanced at each other as though we didn't believe it. Then we grabbed our books and took off before she changed her mind. I raced out the side door. It was still like summer. I stuck my thumb out to a guy in a black Plymouth parked along the curb but he only gave me a dirty look. After a few cars, a guy with buckteeth picked me up in a plumber's truck and gave me a ride to Snelling. There were a few kids still around on the playground at Gordon, but Stewy was nowhere in sight. I went in and found the kindergarten room and the teacher said Stewy had left with the other kids. Then she asked me why Stewy kept calling her Mrs. Sawyer.

Criminy, I circled the building, called his name, and

wondered if I should start for home. On the back side of the school I heard Stewy calling but I couldn't find him.

"Donny, Donny!"

Then I looked up. Stewy was twenty-five feet above me, squatting in a Dutch elm, well hidden in the leaves. He could climb a tree like a squirrel. The only problem was, like a cat, sometimes he couldn't get down.

I climbed up to meet him and helped him find branches with his feet. He was half crying and half laughing.

"I was afraid Miss Doomsday would find me," Stewy said.

"Don't you worry, Stew, I won't let her get you. You did good to hide in the tree. She'd never find you up there."

We headed for home down Marshall. Stewy liked it when I held his hand. He jabbered like a bluejay as we walked.

I'd met a new girl in school, Mitzi Fitzsimmons. She'd gone to Summit, a private all-girls' school for rich kids, and had transferred to Central her senior year. She didn't know many kids and I hoped I could help her get acquainted. She ended up in my homeroom and she was only five foot even. When I stood by her, I stretched up on my toes. With Mitzi there was the chance I might catch her and pass her if I ever started growing again. She said she might be at the football game, and I figured Reggie and I could find a way to sit by her.

Reggie was my best friend. He weighed close to two hundred pounds and he was five foot six. We got to be friends because we were always the last ones picked when kids divided up sides for baseball or football. Some kids called Reggie fatty and fatso and things like that. He'd just laugh. Remember in grade school you learned to say, "Sticks and stones may break my bones, but names can never hurt me"? That's a lie. I could tell they hurt Reggie. Kids would call me midget and dwarf and runt and pipsqueak. It hurt, but I'd never let them *know* it hurt. The kids I knew at Central were swell. They called me Donny.

Reggie and I would wrestle all the time for the fun of it. We'd just start wrestling for no reason. He was big but I was fast. When Reggie'd get the best of me, he'd make me say "uncle" and I'd do the same to him. I could always get him to hold off a minute so that I could set my glasses someplace safe. Then, before he was ready, I'd jump him. I didn't wear my glasses a lot. It was bad enough being short but to be a four-eyes too didn't leave much hope. I'd keep my glasses in my shirt pocket a lot and only use them to see the blackboard or at a movie and stuff like that. I'd wear them in the halls because Central was a huge building with long halls and I wanted to see who was coming. When I'd spot Mitzi, I'd slip my glasses in my pocket and get on my toes.

When Stewy and I were a half a block from home, McCoy ran to meet us. McCoy had been our dog for as long as I could remember. A large, black Lab with a touch of mutt in him, he loved everybody. He was a big, old cub bear in disguise. He'd retrieve a pumpkin if you threw one. He'd go up to strangers with his tail wagging and never bark, like he didn't want to scare them. He tried to climb trees with Stewy and followed him around like a bodyguard. Stewy learned how to walk hanging onto a handful of McCoy's hair and when he'd fall, McCoy would stand and wait for him to get up. You could tell McCoy knew what he was doing.

When Dad brought him home as a puppy, he said, "This dog is the real McCoy." Us kids didn't know what that meant and we thought it was his name. We started calling the puppy McCoy and my mom and dad laughed. McCoy became as much a part of our family as any of us. Sometimes I'd see him looking down the block, just standing, staring, and I knew he was still looking for my mother, waiting for her to come home.

I did that sometimes. I'd hear her singing. I'd hold my breath and listen. When she was alive, she sang all the time. When I was alone and the house was quiet, I'd swear I heard her, down in the kitchen, in the living room late at night. I'd strain to listen, not move a muscle, and then her voice would be gone.

When Stewy and McCoy and I got home, Irene was jumping rope with neighborhood girls on the front sidewalk. Two girls swung the long rope and one or two and sometimes up to three would be jumping. Once in awhile I'd still jump with them. They were chanting in rhythm.

> *"Down by the ocean, / down by the sea, /*
> *Johnny broke a bottle / and blamed it on me. /*
> *I told Ma, / and Ma told Pa, /*
> *And Johnny got a lickin' / so ha ha ha."*

"Hi, Donny! Hi, Donny!" they all called. They weren't hailing me because I was Irene's brother or because I was bigger than them, because I wasn't. They were flirting with me because I was a senior at Central High School.

"Hi!" I waved. "Is Clark doing the route?" I said to Irene, who was jumping.

"Yes!" she shouted. Then she changed the verse.

> *"Down by the ocean, / down by the sea, /*
> *"Donny broke a bottle / and blamed it on me. /*
> *I told Ma, / and Ma told Pa, /*
> *And Donny got a lickin' / so ha ha ha."*

I broke more than a bottle. But Irene could never tell Ma again.

I hoped my dad would come home in time. It was the first football game of the season and we were playing Johnson and I figured it would be a swell game. I changed out of my school clothes and I called Dad at the station but he didn't answer. Probably busy with a customer. I helped him on Saturdays when I wasn't doing my other jobs. Around six I ran the four blocks down to the station, but it was closed. Dad was gone. I liked it when he walked to the station. He always walked when my mother was alive. Now, when he drove, I was afraid he'd go to some bar and get drunk.

When I got back, I started making supper. I'd fry some Spam and heat up some baked beans. I hoped I could see Mitzi at the game and say Hi. Clark finished the paper route and Irene set the table and my dad wasn't home by six-thirty. We started eating without him. We did that a lot because he might not come home until nine or ten.

"Are we gonna have Spam again?" Irene said.

"Are we going to?" I said.

"That's what I said."

"Our soldiers won the war eating Spam," I said.

"Well, the war is over," Irene said.

"Yeah, the war is over," Stewy said. "I want bacon."

"You eat it," I said, "it's good food. And no slipping it under the table to McCoy."

"You can't tell me what to do," Irene said. "You're not my mother."

"Dad told you to mind me when he's not here," I said.

"You're just my brother and I don't have to."

She was right in a way and I let it go. I was always holding my breath to keep things working. And it irked me that both Clark and Irene were taller than me. Clark about five foot six and Irene about five foot four. It was hard to be in charge when you had to look up to the person you were bossing.

I watched the clock and swept the kitchen floor while Clark and Irene did the dishes. I hoped Dad would come home without drinking. If he was drinking a lot, I'd stay home. I knew Clark was old enough to take care of the kids when I was gone, but with Miss Doomsday lurking like a commie spy I didn't want to take any chances. The Friendly Visitor could report that the children were left all night without adult supervision.

Irene sang "Someday" along with Vaughn Monroe on the radio and Clark hammed it up, mimicking her the best he could. She ignored him, something she could do well if she had a mind to. Like a family trait, she'd picked up my mom's and dad's habit of breaking out in song with the radio or phonograph.

Heck, I called Reggie and told him if I wasn't at Carpenter's Drugstore by seven-fifteen to go to the game without me.

"Your dad drinking again?" he said.

"No . . . he's just working late."

Darn it, my dad didn't show up until after nine. He was happy and a little unsteady. He pulled off his steel-toed boots and tried to get the grease off his hands in the kitchen sink. I was steaming mad. I wanted to lay into him but I'd learned it wouldn't do any good when he was like that—a big, happy clown. He bounced Stewy on his knee and sang "Don't Sit Under the Apple Tree." He ate the dinner I heated up in the oven and then we listened to the radio.

We had a big Zenith console in the living room and we liked to stretch out on the rug and listen. The Zenith had three tuning knobs and a huge dial with a big green eye in the middle that showed when you had it tuned in the best. We listened to *Ozzie and Harriet* and my dad fell asleep on the living room sofa. I put Stewy to bed. McCoy slept in Stewy's bed with him. But sometimes he'd sleep with me, or Reenie or Clark. It was almost as if McCoy knew which one of us was hurting the most. That's the one he'd comfort with his big, warm body.

I got right to bed, too. I had two jobs to work besides the morning paper route. I hoped Central won the football game and I hoped I'd make it to the game next week. I couldn't stop worrying about Dad's drinking and Miss Doomsday breaking up our family. And I thought about Mitzi Fitzsimmons. Most of all, I hoped I'd get through the night without my nightmare.

Chapter 3

When I got back from my paper route Saturday morning, I waved at the milkman who'd left four bottles in the box on the back steps. Dad was eating breakfast with Glenn Miller's "String of Pearls" bouncing on the phonograph. He always liked it loud so you could hear it all over the house. I hoped no neighbors were trying to sleep. Dad seemed normal, finishing a bowl of oatmeal that Irene had cooked for him. She was proud of the fact that she could make it and my dad would smother it with sugar and cream. He apologized three or four times.

"I'm sorry I didn't make it back so you could go to the game, Donny. I don't know what happened, the time just got away from me."

"I saw in the paper Central whipped Johnson 26 to 7," I said.

"That's good. We have to show those East-siders," my dad said while scanning the paper. "Is it Clark's turn to help at the station?"

"Yeah," I said. I swallowed. "Dad, you know we have to be careful with—"

"I know, I know, Donny, and I promise. I'm going to quit."

"Miss Doomsday is sneaking around all the time. Did she come to the station Friday?"

"No . . . I never saw her," he said.

"Where were you?"

"Oh . . . I had to road test a Chevy I put new brakes on."

He didn't look at me. He never looked at me when he was lying.

I had a bowl of Wheaties, the "Breakfast of Champions" that Jack Armstrong drilled into me when I was just a kid, assuring me that I'd be stronger and braver if I ate Wheaties every morning. A guy had to admit he never said it would make you taller.

I changed clothes and headed for Carpenter's Drugstore where I'd do everything except prescriptions. Fifty cents an hour, about four dollars a day. I was the soda jerk and stock boy, and sometimes I'd wait on people at the front cash register. Making change was a snap. I never had trouble with numbers.

Irene and Clark would get to squabbling now and then about whose turn it was to do what. But usually all I had to do was mention Miss Doomsday and what would happen if it looked like we weren't living in a properly clean house and Stewy wasn't getting proper care. Clark was going to help Dad at the station and keep an eye on him. We all knew how to check the oil, the radiator, the air pressure in tires, wash the windshield, and pump gas. Irene would keep track of Stewy all morning while doing housekeeping chores. At noon they'd switch, Clark would watch Stewy and Irene would help out at the station.

Something in Clark went away when my mother died. He'd been a clown, always horsing around, pulling something. He'd keep us laughing and keep us on guard at the same time. That had all changed. He even talked slower, and stuttered sometimes.

About a year ago Clark started feeding gray squirrels from his bedroom window. He'd sit for hours with the window open, coaxing them to come from the oak tree and eat out of his hand. They became so tame they'd run up his arm and sit on his shoulder. They'd sit on his head, find peanuts in his pockets, and finally they'd come in and explore the room. Dad laid down one rule. They could only come into the bedroom, nowhere else in the house.

Clark could identify and name seven squirrels. They all looked the same to me. He called them the seven dwarfs and named them accordingly. I'd ask him who one was and he'd say, without batting an eye, Bashful. He taught them tricks and spent so much time with them they'd let him put them in his shirt or have them jump onto his shoulder from the dresser across the room. We had only one problem. Happy or Grumpy would show up in the kitchen now and then. We might open a cupboard door and out would fly Dopey, or pick up the broom and find a squirrel attached. All Clark had to do was clap his hands and shout "Out!" and the little critters would scamper up the stairs and out the window.

Like a ghost, an albino squirrel showed up in our neighborhood at times. Pure white. But she was more wary than the others and wouldn't come to Clark's window and eat the nuts he left unless the window was shut. Clark sat for hours, watching her, talking to her. She'd come and eat only when the window was down. He named her Snow White and said he would win her over if it was the last thing he ever did. Spending time with the squirrels made Clark feel good, even if sometimes I figured our family had gone nuts.

A little after six I left the drugstore and hustled down to St. Mark's Catholic Church. We didn't go to most of the church stuff. My mother was Catholic and my dad was Baptist and we just kinda wandered around in the middle. Mom always read Bible stories to us and Dad had kept it up after she died. I went through all the sacraments in the Catholic church, baptism and first communion, and going to Mass and all those things. Every Saturday I'd go to confession. *Bless me, Father, for I have sinned. It's been a week since my last confession.* I used to only go once in awhile or when my mother made me, but since my mother died, I hadn't missed except when I was sick in bed with the flu or something.

After confession I walked home to check on the gang. Dad was home with Stewy while Clark and Irene were playing hide-and-peek with the neighborhood kids.

Hide-and-*peek* was an advanced form of hide-and-seek. Whoever was "it" had to count to a hundred at the goal, usually a large Dutch elm on the boulevard. When he was done counting, he yelled, "Here I come ready or not!" The game was timed: thirty minutes. In that time the other kids had to hide and *peek*, which meant they had to *show themselves* to the person who was "it" *once* before they were eligible to try to reach the goal safely.

He could come racing after you, so you had to be a long way off. The minute you were out of sight you could double back, circle around a few blocks, come at the goal from the south when he saw you to the north. If he saw you again, he could tag the goal and call out your name and you were caught. It was the most fun at dusk. Stewy played sometimes. He could hide so no one could find him. Still too young to play with the bigger kids, he never got home within the thirty minutes. But he loved playing.

Seeing that all was well at home, I hitchhiked down Fairview to Highland Park. I'd set pins at the Highland Bowling Center until around ten. My dad said we weren't doing so well with the station and I figured I could help out with the money. He sold our '48 Oldsmobile with Hydra-Matic transmission and bought a '40 Hudson with fifty-two thousand miles on it. I didn't care what car we had. I didn't drive.

I'd get eleven cents a line setting pins, but I had to be quick or I'd get clobbered. You had to be careful while you were picking up pins that were down from the first ball and setting them in the cradle. The second ball could already be on the way. The pins would explode and you had to get your legs high when the ball hit. I'd always get nicked somewhere before I was through.

I spent a dime and rode the streetcar home, but I was dog-tired. I hoped everything went okay at home and I thought about Mitzi Fitzsimmons. When I came in the front door, my dad was asleep on the sofa, Stewy was asleep on the floor, and Cedric Adams was giving the day's news on the Zenith. Irene and Clark were playing Monopoly at the kitchen table with Martha and Willie Winfield, the neighbor kids. I walked into the kitchen and looked in the icebox. Nothing but leftover Spam and beans.

"What did you have for supper?" I said.

"Dad brought home White Castles," Irene said.

White Castles were delicious little hamburgers that I loved
and I really got hungry just thinking about them.

"Darn it, did you eat them all?" I said.

"Yeah. We m-made some popcorn," Clark said and nodded
at a big bowl over on the counter.

I poured myself a glass of milk and ate some cold popcorn.

"Did Miss Doomsday come around today?" I said.

"No . . . we didn't see her," Irene said.

"Was Dad okay?" I said.

Clark glanced at Martha and Willie. "Yeah, he w-was okay,"
Clark said. "He w-worked hard all day. I p-pumped a lot
of gas."

"I bet I pumped more than you, Clark," Irene said.

"No, y-you never. I p-pumped over two hundred gallons."

"Liar, liar, pants on fire, nose as long as a telephone wire!"
Irene shouted.

"Hey! Hey! the cleanest windshields in town," I said.

"The cleanest windshields in town," Irene and Clark
chorused.

Monday morning I got to my homeroom before the second
bell. Miss Rice, the typing teacher, let us talk during homeroom if we kept it down. I was trying to find a way to talk to
Mitzi, but she was yakking with two other girls. She was so
pretty in the morning. They were talking about the sororities
at Central and guessing which ones, if any, would invite Mitzi
to join. Usually kids joined when they were freshman or
sophomores, but when a kid showed up for the first time as a
senior, they made exceptions.

At second lunch, Reggie and I grabbed a seat at a table of
boys in the lunchroom balcony where I could watch Sandy
Meyer. The lunchroom was in the sub-basement and usually
the balcony was mostly boys. If you were close to the balcony
railing, you could watch the girls below. It was my bad luck
that Mitzi had first lunch so I had no chance to see her.

I liked being around Sandy Meyer. She was five foot eight. I know I bugged her sometimes, but she looked so much like my mother, like my mother probably looked when she was in high school. She was the only girl in wood shop and I talked to her whenever I could and kidded around with her. I suppose she thought I wanted to be her boyfriend. Heck, it wasn't that, not that I wouldn't like that, but she was way too tall for me. I'd just hang around her when I could, ride on the same streetcar after school or whatever. I knew it wouldn't bring my mother back, but it just felt good being around Sandy.

Reggie had a secret girlfriend he was in love with, really in love, the kind that hurts. But he'd never tell me who she was. I promised I would never razz him about her or make fun of him but he wouldn't tell. When we'd wrestle and I'd get him in a hammerlock, I'd try to make him tell me her name, but he'd take the pain until I'd quit. I never saw him talking to girls much and I had no idea who it was. There were around eight hundred girls at Central so I didn't bother guessing.

Sandy looked up at me once during lunch and I waved at her. She was nice enough to give me a smile. It was almost like a smile from my mother.

Over the lunch hour the story spread fast about what Hugh Mayer and Phil Costello did when the marching band was practicing on the football field. In full uniform they marched down the field playing the Central fight song. Lester Hambull, the stocky little director with a handlebar mustache, was shouting instructions. Mayer and Costello were the only clarinets in the band. Mayer says to Costello, "When they go right, we go left."

Jackie Pool, the majorette, gave the signal. The band turned smoothly with Jackie out front, going south, and the two clarinets marched north.

"No! No! Stop, stop!" Hambull shouted and blew his whistle.

The band stopped and lined up again, the clarinets in place, and off they went, in step, drums giving them a beat.

Mayer says to Costello, "When they go left, we go right."

They looked dandy in their red and black uniforms, playing away, marching smartly. Jackie gave the signal, the band turned north and the clarinets marched south.

"No! No! No!" Lester shouted, waving his arms and blowing his whistle until his face turned red. The band stopped.

They said that Lester thought Mayer and Costello just didn't get it, that they were slow to catch on. It seemed he never realized they were having fun at his expense.

With the band all lined up along the chalked stripes, Lester waved them on and they stepped out together. As they crossed the fifty-yard line, Jackie gave the signal to turn the band to face the home team's bleachers. Sharply they pivoted, perfectly in step, the band going south and the clarinets going north.

"Stop! No! Stop!" Lester shouted and he actually jumped up and down and threw his hat and whistle into the bleachers.

We'd have given our eyeteeth to have seen it. Reggie did. He'd gotten out of class to help run the chalk lines on the field. He told me he fell down laughing. I about fell down just hearing about it. But in a strange way it reminded me of my life. When the band is going south, I, along with the clarinets, am always going north. Only, unlike Mayer and Costello, I wasn't doing it on purpose.

Chapter 4

Tuesday nights boys show up at the house of the girls who are having one of the sorority meetings. Word spreads all day in school. The Sokos had their meeting at Katie Leahy's over on Laurel and I talked Reggie into going with me. Reggie and I belonged to Delta Hi-Y and we figured, like on the playground, we were picked last when we were sophomores.

I think they picked me because of the time I hid in the janitor's locker in the girls' lavatory. Reggie bet me a dollar I wouldn't. When the bell rang ending third period and the girls came flooding in, two girls started smoking and blowing the smoke through the louvers in the locker in case a teacher showed up. I couldn't breathe. I tipped some bleach on my pants, stooping to duck the smoke. I had to choose between complete humiliation or death.

Finally, I blasted open the door and ran for my life. I got caught for running in the halls by Al Cohen on the traffic squad, but he started laughing at the streak down my pants. It looked like I'd wet them after drinking hydrochloric acid and he let me go. It seemed that everyone in the school knew about it in fifteen minutes. Every so often I'd do something crazy like that, I don't know why. Maybe to make kids laugh, to get their attention, to get them to like me?

Katie's was a madhouse, standing room only. In the jam, kids looked for the reason they were there, their sweethearts, their steadies, or to meet someone new. Girls would hang around in hopes they'd end up with a ride home or a date for the weekend.

Friday night the Minute Men Club was sponsoring the Fall Fantasy at the Saint Paul Hotel, the first dance of the year, and I was working hard on my courage to ask Mitzi. Shoot, the only problem was I didn't drive and Reggie didn't have a date, even though he could get his father's Dodge. There would always be other boys with dates I might hook a ride with. I sure couldn't take Mitzi on the streetcar. I'd found out she lived on Summit Avenue, the boulevard of rich people.

Then I saw her, in a corner of the dining room. My knees got weak. Gosh, she was so pretty she knocked my socks off. She made me wish I was taller and a lot more handsome. Sometimes I'd wish I had a body like Charles Atlas so when some jerk was pushing people around, I could pound him. Mitzi gabbed with two other girls and glanced around the room as if she were looking for someone. I hid behind a taller kid to work up my nerve but I couldn't find any to work up. Kids pushed and shoved through the dining room and all of a sudden I was standing face-to-face with Mitzi. Holy Moses, I stretched up onto my toes.

"Hi, Donny," she said with a big smile.

"Ah . . . hi."

"Do you have a girlfriend that's a Soko?"

"No . . . Reggie and I . . . are you going to be a Soko?"

"Yes, they invited me tonight."

"That's swell."

I wanted to ask her to the dance but I knew it would be shaky. What if Dad didn't come home after work Friday?

"Are you in a fraternity?" she said as we got shoved closer together.

She had on a blue sweater that matched her eyes and a blue ribbon in her blonde hair and I know it sounds crazy, but I was so close to her I could smell pretty blue girl. I was afraid I'd start stammering like Clark did sometimes.

"No . . . I'm in Delta Hi-Y."

"What do the Hi-Y's do?"

"They put on dances and other events during the year, kind of like a boys' club," I said.

"I'm glad I transferred to Central. You have a lot more fun."

"I'm glad you did, too," I said, and, boy was I sweating.

My legs started to ache and I didn't know how long I could keep standing on my toes.

Then Jim Rotter elbowed in and started talking to Mitzi. He was about five foot ten. I stood there and listened until I was slowly being wedged out by taller kids like a midget in a corn field.

"Ah . . . I'll see you in homeroom, Mitzi," I shouted, still on my toes.

"Okay." She gave me a little wave and I slid through the crush with a lump in my chest. But it felt good to stand on my feet again.

I found Reggie, laughing with a couple other guys.

"You find Mitzi?" Reggie said.

"Yeah."

"Did you ask her to the dance?"

"Almost."

A lucky thing I didn't ask Mitzi to the Fall Fantasy. Dad had been good all week and our family life had run smoothly. He came home after work every day and even though I caught a whiff of beer on him a few times, he did nothing to give Miss Doomsday any ammunition. Reggie and I tried to talk ourselves into going to the dance stag. He'd get the car and we could talk a few other guys at school into going with us. Then Reggie said it would be too painful to watch his secret girlfriend romancing with some other guy and he dug in his heels. We agreed we'd go to a movie. I called him around six-thirty and told him my dad hadn't shown up. The car was gone and the station closed.

I got the other kids to bed a little after nine. We'd listened to the *Lone Ranger* and *Life of Riley* on the Zenith in the living room, and we'd catch each other cocking our heads and listening for our car.

"Maybe Dad is helping someone with their car," I said.

"At nine o'clock?" Irene said, and she rolled her eyes.

"He's d-drinking, isn't he?" Clark said.

"He doesn't care if we get sent to an orphanage," Irene said.

"Don't talk that way!" I said. "He almost cares too much. He misses Mom."

"So do we but we don't go drinking booze," Irene said.

"I know, I know, it's going to be all right," I said, and one by one I got them in bed.

The phone rang around ten-thirty. Scary.

Our backdoor neighbors across the alley are the Rileys. Stewy calls Mr. Riley Uncle Ellie-Ellie because he wears a gas mask sometimes. He fought in France in the First World War and got gassed and now he says he always wants to be prepared. He says they'll never catch him off guard again. The first few times Stewy saw him in the gas mask he started bawling. Mr. Riley had to take the mask off around Stewy for a while until Stewy recognized him with the gas mask on. With the gas mask on, Stewy thought he looked like an elephant, only he couldn't say "elephant." He called them ellie-ellies and so Mr. Riley became Uncle Ellie-Ellie. Mrs. Riley's name was Grace and she was like a grandma to us. Somehow, as we grew up, she became Nana Riley.

Uncle Ellie-Ellie had a son who was a policeman. We'd met him lots of times when he was visiting his parents. A few times he showed us his handcuffs and his .38 pistol. *He* was the policeman on the phone.

"Is this Donny?" he said.

"Yeah."

"We have your dad, Donny. He's been drinking up a storm."

"Is he okay?" I felt the glue running through my veins.

"Yeah, he's okay. He's stumbling drunk, but he's all right."

"Will he go to jail?"

"Well . . . I—"

"Please, Sergeant Riley, can you bring him home, please?"

"He's been soaking it up in a bar on University, mooching drinks and money, telling everyone he owns a gas station and can pay them back tomorrow. The bartender called us."

"Can you get him home, please? I'll sober him up."

"Okay, okay . . . I'll drive him home in his car. My partner can pick me up at your house in the cruiser. We can duck the report this time, but . . ."

"Gosh, thanks, *Sergeant Riley*, thanks a million. I'll keep a better eye on him, I promise. Listen, could you have your partner stop in the alley, so our neighbors won't see the squad car?"

Uncle Ellie-Ellie's son parked our car in the driveway and I helped him get my dad in the house. Dad was happy, singing "Ac-Cent-Tchu-Ate the Positive," and I was trying to quiet him down so he didn't wake half of Saint Paul.

When I got Dad in his bed, I walked out in the backyard with Sergeant Riley and thanked him for keeping Dad out of the tank. Luckily, all the neighboring houses were quiet and dark.

In the alley, just before he got in the cop car, Sergeant Riley turned and looked at me.

"You know, Donny, he isn't getting any better."

"I know, but he will. Any day now he'll snap out of it. This isn't like him. He's a good man. He's a good father. He'll snap out of it."

The look on Riley's face said I was just a kid who didn't understand. But I *did*. I understood how terrible it was when you were "hooked" on something like my dad was. I learned it well the summer I was thirteen.

Chapter 5

The summer I was thirteen my father got someone to run the station and took us to the wild country along the north shore of Lake Superior. He'd been doing it every August since I was ten. We always stayed at Sunnydale Cabins, a resort perched along the rocky shore. The lake was so big you couldn't see across it, and the woods ran all the way to Canada and Hudson Bay. I loved that place where wild animals prowled. I could feel their eyes watching me from the underbrush.

Our rustic cabin sat so close to the rocky shore we could feel the lake's spray when the wind was right. From my bed I could hear the waves smashing against the bedrock all through the night. We had only kerosene lamps, a hand pump for cold water at the sink, and an outhouse in the woods. A boy's dream, just being there, hauling wood, pumping water, the glow of the lamps and the warmth of the fireplace at night. I felt as if we were living in the olden days, pioneers I'd see in movies. And like movie stars, my mom and dad acted like mushy love birds the whole time we were there.

The first night at the cabin my mother got out a dozen or more mousetraps she brought along. She had a squeamish fear of a mouse running across her face while she slept. Just before bedtime, my dad loaded the traps with small pieces of cheese and set them. Then, before we blew out the lamps, he'd place the traps along the ledges at the top of the stud wall.

Boy, as soon as the cabin went dark, there were mice running all over the place and mousetraps going off everywhere. I'd hear them in the dark: Snap! and then Plunk. The spring-loaded bar would crack shut on the little animal with such force that the trap would flip off the ledge and hit the floor. The first couple nights were the worst. Snap! . . . plunk. Snap! . . . plunk.

My dad and I would collect the dead mice in the morning and drop them into the outhouse. By the middle of our stay, with the mouse population whittled down, the traps went off less and less until maybe we'd have only a two- or three-mouse night. I figured the people who stayed in the cabin ahead of us must not have minded the mice because our first night was like a shooting gallery. A couple of times a mouse in a trap did a swan dive off the top of the wall and landed on my bed. I slept with my head under my pillow.

We got to know some of the families who came to the Sunnydale Cabins at the same time each year, and sometimes after supper I'd play with the other kids along the shore. One of the kids, Buzzy, was the son of the resort's owner. He was almost fourteen and he'd join in when we'd play capture-the-flag or kick-the-can. They had a garage with a large loft and sometimes, in between other stuff, I'd lay around up there with Buzzy reading comic books.

In the little town of Tofte, a Standard station sat along the highway. While Mom bought groceries, my dad would fill up and compare notes with Lloyd Tollefson, the owner. That summer, Lloyd had gotten hold of a black bear and had him chained beside his filling station. It was a tourist attraction, a "black gold mine," Tollefson called it. He had a big sign, pointing to the bear, and about every other car stopped to gawk.

You could buy a Coca-Cola at the station and give it to the bear and he'd stand on his hind legs and guzzle it. People would take pictures and admire the bear and buy him a Coke or two. I thought it was swell to have a live bear and it was fun to stand just out of reach of his chain and watch him. I'd talk to him. I wondered what would happen if we had a bear at our station in Saint Paul and imagined how rich we'd be.

Then one day, when I was standing there watching the tourists and the bear, I heard a woman's voice behind me. "Isn't that tragic, just tragic! That lovely animal was meant to be free in the forest, living in the beauty of the woods, and he's chained here like a criminal, his life *stolen* from him."

A man's voice added his two cents. "It's disgusting, a crying shame. Let's get out of here."

I turned and saw the man and woman, dressed in city clothes, march off to their '41 Buick Roadmaster and drive away. They left me stunned. I'd never thought about how the bear felt, getting all that free pop and having people admire him and take his picture. I took a good look at him and the circle he walked at the end of the chain. His coat had turned dull and shaggy and dirty. There was a tarpaper house for him, like a big doghouse, but not a tree, not a blade of grass, not an inch of shade.

Riding back to Sunnydale Cabins, I couldn't forget what the woman said. She was right! It was a shame. The station owner was stealing the bear's life. The bear was meant to be free in the woods. Before we got back to our cabin, a plan was forming in my head. Doggone it, *I'd free the bear!* I'd give him his life back. But I'd need help. Who? Clark and Irene were too young. And then I knew. Buzzy. It would be much more of a risk for him. I was a tourist, I could go home next week. He lived here, part of the neighborhood. But he was a stocky, freckled redhead that looked like trouble walking. I couldn't wait to ask him.

When I told him, I didn't have to twist his arm. Buzzy was all for it, and we made our plan. That afternoon we hitchhiked into Tofte and bought eight bottles of Coke. Not all at once. One here, one there. One at the grocery store, one at the restaurant. All we could scrape together was forty cents between us. We stashed the Cokes in a culvert not far from the Standard station. Then we watched the bear for a while as he performed for tourists. I studied the buckle on his collar. The collar went through an iron ring on the chain and there was no way we could cut through the ring. Shoot, we'd have to get the collar off. The tongue on the buckle had an eyelet and Lloyd had run a wire through the hole and twisted it several times so the buckle couldn't come unfastened accidentally. We'd have to untwist the wire and pull it through the eyelet before we could unbuckle the collar.

When no tourists were right on top of us, we talked to the bear. "We're coming tonight, we're going to let you go," I told him.

"Yeah," Buzzy said, "and you can run back into the woods and be happy."

We hitchhiked back to Sunnydale Cabins and got what we'd need from Buzzy's garage: pliers, bottle opener, and flashlight. I got permission from Dad to sleep with Buzzy that night in the loft of their garage. We played games with the other kids along the shore until past dark and then we climbed into the loft.

"How are we going to wake up?" I said as we stretched out on sleeping bags and pillows.

"I brought an alarm clock," Buzzy said.

"Okay, set it for two."

Buzzy wound the clock and set it.

I lay there getting more and more excited. We were going to stage a prison break *with a bear*. I didn't lay there more than ten minutes and Buzzy was sound asleep. I turned on the flashlight and looked at my watch. Ten twenty-two.

The alarm went off at one-fifty. Luckily, we had a moon. We grabbed our stuff and hightailed it for the highway. A few cars and trucks passed while we hiked to Tofte. We could see their lights coming a mile off and we'd pile into the ditch until they went by. Every once in awhile we'd see a bat fly across the moon and we spooked a big owl out of a tree. It took over an hour to get to the station.

The town sat quiet and mostly dark. We found our stash of Coke and we each carried four bottles to the bear's circle.

"Hey, wake up," I said quietly, "we're here to let you go."

We could hear the bear rustling around but couldn't see him in the dark. He was midnight black and before I knew it, he was standing beside me, breathing in my ear.

"Jeez!" I jumped back. "You feed him the Coke with one hand and keep the flashlight on the collar with the other," I said. "I'll work on the buckle."

"Okay," Buzzy said and he opened a bottle. The bear grunted a little hearing the pop of the bottle top. Buzzy turned on the flashlight and held out the bottle. The bear seemed much bigger in the dark. He took the Coke and swilled it. I had barely found the buckle and the first bottle was gone. I didn't know if Buzzy was scared, but the light bounced all over the place. I couldn't get hold of the twisted wire.

"Give him another bottle, but slower," I said, "and keep the light on the buckle."

"I'm trying, I'm trying."

Buzzy opened the second bottle and held it out of reach for a moment. I got the pliers on the wire and started twisting. It was tough wire and I dropped the pliers.

"I dropped the pliers, shine the light down here."

Buzzy turned the flashlight on the ground and the bear put a paw on my shoulder. "Cripes!" I jumped back. I could smell his clammy, fishy breath. I found the pliers. Buzzy fed him the third bottle.

"I've got the wire loose," I said.

I pulled it through the eyelet on the buckle's tongue and threw it aside. I tried to move the thick leather over the tongue but it wouldn't budge. A car came along the highway.

"Turn off the flashlight!" I said.

We froze. The car slowed and then went on north.

"I'm down to two bottles," Buzzy said.

"Slow down, slow down."

The bear was breathing in my face when he wasn't swilling down Cokes and I could barely move the heavy leather. The light was dying, I couldn't see, and it felt like I was dancing with the bear.

"One bottle left," Buzzy said.

"Give it to me," I said. "Go fill some of the empties with water."

Buzzy grabbed some of the bottles and ran to the station's outside faucet. I could hear the water running as I gave the bear his last Coke. Buzzy was back quickly. But now the bear was standing on my foot!

"Keep feeding him the water, maybe he won't notice right away," I said. "Keep the light on the collar."

"The light's shot," Buzzy said.

Finally, while he fed the bear water, I pried the thick leather over the tongue and pushed it back through the buckle. The collar and chain fell to the ground.

"I got it, I got it! Watch out!" I shouted.

For a while the bear didn't move past the circle in the dirt, like he thought he was still chained. Buzzy and I moved around behind him and "shooed" him. Then I realized he was gone. With the moonlight coming through the pines in places, I could see the bear over at the station. Buzzy found me and we tried to chase the bear across the highway. It was like ring-around-the-rosie. We chased him around the station until one time we met him coming back our way and he ran right past us. We were like three kids trying to find the door to the candy store in the dark. I'd think I was moving around the building beside Buzzy and it would turn out to be the bear. I'd think I was meeting the bear coming toward me and it would be Buzzy.

After ten minutes of hunting and chasing and getting scared out of our wits, we herded the bear out onto the highway. We ran at him, shouting, clapping our hands. Buzzy picked up a few rocks in the ditch and threw them. Finally, the bear gave a grunt and rambled down the far ditch and crashed off into the woods. He was gone. We'd done it! He was free!

We grabbed each other and hugged and jumped and laughed in the dark. We were heroes! We couldn't tell anyone, we'd be unsung heroes. We knew we'd be in big trouble if Tollefson found out, or our parents. Even so, I wanted to shout.

We cleaned up the empty Coke bottles and hoped no one would suspect that somebody set the bear free. I took the

collar and the wire with us on the hike home and halfway
down the highway I threw them far into the woods. By the
time we got back, it was almost five, faint light showing to the
east out over the lake. We climbed back into the garage loft
and I fell asleep immediately, imagining the bear halfway to
Canada.

When Buzzy's father was ready to take his daily trip into
Tofte, Buzzy and I were there to ride along. We both had big
smiles on our kissers and we had his dad drop us at the
Standard station.

Inside the station it was like a morgue. Four old cronies
besides Lloyd were bemoaning the loss of the bear. To hear
them talk, the whole economy of the North Shore would col-
lapse, Lloyd would end up in the poor house, and the tourists
would just go roaring by without spending a cent until they
were in Canada.

Buzzy had the guts to say, "What happened to the bear?"

That started another round of complaining about bad luck
and the loss of the bear that laid the golden egg.

"I can't figure it," Lloyd said, scratching his head. "How
could he get that collar through that steel oval?"

"Never heard anything like it," one old crony said.

"Them wild things is smarter than we know," another said
and spit.

Buzzy and I walked over to the circle in the dirt. The chain
lay where it had fallen, the collar mysteriously missing, and
the bear long gone. We looked at each other and smiled.

Buzzy's dad picked us up on his way home and we were
whistling a happy tune. Then I got hit with a two-by-four in
the stomach. Coming down the ditch along the highway was
the *bear!*

"Stop the car! Stop the car!" Buzzy shouted.

We piled out. I ran across the highway and cut off the bear.
I waved my arms and shouted. Buzzy waved his arms and
shouted. The bear just ran around us and headed for town. I
ran down the highway and passed him. I got a ways ahead

and then jumped in the ditch and picked up rocks and sticks and anything I could find. I threw them at the bear. I was really mad and crying at the same time.

"No, no! Go back! Go back, you stupid bear!"

Buzzy caught up and threw rocks. Nothing we did stopped him.

We followed him all the way to town. Tourists hit the brakes and watched this strange scene of two boys herding a wild bear down Highway 61. They jumped out of their cars and snapped pictures. When the bear got to the station, he ran right inside. In about two seconds the four old cronies came flying out as if their pants were on fire. Buzzy and I ran up and watched. Lloyd came out, leading the bear like a mother with a bottle of milk. Lloyd held the Coke high and led the bear over to the circle in the dirt.

He yelled at Buzzy. "Get me more Coke, quick!"

Buzzy didn't move.

"Buzzy, damn it! Get me more Coke!" Lloyd shouted.

One of the old men came hustling with two bottles. They got the chain around the bear's neck and fastened it with a bolt Lloyd had in his pocket. The bear was caught! They all cheered. Lloyd looked at Buzzy, whom he'd known for years.

"What's the matter with you, boy? Can't you hear? Why didn't you bring me more Coke?"

"I was afraid of the bear," Buzzy said.

The four cronies and Lloyd went back into the station, patting each other on the back and celebrating. Tourists were pulling over and stopping again.

Buzzy and I couldn't believe it. We'd saved him, set him free, and he came back to the chain. We walked over just out of reach of the bear. He was sitting in the dirt, looking off across the highway to the forest, sniffing the air.

"Dumb bear," I said. "Dumb bear."

I looked into the bear's eyes and could see his terrible sadness. I knew that deep inside he really wanted to be in the wild. He'd sold out his life and he knew it, hooked on Coca-

Cola. And I realized the terrible power drugs and all that stuff had on people. They were hooked, they were chained prisoners who had sold out.

Now, four years later, I saw that same sadness in my dad's eyes. He was hooked like the Coca-Cola bear, and I didn't know how to get him back in the woods. I'd learned that shouting and throwing rocks wouldn't work.

Chapter 6

Dad had a real hangover Saturday morning, but I got coffee
and some breakfast into him and walked him down to work.
He came home Saturday night right on schedule. Saturday
afternoon I went home before going to confession. Cal Gant,
one of my classmates at Central, delivered our groceries from
Finley's Market. My dad kept Mr. Finley's '41 Plymouth panel
truck going during the war and since then we got most of
our groceries there. We always made a list and either Dad or I
would call it in on Saturday morning.

Cal played football and basketball for Central but he wasn't
stuck up or anything. Once last year, when we were juniors,
some of the senior jocks were making fun of me. There's a
little midget on the radio and on billboards in a bell hop's
uniform advertising for Phillip Morris cigarettes. He goes
around shouting, "Call . . . for . . . Phillip . . . Morreees," with
a real fruity voice. Shoot, sometimes kids would holler that
when I'd walk by. "Call for Phillip Morreees." Well, that day,
one of the big senior football players was about to hold me
by the ankles out over the stairwell on the third floor. If he
lost his grip, I'd be like a splattered bug on a windshield. Cal
stepped in and kidded them out of it. I was really scared. He
saved my bacon that day and those guys never did pull anything on me.

I tried to give Cal a quarter tip that my dad left for him,
but he wouldn't take it.

"I'll see you in school," he said and he drove away.

Sunday morning my dad cooked up pancakes and pork
sausage. He loved making breakfast Sunday morning and we
loved eating it. When I came down, he was bouncing to "In
the Mood" by Glenn Miller. He had all of Glenn Miller's

records and he and Mom used to dance to them all over the house. Mom had her own stack, Frank Sinatra, Jo Stafford, Dinah Shore, romantic songs. Dad didn't play those anymore. They gathered dust in the rack by the phonograph.

Dad had a dishtowel tied around his waist and a chef's hat on his head that he'd had forever. When he wasn't tapping to Glenn Miller, he sang songs like "Old Man River." He could sing real good. He'd deliver pancakes to our plates singing "Shoo Fly Pie" and he'd dance back to the stove. He always made Sunday breakfast, even when my mother was alive, and she told us he did ever since they were married.

We sat around the kitchen table with different parts of the morning paper, tapping our feet to the beat of his song. Irene and Clark usually fought over the funnies, wanting to be the first to read "Joe Palooka" and "Li'l Abner" and "Terry and the Pirates." But that morning Irene was really upset about some stuff she accidentally saw on the front page while she was waiting for the funnies that Clark was hogging.

"It says here that the Germans killed thousands of Jews just because they were Jews. They hadn't done anything wrong, they weren't even soldiers, just Jews," she said. She had the expression on her face she always got just before she started crying. "They killed mothers and babies and little kids and old people. How horrid, how could they *do that?*"

"Sometimes Evil gets loose in the world," my dad said, "brutal, insane Evil."

"How does it g-get loose?" Clark said, looking up from the funnies.

"It finds a foothold in people's hearts and it turns them evil," Dad said.

"Why didn't somebody stop them?" Irene said with her bottom lip trembling.

"We did, Reenie, that's what the war was about," Dad said. "That's why thousands of American boys died."

Irene looked back at the front-page article. "It says that some Dutch families hid the Jews in their attics and basements and root cellars. They hid them for two or three *years*, until the war was over. They saved them. Isn't that super!"

"They were brave people, those Dutch," my dad said as he served another round of pancakes.

Gosh, Irene's eyes shot flames. She pushed her plate away, she didn't want anything more to eat.

"If we lived in Holland, would we hide the Jews?" she said, looking at Dad.

"You betcha, Reenie, you bet your sweet patootie." He shook the spatula in the air. "We'd fill the attic with them!"

Reenie was so worked up I was afraid she'd go out and grab a Jew off the street and hide him in our attic. We had a great attic for hiding someone. It had no windows and if you didn't know where the attic door was, in Stewy's closet, you'd never know there was an attic.

Sunday afternoon, after Dad took a nap, he rounded us up and we piled in the car for a drive to the little town of Afton. My dad loved driving out to Afton, through the farms and countryside to the St. Croix River. We had the black '40 Hudson four door. It was pretty old but Dad kept it in good shape. The Oldsmobile Dad sold had an automatic transmission. No damned-to-hell clutch! Just a gas pedal and a brake pedal. Press on the gas, go. Press on the brake, stop. The Hudson had a stick shift on the floor and a bloody clutch. I wished we'd have gotten an automatic transmission before my mother died, but they were just coming out then. I thought how different our lives would be if we'd had an automatic transmission.

Afton was a little town with great big ice cream cones. We always got double dips and Irene could never decide what flavor to choose. When we got out of the car at the dairy store, open Sunday afternoons for people like us, I noticed the back left fender had been bashed in and the bumper twisted and bent. Dad saw that I'd seen it and I didn't say anything with the kids there. I wondered if next time he'd hit someone head-on or go off a bridge. I knew we walked on thin ice and I tried not to think about it.

Sometimes my dad would get sad when we'd do things we used to do with Mom, but it seemed the drive to Afton didn't do that to him. We'd go whenever the weather was good and Clark and Irene would fight over who got to sit next to Dad. They'd race to the car and just about kill each other scrambling to get in the front seat. Finally, Dad had to make them take turns or he'd think of a number between one and ten and the one who guessed the closest got to ride up front.

Once in a while he'd let Stewy ride shotgun and the other two would complain, "He can't see over the hood anyway." I always climbed into the backseat. It was a swell ride, peaceful, full of things to see. I loved the country.

Clark was in front and he said, "Can I drive today, Dad?"

"Oh . . . not today, but one of these days."

"You always say One of these days, but one of these days never comes," Clark said.

"You're wrong there, son, one of these days will surely come, faster than you want it."

"I'll be fourteen soon. I've got to start sometime," Clark said.

"Donny gets to drive first," Irene said and she smiled at me.

"I'm too short to drive," I said.

Clark was skinny but had grown to be five foot six.

"You can't be *too short* to drive," Irene said and laughed.

"I don't want to drive," I said.

"Why not?" Stewy said. "You could drive us to the zoo."

"Some people just weren't meant to drive," I said and I glanced at my dad. He was looking out at the brown corn field we were passing. I wanted to know what he was thinking.

"We could pull off on a dirt road," Clark said.

"Not today," my dad said, "not today."

That night when Dad was putting the kids to bed I smelled
alcohol on him. I couldn't figure where he got it and when. I
was really bushed and I fell asleep right off. Something woke
me. It was Dad tiptoeing down the stairs. Our stairs creaked
so loudly a ghost couldn't sneak down them. Darn, was he
going for some hidden booze? I lay there for a few minutes
and listened, hoping he was just getting something to eat or a
glass of water. Then I heard the music, faintly, softly.

I crept out of bed and over to the top of the stairs. My dad
was playing "I'll Be Seeing You" by Frank Sinatra on the
phonograph. I eased myself down a couple of steps until I
could see him in the dark. He was slow dancing in the living
room. This wasn't the first time. It was my mom and dad's
song. He'd sing it to her out of the blue, when we drove
along the highway, at the supper table, anywhere, anytime.
He'd just break out singing and smiling at her. That's what he
put on her tombstone, "I'll Be Seeing You."

I could see him in the shadows from the streetlights. It
seemed as if he was really dancing with her, his arm around
her waist, the other hand holding hers up by his head. He
sang the words softly, a duet with Sinatra. I couldn't tell if he
was crying but I felt it coming in my throat and eyes. I'd
become good at holding it back, shutting it off. I swallowed
and shut my eyes hard. I turned to go to my room and leave
the two of them alone when I bumped into Stewy.

"What are you doing out of bed?" I whispered.

"Who is Daddy dancing with?" he whispered back.

"With Mom."

"Did Mommy come back?"

"No . . . she's not coming back."

"Not never?"

"Not never," I whispered and the horror of it hit me.

"Then who is Daddy dancing with?"

"With his broken heart."

"Do you have a broken heart, Donny?"

"Yeah . . . I do."

"Do we all have a broken heart?" Stewy said softly.

"No, yours hasn't been broken yet."

"How will I know if it's broken, Donny?"

"You'll know. C'mon, let's go to bed."

I stood quietly and took Stewy's hand. I had promised myself, knowing I was raising Stewy as much as Dad, that I wouldn't ever lie to him. It made a guy hurt to have to tell a little brother the truth.

When I had him tucked in, McCoy jumped on his bed and curled beside him. Stewy said, "I'm sorry your heart's broken, Donny."

I couldn't get any words out. Darn, my throat filled. I stuffed back tears. My glasses fogged up. I was a young man, a grownup, I wasn't supposed to cry. I didn't want to give Stewy a bad example. I was glad the room was dark.

As I lay in my bed, I held my breath. I could faintly hear my dad once in awhile, still singing, still dancing with the woman he loved who was never coming back. I wished McCoy was sleeping with me.

Chapter 7

The next week things were going swell. Dad was doing good, working all day, coming home for supper, helping with the kids. My hopes were high. Wednesday, in homeroom, Mitzi acted as though I'd just returned from a war. Criminy, I was trying to find the nerve to ask her to go to the football game Saturday night. But every time I opened my mouth to ask her I heard a little voice saying How are you going to get her there? I knew I had to talk Reggie into getting a date first. The bell rang.

"See you later, Donny," Mitzi said as she gathered her books.

"Yeah . . . see ya."

Then in Mr. Thorton's math class we just about busted a gut. Mr. Thorton is a good teacher and perfectly sane. But Jerry Douglas made him wonder. When the weather was nice, the teachers would have the gigantic windows open. Thorton had his class in room 118 on the north side of the building, facing the football stadium. Jerry got to class a minute early and sat at his desk in the first row, right next to the windows. The bell rang, kids settled down, and Mr. Thorton took attendance. He'd put a *P* next to your name if you were present, an *A* if you were absent, and a *T* if you were tardy.

Once attendance was taken, Thorton started in on the day's lesson. And almost always, he'd start by doing problems on the blackboard, which was on the opposite side of the room from the windows. With his back to the windows, the teacher chalked up the equations and explained as he went.

Jerry stepped out the window and edged along the narrow stone ledge over to room 119, which was empty the period we had math in 118. Everyone in the class was trying not to laugh and holding their breath for what was coming. Jerry waited about three minutes and then he came bustling through the door.

"Sorry I'm late, Mr. Thorton," he said as he hurried over and slid into his seat. "I couldn't get my locker open."

Mr. Thorton stood like the Statue of Liberty with a piece of chalk in his hand. He didn't move for a minute. Then he walked over to his desk and ran his finger down the attendance chart. He picked up a pencil and was probably about to mark the chart with a *T* when he found a *P* already there. He looked over at Jerry, who was settled at his desk with a sappy smile on his kisser. Gosh, we were all biting our tongues and nearly gagging. Jerry just sat there like he'd been hatched out of an egg.

Mr. Thorton gazed at the class with an expression that asked Am I losing my mind? His lips were moving but no sound came out, muttering to himself. I knew I was about to bust out laughing and I ducked behind Bill Swearengin who was six foot four and sat right in front of me. Mr. Thorton put down the pencil and walked back to the blackboard, as if he couldn't remember his name. We managed to act normal until the period was over and we were out in the hall. Then I heard Jerry telling some of his buddies that next time he was going to do it twice during the same class. I couldn't wait to see that.

Stewy was learning how to walk home from school by himself. He was home when I got there and Clark was doing the paper route. Dad had been working hard lately, I could tell. Even though I caught a whiff of beer on him a few times, I didn't think he'd been drinking much. I got supper started and left Irene to watch it. Then I ran down to the station to see how Dad was doing. He always wanted to stay open until six, to catch people coming home from work who didn't want to take the time to gas up in the morning.

Dad was under the hood of a '46 Dodge when I got there and I waited on a woman in a new Oldsmobile 88 like we used to have. She had me fill it up and it took almost ten gallons, a dollar sixty-three.

My dad saw that I was taking care of her and he waited in the station, flopped in his greasy swivel chair. He looked like he was wiped out, just dragging around. I didn't say anything because he didn't like talking about how he was feeling, like I was checking up on him or something. I thought I could smell beer.

"What brings you down here?" he said with exhaustion in his voice. "How about supper?"

"I put Irene on it. She'll have it ready on time. I thought you might want some help closing up."

He looked at me out of his kind, grease-smeared face and smiled.

"Donny, my boy, I think you're old enough to close up by yourself. I'll head home and you close her down."

"Really? You're not kidding?"

"Really, I'm not kiddin'."

"Oh, swell, Dad, I can do it. Just watch. I've seen you do it a million times."

Golly, I felt proud that he was trusting me. Closing the station had a lot to it. For a second I suspected he was up to something, that instead of going home he'd hit a favorite bar. But he was walking, he'd left the car at home, and I felt sure it was legitimate. He was giving me the responsibility.

He grabbed his jacket and cap and walked out to the sidewalk.

"We'll keep dinner warm for you," he said. Then he nodded and walked over Wilder. I called Irene.

"Dad's on his way. Walk down and meet him."

Then I turned to the closing. Gee whiz, I had to think. Turn off the outside lights, turn the big sign in the window from OPEN to CLOSED. Haul in the cans and bottles of oil stacked by the pumps. Roll the Atlas tire rack into the garage bay. Gad, I was sweating, working lickety-split, trying not to forget anything. I wanted to show Dad I could handle this grown-up responsibility.

When I hauled the last rack of oil cans into the garage, a

guy was standing in the office door. I hadn't seen him coming. Jeez, in a long, black overcoat and black hat he looked like he just came from a funeral or was on the way to his own. I stopped in my tracks.

"You need gas?" I said.

I looked for a car but there wasn't one.

"Frank Cunningham around?" He was tall and the poor guy only had one nostril. He looked like someone out of a Dick Tracy comic book.

"He's gone for the day. You need some work done on your car?"

"Will he be here tomorrow?"

"Yeah, seven in the morning."

I carried the oil cans to the stack and hoisted them on top. When I turned around, the guy was gone. I walked out to the pumps and looked both ways along Marshall, but the creep had just disappeared like a vampire.

Finally, when I had it all done, I surveyed the station and it looked ready for tomorrow. "It's sparkling, Mom," I said out loud. On the way home I looked back twice, the big STANDARD sign still visible even though the spots were turned off. I felt proud, it was one more thing I could do for my dad.

Thursday, when I got home from the paper route, I found the Friendly Visitor interviewing the three kids at the kitchen table. We'd had no warning, she just showed up. Makes a guy think of the Gestapo. I hadn't had a chance to coach Stewy and I was afraid he'd call her Miss Doomsday or give away the fact that he was going to two kindergartens. I pulled up a chair at the table and Stewy crawled into my lap. I could see that he was scared.

"Well, glad you could make it, Donald," she said sweetly, her voice like cheap perfume.

"I would make it if I knew anything about it," I said.

Her face made a guy think of cottage cheese.

"Well, I was just in the neighborhood and thought I'd get some paperwork done," she said.

McCoy didn't like her either but he didn't bark or growl. He just sat close to her chair and cut the cheese.

"So, Stewart has started school now, has he?" she said to me. I felt sorry for the chair she was smothering.

"Yeah, he's growing up," I said.

"And he's at the filling station in the afternoon?" she said. We glanced at each other.

"Only for two hours," I said, "or he's with our neighbor, Nana Riley."

"And how do you like school, Stewart?"

Stewy looked at her out of the corner of his eye with his head down. I shook him a little.

"It's fun. . . ."

"And what did you learn in school today?" she went on.

I held my breath while Miss Doomsday jotted in her note-book.

"I learned that an ant lives for nine years if you don't step on it," Stewy said.

"Nine years, imagine that."

"If you don't step on it," Stewy said.

"Yes, if we don't step on it."

Stewy was losing his fear of her. "And I have *two* teachers—"

"Irene, you're in seventh grade now?" Miss Doomsday said, missing Stewy's clue.

"Yes, at Longfellow," Reenie said.

I could feel Stewy was about to blurt out something and I gave his arm a squeeze.

"Tell me, children, how has your father been feeling lately?"

I cringed, afraid the cops had written a report on him last week or afraid that Stewy would spill the beans.

"He's been f-fine," Clark said, "not sick or an-anything."

"Does your father go out at night, come home late?" She looked into each of our faces with her beady eyes.

"No," Irene and I said in unison.

"Does he come home late for supper, or miss it altogether?"

"No . . . no, he's here every night to spend the evening with us," I said. "We listen to the radio and play games and he reads to Stewy, Bible stories like my mom used to."

"Yeah, and we play tiger hunt," Stewy said.

"Oh, I don't think I've heard of that game," Doomsday said.

"It's really fun," Reenie said. "We go and hide somewhere in the house and then Dad turns off all the lights and he comes looking for us."

"Yeah, and he growls like a tiger," Stewy said. "I get scared."

"Who makes your supper?" she said.

"He comes home right after work and usually cooks our supper," Reenie said. "We help. I can make Jell-O and oatmeal and macaroni and cheese and Spam and beans and hot dogs."

"Do you have to cook supper a lot?" she said to Irene.

"We all help," I cut in. "It's fun when we do it together."

"Who washes your clothes?" she said as she jotted in her notebook. I wanted to see what she was always jotting, as though she were giving our family a grade.

"We all do," I said. "Dad does a lot of it on Sunday. We take off our school clothes after school and put on our play clothes."

"I see here that your mother died in August of 1946," she said. "How did she die?"

I felt my stomach tighten. Irene and Clark glanced at me. The silence was sucking the breath out of me.

"She went to heaven," Stewy said.

"Oh . . . I'm so sorry," Doomsday said.

"Yeah, and she ain't coming back," Stewy said with authority.

"I'm sure that was very hard for all of you," Doomsday said. "You must miss your mother very much. Did your father drink when your mother was alive?"

"Never," I said. "He's a *good* father."

"Does your father ever punish you by hitting you . . . with a belt or with his hand?" she said.

"No, never," I said. "He spanked us a few times when we

were little kids, when we'd run in the street or do something dangerous like that. But it was for our own good."

She jotted in her notebook. When she looked up, she screamed and almost tipped over backwards in her chair. A squirrel had jumped onto the table in front of her.

"Judas Priest! Get away! Shoo! Get away!" she shouted as she waved her hands at the squirrel. She was petrified.

Clark stood up calmly and clapped his hands and said, "Out!"

The squirrel leaped off the table and scampered up the stairs.

"I left the window open," Clark said, shaking his head.

"You allow that beast in the house?" Miss Doomsday said, still flustered.

"He's tame," Clark said and sat down.

"Was that Dopey?" Irene said.

"Happy," Clark said.

Miss Doomsday looked baffled.

"Darn," Irene said, twisting a pigtail, disappointed that she hadn't recognized Happy.

"He's one of the seven dwarfs," Stewy said, "but Snow White won't come in the house."

Doomsday wiped her forehead and scribbled in her notebook. When she caught her breath, she tucked her papers in a briefcase and went tipping out to her car.

Clark and I started to fix supper and I figured squirrels would show up in Doomsday's report. I wanted to thank the little bugger. Happy had found a way to cut short a Ramsey County Welfare Board's interview and send the Friendly Visitor packing.

Chapter 8

Uncle Ellie-Ellie showed up and played with Stewy and poked around the kitchen as he often did at suppertime. He wasn't wearing his gas mask. He had one lazy eye, the left one. It would look at you for a bit and then go drifting up towards his forehead. All of us but Stewy learned to ignore it. Stewy would look up on the ceiling or into the sky to see what Uncle Ellie-Ellie was looking at. Sometimes Uncle Ellie-Ellie would help with the cooking and then go home to eat with his wife. Sometimes he'd forget and he'd sit down and eat with us. Sometimes he'd eat both places. He'd forget a lot.

He had a trunk full of souvenirs from the First World War. He'd show them to us about once a year when I was a kid. I'd act like I'd never seen them before. He had his helmet and his Springfield 1903 bolt-operated, magazine-fed, .30-caliber rifle. He had a bunch of bullets for the rifle and a bayonet that fit on the end. He had a German officer's helmet with a pointed spike on top, a potato masher—a German hand grenade that he'd let us throw in his backyard. It didn't have any powder in it. He had a Browning belt, a canteen, spats, three different sized shell casings and, of course, his gas mask. When I was a kid, I'd try all that stuff on. Now Clark and Stewy try it on.

Jeez, it was scary when he told us about the gas the Germans used. Chlorine gas. If you breathed it, your lungs would make too much fluid and you'd drown. It was horrible. Without a lake or river in sight, you'd drown.

He had a large, wood-framed plaque on his living room wall, enclosed in glass. It had a photo of him with two of his Army buddies in France. It had his brass U.S. Army pins, one of his rifle bullets, his division shoulder patch, the 77th, and his sergeant first class stripes. He'd get choked up when he looked at his two friends. They were both killed in France.

One Fourth of July we were bemoaning the fact that we didn't have any fireworks. They were outlawed in Minnesota. Uncle Ellie-Ellie must have heard us because he took the gun powder out of all his rifle bullets and made firecrackers for us. We had a wing-ding of a war in his backyard. He blew one empty bean can over the house that we never did find. Sometimes, only a week or two after I'd looked at all his war stuff, he'd ask me if I'd like to see his souvenirs. Sometimes I figured he was living back in those First World War days in his mind.

I couldn't wait for Dad to get home, to hear his praise for closing the station so well. I started to worry when he was late. I was wishing I'd gone down to check on him, when he came in the door. He was happy. I hoped the kids wouldn't smell it on him, and I was glad Miss Doomsday wasn't still hanging around. As usual he tried to get the oil and grease off his hands at the kitchen sink and he visited with Uncle Ellie-Ellie. When Uncle Ellie-Ellie went out the back door, Dad wanted to know what Miss Doomsday asked us. Everyone was chattering like chipmunks so I figured I'd wait to say anything.

When we were done eating and had heard all about Stewy's adventures at school and Irene's scraped knee at recess and Longfellow's upcoming football game with Ramsey, my dad pushed back his chair and used a toothpick.

"Donny," he said, "you did a fine job closing the station last night, a very fine job."

"Thanks, Dad."

"Only one suggestion I'd make." He paused and looked me in the eye. "Next time it would be a good idea if you'd lock the *front door.*"

Holy Moses, I'd forgotten to lock the *door!* Every robber and crook in the city could be roaming through the station all night, stealing everything but the concrete floor. I felt my face flush. Criminy, forgot to lock the door, the most important thing of all.

"Was anything stolen?" I dared to ask.

"Not a nut or bolt." He laughed. "At least you didn't leave the door *open*."

He was happy. There was no judgment or reprimand in his voice. Then, as I thought about it, I started laughing, then Stewy, until we were all roaring.

We'd made it through another day.

But not another night. McCoy settled in my bed, but he couldn't prevent the nightmare from finding me. In it Dad and the kids are running down a road through a woods and they're falling apart. Their arms and heads and shoulders fall off and I pick them up and try to put them back together. Even Dad is falling apart, his nose or his leg. I yell at them to stop, but they are running away from me as fast as they can run. I can't even catch up to Stewy. I pick up Dad's nose or Stewy's hand and try to catch them. McCoy is running with me and barking, but I can't keep them all together, and little by little they all fall apart and disappear and I'm running alone on the road through the woods.

I woke up covered in sweat, shouting for them to stop. I wondered if I had awakened any of my family. Were they fighting their own nightmares? In the shadows, McCoy looked at me as if he knew I was in trouble.

Every day I held my breath, trying to keep Miss Doomsday and Dad apart. If we could only get by until summer, I'd be out of school. I could take care of the house and kids for a few years, until they were grown up.

Dad came home on time Saturday night and Reggie and I went to the Murray football game. We searched through the sea of faces in the bleachers and spotted Mitzi with two girl-friends and surrounded by boys. I tried to watch the game, but I kept looking over my shoulder, working up the nerve to go sit by her. At halftime Mitzi and the girls walked around the track where the kids from both schools mingled and flirted or got into fist fights. Reggie and I followed them but stayed out of sight.

When the second half started, I climbed over kids down Mitzi's row and wormed my way in beside her.

"Hi," I said. "Great game, huh?"

"Hi, Donny, I wondered if you'd sit by me."

Geez, I'd wasted all that sweat and fussing and she was waiting for me. I waved Reggie up and he wedged in next to me and we had a swell time. I was so close to Mitzi I could smell something sweet. She had a white Angora scarf around her neck and white Angora ear muffs and she was so pretty it hurt. I wished Reggie had the car, and I didn't know what to do.

Central beat Murray 27 to 12 and we walked the girls over to the parking lot on Marshall.

"That was fun, Donny," Mitzi said and we stood there as if we'd all had brain surgery.

Out of the blue my mouth just started talking.

"Could I walk you home?" I said to Mitzi.

Immediately I wanted to dig a hole or run. *You lame brain, what if she lives down by the River Boulevard?*

"Yes, that would be nice, Donny. Jonna and Virginia are staying overnight with me."

Shucks! I had my foot stuck in my mouth. I'd be walking *three girls* home like a police dog. Then I looked at Reggie. He was trying not to laugh.

"Swell, *Reggie* and I will escort you safe and sound."

Reggie rolled his eyes and I knew he'd jump me the minute the girls were delivered to Mitzi's house.

"Where do you live?" I said, holding my breath.

"Not far. Over to Summit and then down a few blocks," Mitzi said.

We started off, the three girls in front with Reggie and me tagging along. Reggie actually got to talking with Jonna, and by the time we reached Summit, I was walking with Mitzi. We laughed and talked about the game and some of our crazy teachers. It was fun until Jonna mentioned that the Russians had built an atom bomb. A little cloud of gloom came over us and we talked about how scary that was. Then Virginia said she was still afraid of catching polio and the cloud of doom got bigger. By the time we got to Mitzi's house, a stone mansion with an iron fence around it, all hope for any sign of romance had been blasted.

"Thanks for walking us home, Donny, Reggie," Mitzi said.

We stood there, the five of us, and no one knew what to do. Finally, after long sweaty minutes, Reggie reached out and shook Jonna's hand.

"I'll see you in school," Reggie said.

That did it. I shook Mitzi's hand, then Virginia's.

"It was nice meeting you," I said.

Then with great relief, Reggie and I took off down the sidewalk. Someone opened the door for the girls, and when they were out of sight, Reggie got me in a hammerlock.

"Could I walk you home?" Reggie said in a mocking voice. "You putz, she could have lived in West Saint Paul."

We cut over and caught a streetcar on Grand.

Monday in homeroom I scraped up the nerve to ask Mitzi to go to the Homecoming Dance Friday night. We were playing Monroe, and I held my breath waiting for her answer.

"I would love to go with you, Donny. Thank you."

Holy cow! Reggie promised he'd get the car and he was going to ask Virginia. But I knew that wasn't the biggest problem. If everything else worked out, there still was Dad to worry about. I told him about the dance and he promised he'd be home by six-fifteen on Friday, that he'd start closing early.

I was going to the Homecoming Dance with Mitzi Fitzsimmons. I caught myself whistling in the halls at school.

Uncle Ellie-Ellie was helping Irene hang out the wash in the backyard when I got home from school Wednesday. Uncle

Ellie-Ellie had his gas mask on. I checked to make sure my blue shirt was hanging there. We all did ironing, but Irene was the best at it. She promised she'd iron my blue shirt and go over my dress pants. I hadn't outgrown any of my clothes in years. I got that blue shirt for my fifteenth birthday, I'd had those pants for four years. The only way I got new clothes was to wear something into the ground while all normal kids outgrow stuff. We have photos that are years apart and I'm always in the same clothes.

Every day I reminded Dad about my date and he assured me that he'd be home like clockwork. Wednesday I stopped at the nurse's office and had her measure me. No luck, four foot eleven.

"Do you smoke, Donny?" Nurse Armstrong said.

"No, never. My dad runs a gas station and he doesn't smoke. Says it isn't a good idea for a guy who's around gas fumes all day. He promised us kids a hundred dollar bill on our twenty-first birthday if we don't smoke till then."

"There's a theory going around that smoking will stunt your growth," she said, "but I don't think there's anything to it."

I polished my penny loafers until I could see my reflection in them and every time I saw Mitzi in school I could hardly believe she was going to the Homecoming Dance with *me*. I'd stop walking and get on tiptoe whenever we crossed paths. But I didn't want to be walking down the hall like a fairy or something. I figured my toes would ache from dancing on them all night, but it would be worth it. Donny Cunningham, the smallest boy in the senior class, was going to the Homecoming Dance with Mitzi Fitzsimmons. All the taller boys would be scratching their heads and wondering how I pulled that off.

Criminy, I'd be scratching my own head.

Chapter 9

The warm weather continued into late September and Friday, in Mr. Thorton's math class, the big windows were open wide. The bell rang and Mr. Thorton stepped out into the hall. I could hear some of the boys egging Jerry on. He was going out the window again.

Mr. Thorton walked back into the room and checked attendance at his desk. Then he asked if we had done the homework and he began putting the equations on the blackboard. Jerry slipped out the window and out of sight. I wanted to do that and I wished my desk was next to the windows. The teacher turned and we began doing problems at out desks, trying not to bust a gut. But the anticipation of Jerry coming through the door at any moment made it hard to concentrate. The minutes ticked off the clock above the blackboard but Jerry didn't show up.

"That wind is kicking up. Gary, would you close those windows?" Mr. Thorton said to Gary Wollan. Gary closed the first two.

"All of them?" Gary said.

"No, that's enough," the teacher said.

The window nearest the front, the one that Jerry went out, was shut. Gad, after nearly five minutes, Jerry hadn't come through the door. The class went on and kids were looking at each other with question-mark expressions. Then, after another few minutes, I could see Jerry, still out on the ledge, peeking into the classroom through the closed window. Mr. Thorton went over to the window, opened it, and leaned out.

"Would you like to join our class, Mr. Douglas?"

Jerry climbed back into the room like a whipped puppy. He'd been outfoxed. After Jerry checked the windows in 119 and settled at his desk in 118, Mr. Thorton had gone next door and shut and locked all the windows in 119. Jerry was stuck out on the ledge like a pigeon.

"You better spend some time in Mr. Kirschbach's seventh period, Jerry," Mr. Thorton said while making a note on his attendance chart, "but be careful. His classroom is on the second floor."

I could tell Jerry felt pretty dopey and Mr. Thorton had a look of satisfaction on his face, like he knew he wasn't cracking up after all.

Friday night I had my clothes all laid out. Irene had done a swell job ironing, even though she moaned a lot about doing it. I bribed her with five pieces of Dubble Bubble and a Heath bar. I helped with supper and then I took a bath. I put on a ton of deodorant and checked my face for any sign of pimples. I looked like an eighth grader. I couldn't even grow a pimple like most of my friends. I had to call Stewy three times to come and eat. He'd been sitting on the tire swing that hung from the big oak tree in our backyard, trying to coax Snow White to eat out of his hand.

We sat down at six o'clock, bacon and liver and fried potatoes. Stewy didn't like the liver so I opened a can of Spam. McCoy loved liver. We ate, yakking and laughing and listening for the front door.

"Is Mitzi pretty?" Irene said.

"Yeah, she's real pretty."

"How t-tall is she?" Clark said.

"She's a little shorter than me."

"Is s-she a midget?" Clark said.

"That's not nice," Irene said.

"Don't give me any of your guff, *little* brother," I said. "Don't let your height go to your head. I can still pound you with one hand tied behind me."

When we finished eating and the dishes were done and the floor swept, we watched for Dad. I called the station. No answer. I ran down there. Closed and dark. Doggone it, I knew I should've gone down and rode home with him.

I ran back, hoping I'd missed him if he drove up Marshall and then turned at Prior. There was no car in the drive.

"Maybe he'll be here in time," Irene said.

"Maybe he ga-gave someone a ride h-home 'cause he's fixing their car," Clark said.

It was true. Dad gave lots of people rides when they left their car to be greased or fixed.

"Maybe he got lost," Stewy said.

They all knew Dad was a drunk. But we didn't say it out loud, as if we couldn't stand to admit it or we thought Miss Doomsday would hear. I thought of the Coca-Cola bear.

The kids sprawled in the living room and listened to the radio while I got dressed. I called Reggie and told him to pick up Virginia first, to give me more time. The game started at seven and the dance followed in the school gym. I had my dress clothes on, Reggie honked at the curb, and still no sign of Dad. Reggie came to the front door.

"My dad's gone, he promised he'd be home in time, I hate to leave the kids alone," I said.

"They're old enough, Clark's in eighth grade, c'mon."

"Okay, I'm coming, I'll be right there."

I grabbed my good jacket and stopped in the living room.

"Okay, you guys, I'm leaving, no arguing, no fighting. Dad will be here any minute. Remember, if anything goes wrong, call Nana Riley. Clark's in charge. You mind him."

"I'll mind," Stewy said.

"You can have some ice cream before you go to bed," I said.

I was almost out the door when the phone rang. It was the ring of doom.

Don't answer it, don't answer it.

I picked it up. "Hello."

"Hello. Does a Frank Cunningham live there?"

"Yes . . ."

"Well, you'd better come and get him. He insists on driving and the man can barely stand up."

I couldn't breathe for a minute. What could I do?

"Where are you, where is Frank?" I said.

"The Mint Bar, over on University near Prior."

"Okay, don't let him drive. I'll be right there."

"Is Daddy okay?" Irene said.

I couldn't think. I had to call Mitzi. What would I say? I had a lump of dread in my stomach.

"Clark, run out and get Reggie in here PDQ," I said.

Clark barreled out the front door. I dialed Mitzi's number. I'd memorized it with the hope that I'd be calling it often.

"Hello," a woman's voice answered.

"Could I speak with Mitzi, this is Donny."

"Just a moment."

Reggie came in. "C'mon, Donny, we're going to miss the kickoff."

"Hello." Mitzi came on the line.

"Hi, Mitzi, it's Donny. I just got a call, my father's real sick, I have to go get him. If you want, Reggie and Virginia will pick you up and take you with them."

Reggie rolled his eyes.

"Oh, Donny, I'm so sorry about your father. I hope he'll be all right," Mitzi said.

"I'm sorry about our date. If my dad turns out to be better, maybe I can meet you at the dance?"

"Oh, are you sure Reggie won't mind?" Mitzi said.

"Oh, no, Reggie would *love* to have you along with them. And there are always a lot of stags at the dance in case I don't make it."

I was cutting my own throat.

"Well, okay, but I hope your father will be better and I'll see you at the dance."

I hung up. I slapped Reggie on the back.

"Go, go, don't be late. Pick up Mitzi and pay her way." I gave him two dollars.

"Are you coming later?" Reggie said.

"I will if I can, go on."

Reggie hustled out to his dad's Dodge and gunned away.

I got to the Mint Bar after running most of the eight blocks. I'd forgotten to take off my good clothes and I hoped my dad wouldn't puke all over me. I waited outside the bar for a minute to catch my breath. I'd worked up a good sweat and I felt pretty lousy for breaking my date with Mitzi. Shoot, I could see her with other guys, dancing in their arms, maybe falling in love. I hoped I could get Dad home and make it to the dance.

I pushed through the door into the dimly lit bar. People looked at me through the stinking cigarette smoke as if I'd just picked their pockets. A bald guy behind the bar held up his hand as if he were stopping traffic. His face made a guy think convict.

"Sorry, kid, no minors allowed in here."

I stood on tiptoes. I wanted to tell him I wasn't a miner but a carpenter.

"I'm looking for my father."

"Your father? Aren't we all," he said and a bunch of his cronies at the bar laughed.

"Yeah, someone called," I said.

"Called, you mean on the phone?"

I hated admitting I was his son. "Yeah."

"Oh, you're looking for Frank. Why didn't ya say so, he's in the back."

I walked past bar stools and booths and there, babbling in a booth with another man, sat good ol' Dad. I was about to rip him from wall to wall when I reminded myself why he was like this. I held back the anger flooding through my veins and settling in my fists.

"C'mon, Dad, I'll take you home."

"You his boy?" the stocky red-haired man said.

"Yeah, I'm his boy."

He handed me the keys to our car. "We took these away from him. He's in no shape to drive."

"Thanks."

My dad looked at me with bloodshot eyes. "We have to get home, Donny, big date tonight, we got to hurry home."

I helped him stand. He stank like a brewery.

"You drive him home," the guy said.

"I don't drive. We'll take a cab," I said.

The stocky man called, "Hey, Mike, call a cab."

On the way out I thanked the convict for not calling the cops. With Dad's arm over my shoulder like an injured football player, we shuffled out onto University in the glow of the neon sign. Some of the people in the bar shook their heads as we stumbled by.

"We got to hurry, Donny, big date tonight."

I had the cab drop us at the end of the alley. I had just enough money, a dollar twenty. I half carried Dad up the alley so our neighbors wouldn't see the cab at the house. Once I got him in the back door, I wrestled him upstairs and laid him on his bed. He'd thrown up on himself a while ago. It was dry and caked onto his shirt. I wrestled his stinking clothes off him. Like a family of raccoons the kids watched from the hallway. They didn't say much and then drifted back to the radio in the living room.

With his bathrobe on, my dad insisted on getting up. He staggered down the stairs and into the kitchen. With his hand on my shoulder he said, "What are we going to do, Donny, what are we going to do?"

I made coffee and persuaded him to drink some, black. He was more stirred up than usual, singing and warning me that I'd be late for the dance. He finally fell asleep on the living room sofa, listening to the radio with the kids.

"Are we going to be sent to a foster home now?" Stewy said.

"No, we'll be okay," I said. "Miss Doomsday won't find out about this. We're going to stay right here, together."

Irene and Clark glanced at each other as if I was as gullible as Stewy.

I looked at my watch. It was nine-fifty. I looked at my clothes. My blue shirt was smeared with my father's mess. I'd never get to the dance until after eleven. I took my shirt off and put it in the hamper. I tried not to think about pretty Mitzi Fitzsimmons dancing in another boy's arms, but it was no use. That desperate feeling I'd had before flooded over me, hollow and black inside, a stone in the chest, hard to breathe. I was ten and I knew I had missed a once-in-a-life-time chance. Only that time it was with a fish, the biggest, most beautiful trout I'd ever seen.

Chapter 10

It's funny, but I hear my boyhood sometimes. It comes to me out of darkness on puppy dog paws and the taste of jaw-breakers. It tiptoes out of quiet moments in knotted high top tennis shoes and corduroy knickers. It wings on the call of a crow or the smell of pine, sunlight reflecting off a lake. It won't lie down; it won't let me forget.

I hear my boyhood sometimes like a chum calling me to come out and play. It tells me to remember, to speak of moments that flew away, that are flying now out towards the stars, ripples across an unending sea. My boyhood tells me to remember those things, those times, to bring them back to earth. Say them out loud or write the words on paper, keep them from being lost out beyond the sun. But sometimes I don't want to remember, I don't want to write them down, I want to forget.

My boyhood won't relent. It paces somewhere behind my heartbeats; it won't go away. It is unfinished. Remember, it tells me, *remember.* Write it down. It will happen again in the hearts of those who read. No one warned me how swiftly it would fly away. My boyhood comes to me and warns me, tells me it will be gone forever, as though it never happened.

I hear my boyhood sometimes.

It tells me about the first time I pushed the willow brush aside and found the pool. Water tumbled over a rock ledge, fell six or seven feet into a deep pool, and sang its secret song. I shivered. I could feel a great trout dwelling there and I hoped no other fisherman had ever stumbled into that hidden place.

I was ten that first August my father took us to the north shore of Lake Superior, three years before Buzzy and I freed the Coca-Cola bear. We had the same rustic cabin each summer and the first night, before my mother came prepared with

mousetraps, was a circus and a zoo. When we put out the
kerosene lamps, happy little mice played tag and hide-and-seek
and held a track meet. We could hear them running in every
direction. My mom slept in the car. Twice I felt one run across
my chest and I wondered what went on while I was asleep.

Our first summer on the North Shore the world was at war,
1942, though it seemed far away from a boy's life in St. Paul.
It invaded my life over the radio, from the front pages of the
newspaper, in newsreels at the movies, and through the con-
versations of my parents. I remember the first question each
morning would be How is the war going? Are we beating the
dirty Germans and those sneaky Japs?

Gasoline was rationed, I could understand that, and I often
thought how wonderful it would be if we were up on the
North Shore and ran out of coupons. We'd have to stay for
awhile. My dad had a 'B' sticker on the windshield of our
1939 DeSoto and that wasn't bad. It meant he got a larger
ration of gas because, being a gas station owner and
mechanic, he made his living with his car.

That warm August day I discovered the pool, I fished a
small creek called the Onion River. It tumbled out of the forest and down the rocky outcrops into Lake Superior. Alone, I
had fished my way up the river most of the day and had my
pockets stuffed with brook trout. When I'd catch one, I'd
wrap it in grass and stuff it in one of my pockets. To fish the
Onion River you had to climb over bedrock, bushwhack
through underbrush, and fight off headhunting mosquitoes.
The river hurtled downhill in leaps and cascading waterfalls,
slowing at times in quiet pools.

I was worn out and about to turn around. I shook the
Prince Albert tobacco can and saw that I had one more
worm. Ahead, the river disappeared into thick brush. I figured I'd use the last worm and then head back to the cabin.
Bringing home dinner, like a pioneer boy, made me happy.
Mom and Dad loved fresh-caught trout and they'd cheer
when they saw me coming.

If he noticed it, any respectable fisherman with fly rod and creel would pass up the Onion River, overgrown as it was with thick brush. It constantly forced me to duck and crawl under, through, or around to reach open water. The fact that it flowed under the only road it crossed through a crummy culvert, without so much as a signpost to show that it was there, may explain why I usually returned with my pockets bulging with small trout and my heart bulging with happiness. I loved that place.

In a crouch I followed the water into the underbrush and tried to keep my short willow pole out of trouble. Fishing the Onion, I often spent half of my time untangling my line from brush that reached out and snagged it. When I worked my way through, I discovered the pool surrounded by tangled undergrowth and pine trees. I felt my heart thumping with anticipation.

The tear-shaped pool was about eighteen feet long and maybe ten or twelve feet across. I could tell that it was really deep below the ledge. At the lower end, where I crouched, the pool tapered towards me and became shallow. I could see the bedrock where the water ran thinly over the lip. The hairs on the back of my neck rose as I imagined the lunker that hid there.

I crept back the way I'd come and planned to let my worm float to the fish from upstream. I bushwhacked through the brush and arrived at the head of the pool with my chest heaving. I shook that last worm out of the tobacco can and carefully baited my hook, leaving a portion of the worm's tail hanging free to wiggle deliciously in the trout's hungry face. Gently I flicked the worm into the turbulence of the falling water. With the line following slackly, the worm drifted slowly into the clear iron-colored water and disappeared. I held my breath.

Suddenly the line straightened, my pole bent to the water, trembling. Holy cow, I had him on! There wasn't much room to play him, let alone stand. The line zigzagged through the water like Zorro's sword. My best hope was the far end of the pool, but I had no idea how I'd get there with a whale in tow. I tried to keep him from wheedling any slack as I stepped into the water and slid my feet sideways along a narrow shelf just above the deep. While ducking overhanging branches, I tried to keep my balance and play the fish.

Then I caught a glimpse of him and thought I was seeing things. Holy cow! he scared the sap out of me. I'd never fought a fish his size. Every fisherman knows the dread you feel when you've seen the fish you've hooked, a beauty, and it's running strong at the end of your line, the outcome still undecided. The dread of losing it takes your breath away. In your mind you're already describing the huge fish to your friends and family, afraid you'll never bring it to land. The dread gripped me as I inched my way to the outlet of the pool.

The trout tugged with less force, content to hold his ground, turned upstream and away from me. I decided to risk it all immediately, before some unforeseen disaster struck. Slowly I inched the fish up the smooth-worn bedrock at the end of the pool until he was dry-docked; his flaming gills fanning to hold onto his evaporating life. It was a trout. But his skin glowed a shimmering gold and his fins were slightly tinged in red. I'd never seen a trout like it before. Not only the largest trout I had ever caught, it was the largest trout I'd ever seen, except maybe those rare specimens stuffed and mounted on some bait store or restaurant wall. My pockets were stuffed with six- or eight-inch trout at best, fingerlings by comparison to that beauty. He had to go sixteen inches at least and weighed close to two pounds.

Shaking with excitement, I knelt on the slippery rock. When I slipped my fingers into his gills to have him in hand, he flip-flopped, taking me by surprise. The hook flew from his lip and my heart leaped from my mouth to join the worm-less hook in midair. I grabbed for the thrashing trout, had his slippery body in my ten-year-old hands, and came up holding fisherman's dread and fish slime.

I caught a reflection off the escape artist's shimmering side as he darted for his bottomless world. Instantly that wondrous place was as it had always been, as though the battle had never happened: The water cascaded into the pool from above, drifted idly to the far end, and poured smoothly over the rock lip. I blinked, listened, unsure that it had ever happened. I rubbed my fingers together and felt the slithery evidence. When I examined my hands, I expected them to be golden.

Time to head back to the cabin, I hesitated at the edge of the pool and listened to its quiet sounds. I imagined, as hidden and camouflaged as it was, that no one else had ever found it. Even at ten, I felt a strange peace there that was like nowhere else, a remoteness, a loneliness that I couldn't explain. I shivered as if I were cold.

"How many fish, Donny?" my dad asked from the porch of our cabin. Waves crashed on the rocks along the craggy shore, driven by a steady wind out of the southwest. Clark and Irene came running to see the fish. I began emptying my pockets onto the grass with no idea how many I had taken.

"Gosh, these are nothing compared to the one I almost caught. You should have seen it, Dad, he was gold!"

My dad came off the porch and examined the eight trout I uncurled from my britches. "Well, these are the best eating," he said.

"His fins were kinda red. I'll know if I catch him again."

"He'll be bigger next time, too," my dad said.

The fish would be safe for another year. We were returning to Saint Paul in the morning, vacation over, school starting.

"Helen, Donny has a mess of trout for supper," my dad said as we carried the fish into the cabin's tiny kitchen.

"Oh, wonderful. That's my boy," she said.

"Darn, I lost a big one, Mom, bigger than all these put together and it was gold."

"Golden," my mother said.

"Yeah, golden."

Irene wanted to play with the dead fish. "A goldfish in the river?" she said.

"Not a goldfish, ninny, they're orange."

"No they're not," she said, "they're gold."

"Well, Donald, it's just as well you left it in the river if it's that big," my mother said. "He's probably the daddy of all these."

She took the mess of trout to the shallow porcelain sink. "He sounds like a splendid fish."

"He is," I said, thinking about that word. "He is splendid."

"Can I go fishing with you?" Clark said.

"Maybe next year," I said and I worked the hand pump to wash water over the trout.

But I remembered that desperate feeling then, thinking I'd missed my once-in-a-lifetime chance to catch that trout. Lying awake, unable to find any comfort, reliving how I lost him in my mind. It was the same ache in the chest I had now. My once-in-a-lifetime chance with Mitzi Fitzsimmons, missed, lost.

From that day on, I called that golden trout "Splendid." Whenever I thought of the North Shore and the Onion River, I thought of that pool, Splendid's pool, and I would count the days until we would come back.

As I lay in bed and traced the shadows on my bedroom ceiling, I could remember that night on the North Shore in that little cabin. I could hear my mother's voice as she happily washed the trout and sang, "Mairzy Doats."

I didn't want to remember more. I knew my boyhood was over.

Chapter 11

Saturday I went to work at the drugstore. My dad was remorseful as always and almost broke down telling me how sorry he was for making me miss my date. I felt ashamed to have ruined Mitzi's first and only high school homecoming dance. Thank goodness it was a weekend. I knew I wouldn't be able to face her on Monday.

A funeral procession came down Marshall, the long, black hearse out front, a string of cars with their lights on. I hated funerals. I cut through a yard and came out in the alley. I was safe. I'd never met a funeral procession coming up an alley.

The store was busy and for the bicarbonate and aspirin that went out, I'd guess my dad wasn't the only one with a hangover. I was really dragging. I didn't get much sleep worrying about Mitzi. And I really worried about Dad. I had to admit he was getting worse. Miss Doomsday was bound to catch him again and the Ramsey County Welfare Board would relocate the kids like scattered sheep.

Another thing nagging me was that Dad didn't have money anymore as he should have, cash for everyday household things. He had a good business, a lot of people who brought their cars to him. Many told me they wouldn't think of taking their car anywhere else. And with gas rationing over, we pumped a lot of gas. Where was the money going? We kept putting Mr. Finley off for our grocery bill. I started giving Clark and Irene their fifty cents allowance every Monday and telling them it was from Dad. I gave Stewy his nickel so he could buy penny candy at the corner store. We started getting lots of letters from the First National Bank. Ben, our mailman, brought them regularly. My dad said they were nothing but I opened one and it said we were behind on our house payments, three months behind.

I knew drinking could soak up a lot of money, but it

seemed it was something more. I knew Dad wasn't good about collecting money owed him, but at least he'd learned not to do any more work on a car until the owner was paid up. I tried to work as much as I could to help out with the money.

I couldn't wait to talk to Reggie and yet I dreaded it. I knew he'd show up at the drugstore Saturday afternoon when I was working. He loved the green rivers I made him in the big soda glasses. When he got to the bottom with his straw, it sounded like you'd pulled the plug on a sink full of soapy dishwater.

"Hi, Donny, working hard?" Reggie said as he climbed up on a stool at the soda fountain.

"I'm bushed," I said and held my breath.

"How about a green river?"

I'd already started to make it. Mr. Carpenter was working the front cash register and things were slow. I slid the green river over to Reggie and waited. He pushed a nickel across the black and white marble countertop and sucked on the straw. When he finished half the green river, he came up for air.

"How's your dad?"

"He's fine. How did your date go?"

"It was something to behold. See, sometimes I didn't know if I should fight or run," Reggie said.

"Criminy, what do you mean?"

"Virginia and I picked up Mitzi and went to the game, see. We sat with a lot of other couples, but guys shoved in around us. Some of them thought Mitzi was *my date* so they started flirting with Virginia. Jeez, I was fighting on two fronts. And then, worst of all, we ended up tying Monroe."

"I know, I saw the papers this morning. What happened at the dance?"

"Well, see, the funny thing happened when we were hanging up our coats and finding a place to sit in the gym. Virginia whispers to me to be sure and dance with Mitzi so she doesn't feel like one left shoe. Holly smoke! When the boys found out Mitzi didn't have a date, see, it was like flies on a dead skunk. I never got the chance."

"Did she say anything?"

"She said she hoped your dad would be all right. And I noticed her glancing over at the door while she was dancing. When it got too late to expect you, she looked kinda down."

"Well, thanks for taking her for me. At least she got to be there."

"Yeah, and the gym looked swell with lots of red and black crepe paper and everything. The place was jammed. There were even some college kids and some older people, see, alumni, I guess."

Two girls ordered chocolate malts and I whipped them up. The malt glass with whipped cream and a cherry on top and the malt can still half full. I moved back to Reggie.

"I'll have another green river," he said.

Reggie had neighbors who paid him to mow their lawns, rake their leaves, put up their storm windows, shovel their walks, so he could work whenever he wanted. He pushed another nickel at me when I gave him the green river.

"Was Mitzi really mad at me?" I said.

"Gosh no, see, she felt bad for you, missing out on all the fun."

"Really?"

"Really. She said that four guys had asked her if she wanted a ride home."

"I didn't dare call her today. I suppose I should. How do you like Virginia?"

"She's a neat girl, but. . . ."

"But, I know, I know, she doesn't measure up to your Juliet, whoever she is."

Reggie nodded and then sucked his green river dry, making the girls two stools from him stare. A grumpy-looking old guy at the end of the counter was ordering cherry phosphates like the world would come to an end before sundown.

On the way home I stopped at the church and gave my confession. *"Bless me, Father, for I have sinned. It's been a week since my last confession."*

My dad came home from work on time and apologized again for ruining my date. He was remorseful as always and said he'd run the ship with the kids until bedtime. When I left, he was fox-trotting with Irene to Glenn Miller's "Begin the Beguine."

I rode my bike over to Highland Bowling Center and set pins for three hours. My mind wasn't on the work and I just about got clobbered more than once. I figured my hopes for Mitzi were a gutter ball; I'd never be able to ask her out again, especially with all the tall boys interested in her.

When I was done around ten o'clock, I came out of the bowling center and saw Doug Smith, a friend from school. He stood around gassing with Peewee Meier and Bill Hann and Steve Holland.

"Hey, Donny, what are you doin'?" Doug called.

The others looked over at me and smiled.

"Donny'll do it," Peewee said.

I walked over, knowing they were up to something.

"You want to have some real fun?" Bill said and I had the feeling I ought to head for home. But these were swell kids, not juvenile delinquents or anything, popular guys at Central.

"Sure," I said. "What are we going to do?"

"Just follow us," Steve said and he laughed.

I hoped I wasn't going to be the guinea pig for one of their pranks, like snipe hunting. With Steve Holland you could never be sure. But for the time being, I was one of them, and that felt good.

We hiked across Cleveland and wove through the Highland Village apartment buildings, heading towards the river. At the back side of the apartments we came to a high wire fence, property of the Ford plant. Peewee had a pair of leather gloves, and he pulled himself up first. Strands of barbed wire ran along the top and Peewee used the gloves to hold onto them without getting cut. When he hit the ground on the other side, he tossed the gloves over to Bill. I could see a big NO TRESSPASSING sign down a ways on the fence and I wondered what I was getting into. But I knew these guys and I knew they wouldn't steal anything or bust up something just for the fun of it.

I got over the fence with no problem and realized we were standing on a road.

"C'mon," Doug said and we ran down the road towards Ford Parkway. Then the road curved and I could see from the faint light of the village that there were hundreds of new Fords parked perpendicular to the roadway. The boys each ran to a car and lifted the hood.

"Can you hot-wire a car?" Doug said.

"Sure, my dad showed me how a long time ago."

"Well, pick out a car and follow us," Doug said as he got a blue Ford coupe started, slammed the hood, and jumped into the driver's seat.

"Are you *stealing cars?*" I said.

"No, no . . . just driving them around a little. C'mon."

"I don't drive!" I shouted. "I don't drive, I don't know how!"

"You don't *drive?*" Doug said as he slammed his door and rolled down the window. He hesitated, revving the engine. "Okay, okay, jump in with me. We were hoping to have five."

I hopped in and Doug pulled onto a huge oval track that must have been at least a mile around.

"What is this, a race track?" I said.

"Yeah, kind of, they used it to test the personnel carriers they built during the war."

I could make out three cars ahead of us in the faint light from the plant. In a few seconds, Doug had the Ford going fifty while we circled the track. He could really work that clutch. In the shadows, I wondered how he could see well enough to stay on the track. When we caught up, the other three cars were lined up, windows down. Doug pulled up beside Steve. They revved their engines and started counting.

"Five! Four! Three! Two! One!"

The four new Fords jumped ahead like race horses. Wheels screeched, rubber burned, cars fishtailed, and we were off around the track. I was scared stiff. I wanted Doug to let me out but I didn't dare say anything. Sometimes the cars were so close I thought they'd touch. On the banked curves we didn't slow down and Doug's shoulder was pressing against mine and mine against the passenger door. It felt as though we were tipping, running on only two wheels. I was sure we'd roll. I could feel the back wheels of our car sliding sideways in the curves.

The boys were shouting at each other as they passed and I was just shouting. "We're gonna die! We're gonna die!"

In that moment I thought how strange it would be if I died in a car accident. Steve cut in front of us in a four-door sedan and then Bill caught up to us on the inside in a two door. Doug shoved it into second when we were going forty-five and I thought the transmission would drop out. He laughed, loudly, enjoying life, and I started laughing with him. Doug held Bill off but couldn't catch Steve. A drag race with your father's car was one thing. But this, with brand new Fords and brand new V8 engines, was a kid's dream come true.

Peewee won the first race and Bill won two. Doug and I would have won the fourth if the plant guards and St. Paul cops hadn't been waiting for us on that lap. They blocked the track with their squad cars and grabbed the boys when they tried to run. A guard opened Doug's door and grabbed him by the arm and pulled him out. But I was so short, the guard didn't see me. In the confusion, I opened my door quietly and crawled behind the Ford coupe that I thought would be my coffin. Glad to be back on the ground, I crawled between the parked cars and stood up, ready to go over the fence.

"No, not here," Steve whispered. "C'mon."

I followed him along the fence until we were far to the south end of the plant property. We went over the corner fence faster than we'd come and without Peewee's gloves. I ripped my pants on the barbs and the first thing that popped into my head was What will I tell my mother?

"Take off," Steve said, and he slapped me on the back.

Back at the bowling alley I climbed on my bike and headed for home. It was almost midnight. When I came in the front door, everyone was asleep and things looked normal. I crept in my dad's room and bent low, sniffing his breath. I could smell beer. But he was home, safe. In one hand, lying close to his face, I could see the lock of my mother's hair he held tightly. Tied with a blue ribbon, he always kept it on his pillow.

When I lay awake, I couldn't help laughing at what those crazy guys had been doing. Doug said they'd driven the Fords three times. The first time they only dared drive one car. But I thought how disastrous it would have been if the police caught me, out driving stolen new Fords at eleven o'clock. It would be enough for Miss Doomsday to prove Dad was an unfit parent, that we had a troubled family. Darn it, I had to be more careful. It was already tough enough staying one step ahead of Doomsday.

Monday, Peewee and Bill and Doug had to go to juvenile court with their *parents,* as close to certain death as the boys could come. The Ford Company must have been lenient because the judge just warned the boys that if they ever showed up in his court again he'd throw the book at them. Then he turned them over to the supervision of their parents. They were good guys. They never ratted on Steve or me, even though the cops knew darn well one driver had gotten away.

Monday, when I climbed the front hall stairs to the second floor, I felt like I was about to be tested on a book I hadn't read, on a book I'd never heard of. How do you tell the girl you're trying to impress that your father is a drunk, that he has to be carried home like a baby who wet his pants and puked on himself? I hoped Mitzi would turn up absent. I held my breath and walked in. All the desks in 210 had covered typewriters on them and we could sit wherever we wanted for the ten-minute homeroom period. I couldn't help but see Mitzi. She was so pretty in the morning, in a blue sweater with a blue ribbon in her hair.

I slunk to a desk back by the windows, hoping she wouldn't notice, but she came bouncing over and sat beside me.

"How's your dad? Is he going to be all right?"

She was as bright and kind and warm as a puppy. I forgot everything I'd been practicing to say all day Sunday and on the way to school. The P.A. belched announcements.

"He's fine," I whispered, "all over whatever it was. I'm sorry—"

"I'm so glad. I thought of all the terrible things that could have been wrong with him."

"Yeah, well, he threw up a lot and had a splitting headache and I think a high fever."

"I even thought of polio," she said. "But it seems only us kids can get that."

"Yeah, when I did my route this morning I saw in the paper another kid in Minneapolis got it. He's sixteen," I said, steering away from the subject of my dad.

"Do you have a paper route?"

"Yeah, me and my brother."

"You must get up awfully early."

"Yeah, around six."

"Does your mother wake you?" she said.

I didn't know what to say. Most kids at school didn't know about my mother and I liked it that way. She died when we were still in grade school. Kids didn't talk about parents much. I guess everyone figured we all had a mom and dad like a bike and dog. What could I say?

"My mother died," I whispered, "four years ago."

"Oh, I'm sorry. That's why you had to take care of your father?"

"Yeah, that's why."

"Do you miss your mother?"

I wanted to change the subject fast.

"Yeah, but listen, I'm sorry I missed the dance."

"Oh, I'm sorry you did, too, but I met lots of nice boys. It was as if they knew you couldn't make it and they danced with me to make up for it. You must have lots of friends."

Yeah, all those nice boys doing me a favor and forcing themselves to dance with Mitzi Fitzsimmons. Great!

The bell rang for first period and we grabbed our books and headed out the door.

"See you later, Donny," she said with a little wave.

"Yeah, see you later."

She scrambled down the front stairs, out of sight. I felt as if I'd waved good-bye to a girl who left on a train that would never come back.

Chapter 12

One summer my mother and I rode the streetcar from downtown with the window wide open and the wind blowing in my face. Out of the blue my mother said to me, "Donald, your whole life is an adventure, every single day. Don't miss one minute of it." I remember I didn't understand what she meant. But riding the streetcar with my mother, with the big wide world going by, seemed adventure enough for me. I think I was ten.

For a week Dad had toed the line pretty well, though he always had the perfume of beer on him. I never saw him drink. I didn't know where he kept it. When I found it, I poured it out. But all week he was happy, with the stink of alcohol on him like aftershave.

We had a game with Mechanic Arts on Thursday night and there was a dance, the Columbus Day Cruise, on Friday. I'd been trying to build enough confidence to ask Mitzi to the dance, especially with Dad doing better. But homecoming left me gun-shy and Thursday came too fast. I knew I'd put it off too long, that she probably had a date by then and it would be too painful to have her turn me down.

Thursday night Clark and Irene and I were making supper, expecting Dad at any minute. What we got was a Chinese fire drill.

"Clark's in love with Marcia Lane," Irene said.

"Not so."

"I saw you chasing her around at school," Reenie said. "You're sweet on her."

"Not so, n-not so, not so," he said and took a swipe at her with a hot pad.

"Okay, quit horsing around," I said.

"Clark's got a girlfriend," Stewy said and clapped his hands.

"He has lots of girlfriends," Reenie said, "he's always flirting with someone."

The doorbell rang. I went, with the kids right behind me, and opened the door. A man with graying hair and a nose like a clown smiled at me. I figured he was an encyclopedia salesman.

"Is your father home?"

"No . . . not yet. We expect him any minute," I said as Stewy pushed his way to the front.

"Well, I was going by and wanted to say hello. Would you be sure and tell him that Doc stopped by."

"Doc?" I said.

"Yes, Doc. Tell him I'll catch him another time."

The man turned and walked back to his car, a tan 1948 Pontiac. We watched for a minute and then hustled back to get the dinner made. It wasn't a minute later when the doorbell rang again. I went to the door with Stewy. A big muscle-bound man in a black turtleneck sweater and black trousers stood there, about six foot two, bald as an egg. He could have been the wrestling coach from the university or a bouncer on Rice Street.

"Is your dad home?" His voice sounded as if he had gravel in his throat.

"No . . . not yet. Should be here soon," I said.

"Are you a doctor?" Stewy said.

"Well, tell him he owes us money." The man growled the words. I figured he hadn't smiled since first grade.

"Owes *who* money?" I said, "Benson's Auto Parts, the Standard Oil Company . . . ?"

"Just tell him, kid. He knows WHO."

The guy looked at me as if I'd stolen his girlfriend.

"You sure he ain't here?"

"His car is gone, see," I pointed at the driveway. He turned quickly and marched off to a black Chevy across the street and drove away. The Chevy needed a ring job.

I closed the door and went back to the kitchen with Stewy.

I told the kids it was a guy about Dad's work. Then the door-bell rang.

This time I recognized the caller. The porch floorboards creaked under the Friendly Visitor. Shoot, she must work twenty-four hours a day. I thought welfare workers went off duty at five. She came on like gangbusters and it seemed to be her mission to nail Dad. McCoy stood beside me but he wasn't wagging his tail.

"Hello, Donny, I stopped at the station but it was closed. Is your dad home?"

Gad, she had him. He must be drinking. I had to think fast.

"Ah, yeah, he's home . . . but he's busy . . . ah, he's taking a bath, came home pretty grimy."

"He is?" Stewy said.

"Oh . . . well, I just want to ask him a couple of questions."

Like an avalanche, she moved into the house without per-mission, outweighing me by a hundred and fifty pounds. I hated pushy people.

"How long will he be?" she said.

Stewy ran upstairs.

"Hard to tell. He likes to soak in a hot tub after a day's work. Sometimes a good half hour. We don't like to interrupt his baths. I can give him a message, or I can tell him you're here if you have the time to wait."

"Humm . . . well, maybe I'll wait a spell."

She moved into the living room and spread out on the window bench. The bench was built along the wall below the windowsills. It had padded cushions for sitting and the mid-dle section opened up like a toilet seat. We kept games and books and all kinds of stuff in there. It was about ten feet long and once when we were playing hide-and-seek, my mother hid in there. It was as if Doomsday knew the window bench was the only furniture sturdy enough to hold her.

She had her notebook. "I didn't see your father's car."

"Oh, he probably left it in the station. I think he's fixing something on it. He walks to work most of the time."

"Are all the children home?"

"Yep, we're making supper. Dad was in charge until his bath water was ready," I said. "Excuse me for a minute."

I caught Stewy coming down the stairs and put my hand over his mouth. I hurried into the kitchen.

"Dad's not taking a bath," Stewy said.

"I know, we have to fool Miss Doomsday."

I whispered to Clark. "Can you get a squirrel in here?"

"No, it's dark, they're bedded down in the trees."

I pulled Reenie and Clark together and whispered.

"I told Doomsday Dad's taking a bath. You two sneak out the back door. Clark, go down to Prior and watch for him. Irene, go up to Howell. When you see him, flag him down. Tell him Miss Doomsday is here, that he'll have to park in the alley and sneak in the back door. Hurry, go, go."

They crept out the back and away into the darkness. I turned down everything on the stove. I took Stewy by the hand and hurried into the living room.

"I put dinner on hold. It'll be okay for a *few* minutes," I said. "I'll go up and see how Dad's coming."

I took Stewy with me. McCoy seemed to know something was up. He sat at the bottom of the stairs, staring into the living room at Doomsday. In the bathroom I put in the plug and ran the water. I told Stewy to splash the water once in awhile and I left the door to the bathroom open. Then I hustled back down to the living room where Doomsday was going over her notes.

"He's scrubbing up," I said. "I told him you were here. He said he'd only be another *fifteen* or *twenty* minutes."

Miss Doomsday narrowed her eyes above her pouchy cheeks. Made a guy think of gun slots on an armored car. Did she know I was pulling the wool over her eyes? She looked at her watch.

"I'll wait," she said with irritation in her voice and she went back to thumbing through her notebook.

"I better look after dinner," I said and crossed into the

kitchen. There, to my thankful relief, came Irene with Dad, tiptoeing in the back door. He was filthy with grease and grime and I could smell his Hamm's aftershave.

"Darn, we have to get him upstairs," I whispered to Dad as I held my finger over my lips.

"How are we going to do that?" Reenie said. "She's in the living room."

"Reenie, go turn the lights on in Doomsday's car," I whispered. "I'll get her to the front door and, Dad, you sneak up the stairs. Be ready."

Dad smiled, he was happy. He acted as though we were playing one of our family games. I went back into the living room and gave Reenie time to get to Doomsday's car.

"Miss Boomray," I said as I looked out a living room window. "I think you left your lights on."

I started for the front door. She heaved herself off the window bench and tagged along like a puppy dog. I opened the front door and went out onto the porch.

"There, isn't that your car?" I said.

She came out onto the porch and squinted over her little wire-rimmed glasses. I glanced back over her shoulder and there, not ten feet away, Dad snuck up the stairs, Santa tiptoeing on Christmas Eve. When he was about to step on the stairs that squeak the loudest, I raised my voice.

"Wear down your battery fast."

"Humph," she said, "I'd swear I turned them off."

I didn't offer to turn them off for her and let her waddle over and do it. Back in the house, she trundled over to the window bench.

"How much longer will it be?" she said with a sigh.

"I'll be down in a minute," my dad called down the stairs.

I knew he was washing like crazy, but what about his breath.

"I'll go see if I can hurry him," I said and I climbed the stairs.

Irene had him in fresh work clothes and a clean face and had even found some talcum powder, but his breath stank like a brewery. I found an envelope of Sen-Sen and poured about ten in his mouth. One knocks me out, and his breath turned to fire.

We were ready. I went down first.

"He's done, Miss Boomray, he'll be right down."

Clark slipped in the back door and caught on quickly. Dad walked down the stairs deliberately, smiling and smelling like a newborn baby.

"Sorry to keep you waiting, Miss Boomray, but I need a long bath after a hard day's work."

She pried herself off the window bench and moved up close to my dad. She studied him with one raised eyebrow as if she were picking out a new dress. They shook hands and I could almost see her nostrils going over him like our vacuum. Dad stood steady and pumped her hand.

"Sorry to keep you waiting."

Off in the dining room, Stewy marched around the table, calling in cadence,

"You're in the Army now,/You're not behind the plow,/
You'll never get rich,/You son of a bitch,/
You're in the Army now./"

"*Stewy!*" Irene said as she hurried into the dining room. "That's a *naughty* word. We don't talk like that in our family. If mother was here, she'd wash your mouth out with soap."

Stewy said, "What word?"

We stood there, frozen, glancing at Miss Doomsday. I didn't know what to say. Then Dad found his voice.

"Never heard him say that before," he said. "Would you like to stay for supper?"

"Oh . . . well . . . no thank you. I have to be on my way. Just stopped by to see how you all were doing."

Just stopped by to catch my dad drunk and tear up our family.

"You had some questions for me?" Dad said.

"Oh, nothing that can't wait. You folks are right in the middle of your supper."

She gathered up her notebook and waddled out the door. After we watched her drive away, we all blew a big sigh and turned on Stewy.

"Where'd you learn that rhyme, Stewy?" Dad said.

"I can't tell, I promised."

"Was it Uncle Ellie-Ellie?" I said.

"He made me promise not to tell."

We laughed with relief, free for the moment from the black cloud the Friendly Visitor hung over us. We'd saved the dinner and our family's life together, although our family swearing would surely appear in Doomsday's notebook. Right in the middle of the meal I remembered.

"Oh, Dad, two guys stopped to see you, I almost forgot."

"What did they want?" Dad said, buttering his mashed potatoes.

"The first guy just said to tell you he stopped to see you."

"He was a doctor," Stewy said.

"No, I don't think he was a doctor," I said. "He said Tell him Doc stopped to see him. He had a nose like a golf ball."

"Doc? I don't know anyone called Doc," my dad said.

"Doc is one of m-my squirrels," Clark said.

"The other guy said we owed them money. He was a sour musclebound guy. I asked him what we owed him for and he just said you'd know."

"That's strange. I don't know who either of them could be. Maybe they got the wrong house."

I looked at Dad's eyes and I figured he was telling the truth; he didn't know who the two men were.

I came down after doing some English composition that was due in the morning, two full pages, and found them curled up together. Dad in the big stuffed chair, Irene on one side of his lap, Stewy on the other, and Clark sprawled on the rug. They were listening to Dad read one of their favorite Bible stories, "David and Goliath." Dad acted out the Goliath part, hamming it up, growling and hissing, and the kids laughed at all the familiar spots. I wished Miss Doomsday could see them like that.

Irene raised her hand as if she were in school.

"What?" my dad said.

"Well, if in the beginning there wasn't anybody but God," Irene said, "how did He know He was God?"

We glanced at each other during a long silence, thinking like crazy. Finally my dad said, "That's a good question, Reenie. I don't know. There's lots of things we can't understand."

When I least expected it, Irene surprised me like that. She'd become a pretty sharp cookie. But when I tried to sleep that night, it wasn't Stewy's swear word that worried me. The brick in my stomach had me wondering how much Miss Doomsday picked up on Reenie's slip, "If Mother was here." It sounded as if Reenie were admitting we weren't getting a good upbringing without Mom.

If Mother was here, but she wasn't.

Chapter 13

The night of the Columbus Day Cruise, Reggie and I met at Carpenter's Drugstore. We didn't know what we'd do, but when I didn't have a date for the dance, Dad came home on time and sober. Cripes, I wanted to yell at him. Why didn't he tell me on Monday I could count on him for Friday! It made a guy crazy. I was feeling pretty much left out when I met Reggie.

Reggie had a surprise. He'd sent out of state for fireworks last summer. He still had one large rocket and he had in mind where he'd set it off. As Selby approaches Snelling from the west, it goes up a slight hill. Selby and Snelling is a busy intersection, even around seven o'clock on a Friday night. We walked up Selby.

"We can't shoot it off here, you nut," I said. "Too many cars and people."

"I figure with the slight rise, see, it might take off," Reggie said.

"It'll just go flopping all over like a landed fish, for cryin' out loud."

"Not if I lay it in the streetcar track."

"You're going to shoot it up the *track?*"

"It's perfect. People seeing this rocket coming at 'em will be jumping around and running for dear life."

"Could it hurt someone?" I said.

"Nah . . . just scare the heebie jeebies out of them."

I was thinking this wasn't such a good idea. We stopped at Fry, the cross street one block down from Snelling. We waited until no streetcars rolled along Selby and only a few cars. Reggie laid the rocket in the streetcar track.

"You ready?" he said with a big grin on his face.

"Yeah." I was scared spitless.

Reggie had the first two matches blow out on him. The

third one lit the fuse. The fuse shot sparks as it worked its way to the base of the rocket. We backed away and I held my breath, ready to run to beat the band. The rocket lit, flame shot out the back, and it started up the track, slowly for a second. Then it roared away, straight as an arrow, flaming bright, headed for the intersection.

We were laughing and hooting when a car turned off Snelling and drove towards us. It came straight for a second or two and then it swerved across the tracks. The rocket must have glanced off a tire, because it ricocheted ninety degrees to the left and shot right in the open door of the Park Theater. Then, in a few seconds, people came swarming out of the movie like a cattle stampede, out onto the sidewalk and into the street. We stood there, frozen in our tracks. When we heard the fire trucks, we ran.

We ran all the way to Summit, almost killing Reggie, before we settled into a walk. Ready to duck into a yard or alley at any sign of the cops, we couldn't stop laughing. It was like a fox bombing into a chicken coop.

"How'd I know it would go sideways into the theater?" Reggie said.

"We're lucky it didn't kill someone," I said.

"Maybe it did."

"That's not funny. I gotta quit letting you talk me into doing dumb things."

I jumped him and got him into a half nelson.

I thought how bad it would be if Doomsday got word of me doing something crazy like that. I promised myself that was the last prank I'd pull, no matter who wanted me to.

We hiked over to the Highland Bowling Center and they talked me into setting pins for a while. I figured it would be a good alibi. Reggie wasn't quick enough to set pins. The manager said Reggie was too "chubby" when he meant "fat," but Reggie didn't give a hoot. He didn't want to set pins anyway.

He bowled a few lines while I set pins and we went to the

late show at the Highland Theater. We hiked home along Fairview. Everytime one of us brought up the rocket we started laughing. Then, he hinted that sometime that night we'd been near the house of the girl he loved. Big clue. We'd only covered half of the Midway and Highland Village. But I could tell he was feeling sad and I didn't know what to say. When we reached St. Clair, he waved and cut across the deserted street.

"See ya," he said.

"Yeah, see you in school."

I took off running. I ran most of the way home so I didn't have as much time to think about Mitzi, dancing in some taller guy's arms.

When I did the route in the morning, I thumbed through the paper. I found nothing about a rocket blasting its way into the Park Theater without a ticket.

The Minnesota Education Association gave us a four-day weekend. The teachers went to meetings and we had the last Thursday and Friday of October off. The sororities used that time every year to have their house parties. The Sokos and Debs decided to have theirs together at St. Croix Falls. They rented cabins along the river and played for three days.

I helped my dad at work Thursday, mainly pumping gas so he could keep working on repairs. I could fix flats and mount tires as fast as Dad, but I hated doing it. We always had some kind of Atlas tire sale going. I measured how much gas we had and the underground tank echoed on empty. Dad usually kept a sharp eye on that and he immediately put in an order for a tanker.

Thursday morning at the kitchen table, I gave Clark and Irene my usual lecture on schoolwork.

"You have to get good grades or they'll say Dad isn't a good father. You have to bring home homework even when there isn't any. You have to do extra-credit work, be the top kid in your class. You can't give Miss Doomsday anything to use against Dad."

"Is she a c-commie?" Clark said.

"I don't know, but she's out to get us. Make sure you wear clean clothes to school every day. No cussing at school, no fighting at recess, they'll say it's Dad's fault."

"Why is she after us?" Reenie said.

"The first time she showed up and told Dad that the welfare board had him under observation, he almost threw her off the porch," I said.

"He c-couldn't," Clark said and laughed.

"Well, he could shove her," I said. "Ever since, she's had it in for him, he got on her wrong side."

I got everything lined up so I could go to the house parties on Friday. Reggie called around and found a ride with Bill Hann. You had to find a guy with a car who was interested in a girl in the right sorority to end up where you wanted to be. Reggie and I met on Fairview and Grand, and Bill picked us up with four other boys crammed in the '46 four-door Ford. We each kicked in fifty cents for gas.

The girls rented cabins on the bluff overlooking the St. Croix River. When we arrived, a bunch were already out playing in the sun. I found Mitzi with some kids who were hiking and climbing around on the rock cliffs and exploring the caves. She seemed glad to see me. The mothers they'd picked for chaperones were swell and they fed a lot of boys lunch. In the afternoon, about twenty of us decided to play touch football on a field cushioned with fallen leaves. Two captains chose players and Reggie and I were picked last. It was perfect, because Mitzi ended up on the other team, just what I hoped for.

We went back and forth, chasing, throwing the ball, tearing around. It was fun. I managed to cozy up to Mitzi several times by blocking her away from our ball carrier. And it seemed she came after me when our team had the ball. Then what I was praying for happened. They pitched the ball back to Mitzi and she took off around the end lickety-split.

Shoot, she could run. But I could use the one thing that kept me ahead of the taller boys. I played back aways, and when Mitzi outran our front line, I used my speed to be the first one to her. She sprinted down the side of the field and I thought of letting her outrun everyone on my team and score a touchdown. But I couldn't, couldn't miss the chance to hold her. When I caught her, I didn't just touch her. I don't know what got into me, but I wrapped my arms around her, slowed her down, and then gently pulled her onto the ground on top of me. Everyone shouted and laughed. Mitzi laughed. Both of us were out of breath.

"You got me," she said with her face close to mine.

"I hope so," just popped out of me.

For a moment I held her there in the soft grass and colored leaves, our faces almost touching. We panted and laughed quietly and for an instant, like the blink of a star, I felt really happy, overwhelmed, so happy that I realized I hadn't felt that way in a long, long time. Then kids grabbed the ball, we rolled away and got up, and the game went on.

That night, down along the river, we had a big bonfire. Kids sat around the fire and I crowded up close to Mitzi. Ed Miller crowded up to her other side. He was about five eleven. We sang songs and roasted marshmallows and it reminded me of our campfires on the North Shore. Some kids necked and some couples were off exploring the caves. I wanted to be off exploring caves with Mitzi, but I didn't know how to give Ed the slip.

When the mothers rang the curfew bell, there were plenty of hurried good-night kisses in the shadows. I planned to kiss Mitzi, but Ed acted like her Siamese twin right up to the door. Shoot! The girls disappeared into the cabins and the boys reluctantly piled into the cars for the long ride back to Saint Paul. I fell asleep quickly in the backseat, feeling all mixed up about the beautiful day and pretty Mitzi Fitzsim-

mons who would be chased by someone else tomorrow. I
tried to call up the happiness I felt with Mitzi in my arms, but
I couldn't.

Bill dropped me off at my house and my stomach flipped. A
strange Plymouth sat in front and all the downstairs lights
were on. At least it wasn't Miss Doomsday's car. I shook off
my sleepiness and found Dad all hung over in the kitchen
with a stranger. Dad, in his underwear, had a blanket
wrapped around him and the coffee pot sat on the table. I
could smell the puke.

"Hi, I'm Bob. You must be Donny," the solidly built man
said.

He must have been around my dad's age and had a big,
round face. Made a guy think pancake. He seemed calm and
steady and he had a space between his two front teeth.

"Yeah, did you bring Dad home?"

"Yes."

"Did the cops get him?" I said.

"They took down his name, but I talked them out of
throwing him in the tank."

"Gosh, thanks, mister, that would have been terrible."

My dad looked pale. He stood up and barely made it up
the stairs to the bathroom. We could hear him puking.

"Were you drinking with Dad?" I said.

"I don't drink."

"What were you doing in a bar?"

"Just talking, visiting with people."

"Why did you bring him home?"

"I didn't want to see him arrested, spend the night in jail."

"Golly, mister, I can't thank you enough. The welfare
people are watching Dad; he's on probation or something.
They're trying to bust up our family, they say he isn't fit to be
raising us."

"How long has he been this bad?" Bob said.

"My dad misses my mother something terrible. He never drank a drop when she was alive. He started drinking a little to feel better, or to forget, and he got hooked. I try to make him stop drinking."

"That won't work," Bob said quietly. "He has to want to quit. He has to be so bad that he sees he's killing himself."

"Sometimes I think that's what he's doing, and it makes me mad. We need him, Stewy needs him, Clark and Reenie need him."

"He has to decide. No one can do it for him," Bob said.

I knew that. I remembered trying to chase the Coca-Cola bear into the woods by throwing rocks.

We finally got my stinking dad to bed and to sleep. Back down in the kitchen, Bob pulled on his worn leather jacket.

"If you're not too tired, I'll drive you to your car and you can drive it home," he said.

"I don't drive. My dad will get it in the morning."

Lying in bed I prayed the policeman who wrote down Dad's name wouldn't do anything with it and it would get lost in the paperwork before it ever found Doomsday's desk. I felt hopeless thinking about Mitzi. I could see her lying beside me in the leaves and grass and hear her laughing in the sunlight. I don't know why, but it brought me back to the North Shore where I had been so happy.

Chapter 14

The next summer, it had seemed that August would never come. But it did, and the dark green '39 Desoto with the 'B' gas ration sticker on the windshield carried us back to the North Shore. All I could think of was catching that fish.

But darn, the day we arrived at the cabin it rained, one of those lousy, unending downpours like Noah ran into. I tried to talk my mother into letting me go anyway but she wouldn't hear of it. Instead we played cards and read Superman and Batman comic books and ran like crazy when we had to go to the outhouse.

The first night, mother got out her mousetraps and put Dad to work setting them. It had become a personal war between her and those little beggars and I figured they'd get the word out that we'd arrived at the cabin. I fell asleep listening to raindrops dance the fox-trot on the cabin roof.

The following morning there wasn't a cloud in sight. I left early, passing some of my favorite spots without fishing, puffing to reach that glittering pool after a year of going over it in my mind. It seemed to me, as I followed the familiar creek through the brush and pines, that I had been there only a few days before, a few hours. The dampness of the forest, blended with the sun's heat on the rock, made a familiar aroma I'd never forget. Sometimes, back in the city, I could close my eyes and smell it.

I couldn't pass up some of the good water and I took several small trout on my way. When my parents first let me go off into the wilderness alone, with no roads and thousands of square miles of forest in which a boy could disappear, it seemed they never worried that I'd get lost or hurt. Though I didn't know it at the time, I grew a lot of confidence from my wilderness roaming. I always found my way home.

When I reached the pool, gasping for air from the climb,

the sun hung high above me. I crept to the head of the pool, careful that my shadow never projected over the water. The falls roared with yesterday's downpour. The sound of the falling water and the expectation of hooking him gave me goose bumps.

Carefully, I sent my worm hunting under the swirling, bubbling water. Expecting a strike any second, I forgot to breathe. The line floated limp. Nothing. The worm washed over the rock lip at the far end of the pool. I retrieved it slowly and tried not to spook the trout. Going against experience, I fished the pool off and on all afternoon, having discovered by trial and error that if you didn't draw fire in the first few minutes in water like that, you might as well move on.

I had daydreamed about that moment all year, and as I wore out several worms dragging them through the water, I couldn't accept the fact that Splendid might have died, or worse, been caught by someone who also believed he was the only one to discover the hidden pool. The only thing greater than my gloom was my stubborn plan to string that huge fish on a willow fork and pop my dad's eyes out with surprise.

Hungry mosquitoes and the lengthening shadows reminded me to start back. I felt terrible after a whole year's wait. Maybe tomorrow, if I reached the pool earlier and if I brought some hoppers, I'd hook him. Hiking to the cabin, I turned it over and over in my mind, every imaginable ruse I might use to entice and hook that wary fish.

The Jacksons arrived that day, a family who spent their vacation at Sunnydale Cabins about the same time each year. I knew if I didn't skedaddle early, I'd get caught up in hikes and picnics and a trip to the swimming hole in the Temperance River. I'd be stuck playing with Sarah Jackson, or worse, having the skinny tomboy tagging along, keeping me in the lower stretches of the river all day and keeping me from hooking Splendid. Troubled and without patience, I fell to sleep with the sounds of the thundering waves crashing over my bed.

When I awoke, I dressed quickly and grabbed what I could for breakfast. Out the door, I glanced over at the Jackson cabin, and to my relief, there was no one in sight. I left for the river without my mother's pancakes and without Sarah Jackson.

I suspected at the time that those days were special, a gift, never to come again. I knew how lucky I was just to be there in that wildly haunting place. At times I would try hard to see across the lake but could. Other kids who stayed at the resort, together with a few of the local gang, played hide-and-seek and kick-the-can in the evenings for hours, running and shouting until after dark.

Sometimes at dusk, while hiding, I'd lie in the soft ferns and plants under the spruce and tamaracks. I'd hear the kids' voices off in the distance like secretive crows searching for me. I absorbed a sense of life lying there, unaware of how much I took in and wrote down on the blackboard of my memory. With my knack for blending into the underbrush, the other kids seldom found me before I'd appear like a wild animal, silent and safe at the goal, home free.

I crossed the highway in darkness and climbed through a flaming sunrise, reaching the pool earlier than ever before. The sky had gone to gray overcast; there would be no shadows to spook the fish.

The worm sank slowly, lulling me momentarily into a trance, until I sensed a split-second movement somewhere in the deep. The line snapped taut like a metal rod and the contest began. When I played a fish, everything seemed to blur, and when it was over, I couldn't remember much or put it back in sequence. But I knew Splendid broke water at least twice, and I broke water once, slipping off the ledge into the freezing water up to my neck. Criminy, I threw my pole into the brush as I went down and scrambled dog-paddle fashion back up the slippery rock. I nearly lost my glasses. I untangled the pole, took up the slack, and I couldn't believe my luck. The trout was still on the line, going against every theory of how to play a fish.

After several minutes in which each of us did his best to outwit the other, I landed Splendid on the shallow rock lip. Holy cow! I gawked. He was so big he was scary. He puffed and flipped and tried to throw himself back into the water. I had him, by golly, I had him! I felt happy. Hadn't used a net, either.

The fish had grown, a humdinger with strange coloring and markings. He had a chunk out of his dorsal fin, probably bitten out when he was smaller. I broke off a forked willow branch. I couldn't wait until Mom and Dad saw him, and the Sunnydale gang. Cars would slam on their brakes and people would gawk when I crossed the highway with him. I started to slide the willow through his gills for the journey down the hill.

I hesitated.

For only a second but it changed everything. I looked at Splendid, still hooked. He flipped and struggled and looked up at me with a pleading eye. I ran my eyes over the pool. If I took the fish, it would never be the same; our trip each August would never be the same, the North Shore would never be the same, not to me. The mystery of this wild place would be gone. I scolded myself for thinking childishly. Holy cow, this is what fishing is all about. Shivering in my wet clothes and unable to make up my mind, I felt stupid. Jeez, how could I explain this, even to myself?

I had to decide, I was killing him keeping him out of the water. I worked the hook out of his lip. No blood, no real damage. I kneeled at the edge of the pool and held him upright in the water, steadied him when he started to roll. He fanned his gills and slowly moved his fins. I loosened my grip and he stayed between my hands for a moment more. He'd gained his equilibrium. Then, with a powerful thrust of his tail, he was gone in a streak, down, out of sight, safe in the hidden places of that enchanted pool.

What had I done! Criminy, I'd let him go!

I'd caught probably the biggest trout in all the North Shore tributaries and I *let him GO! What a sap!*

To make up for my day on the river, I fished on the way home. I filled my pockets with small trout and air-dried my clothes as I went. When I delivered my catch for the evening meal, I never mentioned Splendid. Sure that no one could understand, I'd never tell anyone that I'd released that stupendous fish. Besides, it would sound like just another fish story.

I climbed back to the pool the day before we were to leave the Shore. I walked openly to the edge and perched on a rock ledge. I loved that wild place, what I felt there, what I heard, what I had come to know. I couldn't find words for it, and I knew that I couldn't explain it to anyone.

I tried to capture it, inside of me where it would not fade, as though I were buying a souvenir in Duluth, a birch bark canoe or one of those little cast-iron lighthouses to get me through the winter in the city. I stored whatever I could of it like an autumn squirrel, the sounds and scents and sights, but most of all, the quiet. And the special way I felt.

Next year I'd come back and catch him, but I'd never take Splendid from his wilderness world. Only to see him, to know he was there in that shadowed pool, would be enough. As I headed for the cabin and another year, I wondered how many years were allotted to brook trout, how many Splendid had already lived to reach his astounding size? I wondered if he remembered me, the giant creature who snagged him every year in the late summer? The trout, in a strange and mysterious way, had become a friend. My life, at age eleven, seemed strangely intertwined with the life of that splendid fish.

Chapter 15

On Monday I took Stewy around trick-or-treating while Dad gave candy to the kids who came to our door. Stewy wore a Shirley Temple wig with a scarf and one of Irene's old wraparound skirts. Irene did up his face with rouge and lipstick, and he sure looked like a little girl.

Irene insisted that we give out Fleers Dubble Bubble gum, something she loved and hoped there would be a lot left over. They were a big chew for a penny and Irene saved the wrappers that were covered with funnies and fortunes and stuff like that. She told Dad to just give one to each kid, but knowing Dad, he probably gave a handful to every ghost and goblin that showed up on our porch. When we stopped at the Rileys', Uncle Ellie-Ellie had his gas mask on under the German helmet with the shiny point on top. He held his rifle with the bayonet fixed and stood at attention just inside the door.

"Trick or treat," Stewy said.

"I know who you are," Mr. Riley said with a deep voice from under his gas mask.

"I know who YOU are," Stewy said.

"Whooo am-m-m I-I?"

"You're Uncle Ellie-Ellie. You can't fool me."

"Aw, shucks," Mr. Riley said. He pulled off his gas mask and got down on one knee. Stewy looked at the ceiling to see what Uncle Ellie-Ellie's lazy eye was gazing at. Uncle Ellie-Ellie handed Stewy a fistful of Tootsie Rolls.

"Give some to your brothers and sister." He put a hand on Stewy's shoulder. "You're in the army now."

"You're not behind a plow," Stewy said.

"You'll never get rich," Uncle Ellie-Ellie sang.

"By diggin' a ditch," Stewy sang.

"You're in the army now!" they sang together.

They'd cleaned up their act.

As we left, Stewy said, "Thanks for the Tootsie Rolls," and he glanced at the ceiling.

At lunch hour Thursday, I waved at Sandy when I caught her eye. As usual, Reggie complained about his lunch.

"Peanut butter sandwich, peanut butter sandwich, I get so sick of these dang peanut butter sandwiches."

I wasn't the only one who was tired of hearing him.

"Look," I said to Reggie, "why don't you tell your mother to make cheese or baloney or something different."

"You leave my mother out of this, see, I make my own lunches."

I stood up and got him in a hammerlock, but I quickly let go, afraid I'd get reported for fighting in the lunchroom and Miss Doomsday would get wind of it. I was walking on thin ice. But most of the kids at the table pounded Reggie in the shoulder or hit him with their half-empty lunch sacks.

When some of the kids had finished and left the table, Reggie slid over close to me.

"Why don't you come out for the swimming team? We're starting practice after school. You're a good swimmer, we can use you."

"I'd like to," I said, running it through my head. "How often do you practice?"

"Every day after school down at the Wilder Pool just off seven corners. We hop the Selby-Lake."

"I don't know, I've got the paper route, and I have to help out at home."

"Clark can do your afternoon route and your sister can watch Stewy."

I had started swimming when I was three. We always got to a lake somewhere in the summer and I really wanted to win a letter while I was at Central. Maybe even Mitzi would come to our swimming meets.

"I don't know."

"You're a heck of a lot faster than me," Reggie said.

"I'll have to think about it."

"It's your dad, isn't it?" Reggie whispered.

"He's getting better. I just have to make sure Miss Dooms-day doesn't get an excuse to farm the kids out to a boarding school or some place worse."

"Well, think about it. You could probably make it even if you miss the first few days of practice."

I headed for study hall and tried to figure a way I could be on the swimming team. I walked up the stairs beside Sandy and she made me feel good. I wondered what my mother would say about the swimming team. But somewhere inside I knew I couldn't do it, not right now with things the way they were. I'd have to forget about earning a 'C' while I was at Central.

We limped through the next two weeks, Dad barely one step ahead of Miss Doomsday. We helped him at work and kept up our routines, and Irene was going to be thirteen. We always kidded Clark at this time that she was catching up to him. When he was younger, he believed it because they were the same age for a couple months. She had passed me in height long ago, my little sister, five foot four and growing. Darn, it really irked me. Not that she kept growing, but that I couldn't. Clark was five foot six, and except for Stewy, I was the pipsqueak in our family.

We threw a party for Reenie after school that included sup-per. She had three girls and four boys from her class and, of course, Clark and Stewy joined in. Clark amused the kids, demonstrating some of the tricks Dopey and Sleepy could do. Though it was against the rules, he had the two squirrels eat-ing out of the kids' hands in the kitchen. The girls would squeal with delight when Dopey or Sleepy would sit on their shoulder and shell a peanut.

Irene had asked Dad that morning. "Please come right home from work, Daddy."

"I will, Punkin, for sure. I wouldn't miss your birthday party for anything."

Anything, that is, but the numbing arms of booze.

The party was a success. Clark and I cooked hot dogs and served them with chopped onion and mustard and potato chips and black cows. I used my soda-jerk talents making the black cows with just the right amount of root beer over the vanilla ice cream so it would boil up with delicious root beer foam. The kids brought some swell gifts and went home around eight. Dad didn't make the party.

Irene hoped. She cut a special piece of the chocolate cake Nana Riley made and scooped out some ice cream on a plate and waited. The ice cream turned the cake into soup. Clark and I cleaned up the kitchen and I put Stewy to bed with a story. I gave Irene a carton of Dubble Bubble gum, enough to last through the winter, and she got a card from Aunt Ruth with three dollars in it. Aunt Ruth was my mother's older sister. She lived in California and the last time I saw her was at Mother's funeral.

When Irene had brushed her teeth and turned out her light, I went in and sat on her bed. She was crying.

"Dad doesn't mean to hurt you, Reenie. He really wanted to come to your party. But he gets to drinking, and when he's had a bunch of alcohol he changes, he forgets everything. It doesn't mean he doesn't love you."

"He promised," she said with a sobbing voice.

"I know, but all the kids had a great time. And what's this about getting a compact and lipstick? I don't know if Dad will approve of that. You're pretty young—"

"He won't even notice," she said softly.

She started unraveling one of her pigtails. I sat there for a minute and couldn't think of anything to say.

"We wouldn't be like this if . . . if mother hadn't died," she said.

"I know, Reenie. You're right."

"We're going to end up in an orphanage, aren't we, Donny?"

"No, we're not."

"If something happened to Dad, we'd be *orphans!*" she said, her voice scared and angry.

"I won't let that happen. You go to sleep now, Dad will be home any minute and he'll probably have a nice present for you."

"I wouldn't make a very good orphan, Donny."

"I know. Me neither. Go to sleep."

When the house was quiet, lights out, McCoy in bed with Reenie, I thought about Aunt Ruth. Why couldn't we have had more family around us, sandbagged against the welfare board? It seemed our family tree was doomed.

My mom's brother, Paul, was killed in France fighting in the First World War. Uncle Ellie-Ellie's war. He was in a long column of American and English soldiers marching down a road toward the front when a friendly reconnaissance plane came over, low. It dropped a message canister and it hit Uncle Paul in the head and killed him. The message in the canister was *The war is over.*

My mother's parents were killed by a tornado that leveled every building on their Iowa farm. Across the road, two hundred feet, their neighbors didn't lose a shingle.

My dad was an orphan. Never knew anything about his parents. Spent his boyhood growing up in orphanages and foster homes. Ran away and lived on his own since he was sixteen, had worked his way up to getting a filling station.

My dad met my mother when he went to the wrong *funeral.* That should have been a big clue right there. He was going to a funeral of a friend's mother and went to the wrong cemetery. He stood there wondering where his friend was. He whispered to the pretty girl standing next to him and they fell in love.

Aunt Ruth lived so far away that she couldn't help. Our family tree had been chopped off near the stump. It was up to us to hang on, with no reinforcements in sight.

When my alarm woke me at six to do the paper route, Dad hadn't come home. I didn't know what to do, where to look. Clark got up and did the route while I fixed breakfast and made my lunch. But I figured I'd better miss school and go find Dad. The kids went off to Longfellow with McCoy. I hiked down to the station. Dad was there, still in yesterday's clothes, unshaven, but open for business.

"Where have you been?" I said as I marched into the office.

"I slept it off in the backseat of the car. I didn't want to ruin Reenie's party."

"Well, you did. She cried herself to sleep waiting for you to come home."

He wiped his hands on a rag and looked at me.

"I'm sorry, Donny, I'm so damn sorry. I planned on going right home. I wanted to go right home."

"Tell that to Reenie."

Dad put a hand on my shoulder. "What are we going to do, Donny?"

"I don't know, but I'm going to school."

I ran up Marshall. I wanted to shout and scream and punch something. It was late and I caught a streetcar that got me to school just in time to make the second bell. At school my life seemed sane.

Chapter 16

Sunday, Dad gathered us around the dining room table.

"I want all of you to know how sorry I am for the drinking I've been doing."

"What drinking?" Stewy said, but no one laughed.

"I want to tell you, no . . . I want to *promise* you that I'm never going to drink again. I've been a fool, putting our family in jeopardy, giving them a chance to separate us and scatter us off to who-knows-where. I'm done. Never again. I'll be home at six-twenty every night like clockwork. I say to each one of you: I'm terribly sorry I've hurt you and made your life miserable. Forgive me."

Dad was as close to crying as I could remember, snatching tears from his cheeks as though he didn't want us seeing them. But he'd told us this before. I knew he meant it, that he'd try. But I remembered throwing rocks and shouting at the Coca-Cola bear.

"Now," he said, "let's drive to Afton for an ice cream cone."

We piled into the old Hudson. First we drove down to the station. He had bought Reenie the brand new bike she'd wanted for a long time. She'd outgrown the one she had. I was the only one in our family who didn't outgrow anything. She rode it back to the house with us following in the car. Shouting out the windows and honking the horn, we escorted her into the neighborhood like a new ship coming out of dry dock. We waited in the car while Reenie rode around the block four times, each time hollering "One more time!"

In the backseat I could smell that familiar combination of alcohol and puke. But it was faint. I rolled down a window and let the fresh air carry it away. As we drove across the countryside in the balmy fall weather, I felt a glimmer of hope.

I tried not to think it, as if thinking it would break it like a mirror. Dad had come home after work for two weeks. No aftershave. He cleaned up, changed his clothes, and helped with dinner. With Glenn Miller on the phonograph, he sang and danced, twirling Reenie until her pigtails stuck straight out. He'd see that we got our homework done, if we had any, and he'd play with the kids and listen to our favorite radio programs. He read to Stewy when he put him to bed.

Sunday we raked leaves. Stewy would run and dive into a pile when we'd get one started. We'd fill a tarp and dump the leaves in the street along the curb. There we'd burn them. I loved the smell of burning leaves. We played touch football and hide-and-seek and Dad would push all four of us on the tire swing. I could tell Dad was getting better, maybe getting over my mother's death. I felt in my heart that if I could just be patient, he would turn back into the kind of father he'd been when my mother was alive; he'd find his way back to the forest. I never gave up hoping and now it seemed as though my father was through the storm.

Reggie missed school Friday. He was going fishing with his dad up on Gull Lake. I wished I'd asked Mitzi to the Hi-Y Dance that night, now that Dad was settling down. I heard her talking in homeroom that she was going with Larry Taylor. Larry was at least five foot ten. We said our usual Hi's but I didn't get a chance to talk with her. She waved at me going out of homeroom like a friend from a passing ship. I felt hollow inside, like my girl was off on the moon and there was no way to reach her.

After lunch, before study hall, I stopped in Nurse Armstrong's office a door off front hall. Some of the boys were competing with their yo-yos, walking-the-dog and other tricks. Nurse Armstrong was pretty nice and I stopped in every few weeks and she'd weigh and measure me.

"One hundred and thirteen, Donny, four foot eleven," she said. I was stuck.

"Thanks," I said and I picked up my books.

"You'll grow, Donny, don't worry."

I did worry and when I swung out of her office without paying attention, I just about knocked Mitzi down in the stream of students. Talk about luck!

"Oh, darn, pardon me!" I said, steadying her with my free hand.

"Yipes! Donny, are you all right?" she said.

"Yeah, sure." I went up on my toes.

"Are you sick?" she said, glancing at the nurse's office.

"Oh, no, I know Miss Armstrong. I stop and say Hi once in a while."

We started walking together in the jam.

"I hear you're going to the dance with Larry Taylor," I said as quickly as I could before I chickened out.

"Yes, I am. Do you want to know *why* I'm going with Larry Taylor?"

"Yeah, I guess so."

"Because he *asked me.* I'd be going with you if you asked me."

"Gosh, I'll ask you. I just thought with homecoming and . . . I'll ask, I'll ask."

Mitzi turned into her classroom and I hightailed it back to study hall. Jeez, I had a date with Mitzi, kind of, for whenever the next dance was. Scary. I hustled to my seat in the auditorium and I felt taller.

I got done with my math in about ten minutes and I started daydreaming. I envied Reggie up fishing on Gull Lake and I remembered that next summer when I tried to catch Splendid.

The first one out of the car, I ran to the shore and jumped across the rocks. The wind blew and the waves crashed and the gulls screamed overhead. I loved it. I was in heaven. I never wanted to leave. But the third night there I felt really lousy about myself and I couldn't tell Mom or Dad.

It could have been a perfect night. It seemed like you could touch the millions of stars on a trip to the woodpile in the pitch-blackness. The crackling fire in the fireplace warmed our cabin against the nippy night air. I was twelve. We had returned for another vacation under the northern lights, but I was down in the dumps, struggling with a sinking feeling that if I didn't do something, all would be lost.

Even with popcorn and root beer, that night made a guy half nuts. I hoped, as I lay churning in that restless bed, that sleep, when I finally gave in to it, would carry me quickly to the morning light.

The next day I tracked every foot of the river, even those tough stretches I normally detoured around. I searched every pool, watching the snags and underbrush overhanging the calmer water, praying I would find nothing. The day before I'd caught Splendid again, but the golden trout swallowed the hook. I didn't know what to do. I was racing with time, the hook caught deep in his throat. I knew he couldn't survive out of the water for long. I cursed the stinking barb that held fast its bloody grip.

Splendid fought bravely, twisting, flipping, clinging to the life we both were afraid was slipping quickly away. With that fear in my throat, I held the fish in the water for a few minutes until it revived somewhat. Then I continued the bloody operation with only my boyish fingers and a dull jackknife and a prayer that Splendid would not die.

The fish couldn't understand that we were struggling against each other with the same purpose. Through tears, I talked to him, trying to explain, begging for his cooperation. Having to tear something inside both of us, it seemed like forever before I freed the lousy metal barb from his throat. When I released him into the pool, he slowly turned on his side and floated like a fish already dead. I shook him gently, desperately, holding him upright under the water, suspended as if between life and death.

"Come on, Splendid, please, you can do it, don't give up. Don't die. Please don't die."

If he died, I knew there would be no one to absolve me

from the choking guilt I felt. No confessional would clear my conscience or ease my pain. I could see a trail of blood moving slowly into the current and over the lip, like a warning to all downstream to beware.

After what seemed like hours, when Splendid was able to keep his equilibrium, I let him loose with a gentle shove. He glided a few feet and then held his ground, his gills working, his fins and tail slowly feathering the water. I watched, hardly daring to breathe, as Splendid began rolling onto his side time and time again, only to right himself at the last moment.

I tried to swallow the sobs spilling out into the silence. I never blinked, and inch by inch the fish worked its way deeper and deeper into the pool. It took me a long time to realize Splendid was out of sight, leaving me staring at a shadow. For an hour I hung around the pool, squinting to detect some movement, some sign of life, but I found only mirror images and shadows in the iron-colored water.

The next day, I searched every pool and backwater that might hold the body of a dead fish, dreading a discovery I hoped I'd never make. I flinched at any piece of driftwood or rock resembling a large bloated fish. My sadness turned to hope when I reached the pool without finding a thing. I hung around the pool most of the day, not knowing what I expected to find, hoping, in fact, to find nothing. I went higher to the beaver ponds and filled my pockets with trout, returning to haunt the pool for another hour or more. When I started back, I felt both relieved and terribly worried, not knowing if I'd killed Splendid or not.

During those friendly days of August, I never caught sight of Splendid again. I returned home and lived through a year without knowing. I didn't spend that year moping about that tormenting day. But whenever my mind wandered north to our summer days at the Shore, I did wonder if Splendid was there, in that enchanted pool, doing whatever it is that trout do during the long, frozen winter.

Chapter 17

I didn't wait until the next dance to ask Mitzi out. With no dance scheduled on the coming weekend, I asked her to go to a movie.

"I'd love to, Donny," she said outside homeroom on Tuesday and without thinking I went up on my toes.

Reggie had his father's Dodge and a date with Virginia. He still wouldn't tell me who his heartthrob was. He picked me up first and I was feeling good. Dad came directly home from work, ate supper with us, and was playing Sorry with the kids at the kitchen table when I left.

"Why don't you come out for the swimming team?" Reggie said as we drove down Cleveland. "It's not too late and we could use you in the relay. It's your last chance to earn a letter in high school."

"I know, I know. I'd like to but I have to help my dad at the station."

I wished he'd quit asking me. It only made it hurt more.

After we got Virginia, Reggie pulled up in front of the brick and stone mansion on Summit. I opened the black iron gate into the yard and climbed the four stone steps to the huge front door. Scary. I banged away with a big brass knocker and got up on my toes. I took a deep breath and wiped my sweating hands on my pants. The door swung open and a woman in a uniform with a little white apron smiled at me.

"I'm here to get Mitzi," I said.

"Come in, Donald," she said and I stepped into a large entryway. She closed the door. "May I have your jacket?"

"Oh, no . . . I'm just here to pick up Mitzi."

The maid smiled. "You can wait in the den," she said and motioned to an open door off the entryway. "Mitzi will be right down."

She scurried off into the house and disappeared. I crept into the den, a large room lined with books, a pool table, and a fire going in the fireplace.

"Good evening," a man sitting behind a huge desk said, scaring the bean juice out of me. I thought I'd stumbled into *Inner Sanctum.*

"Oh . . . hello," I said with a squeaky freshman voice.

The man stood and walked slowly from behind the desk. About five foot ten, he had a shock of gray hair and a gray scrub-brush mustache. He was dressed like he was on his way to a wedding.

"You must be Donald. I'm John, John Fitzsimmons, Mitzi's father."

Oh boy. He held out his hand, I stretched up on my toes, and we shook. He almost mangled my hand. I figured he was showing me he could beat me up if I touched his daughter.

"Hello. It's nice to meet you," I said the way my mother taught me.

"Going to a movie, huh?"

With one eyebrow raised, he looked at me like I was planning on ruining his daughter. His voice was the "Let's-be-pals" that grownups use on kids, but it felt like the hidden muzzle of a sawed-off shotgun.

"Yes, sir."

"Sit down, sit down," he said, waving a hand at a deep leather sofa that could swallow six people. I sat on the edge with my hands on my knees. He settled in a huge matching overstuffed chair. I had the feeling I was taking a test.

"It doesn't seem so long ago I was going on a high school date."

Criminy, the guy must have a great memory because he looked pretty old.

"I wasn't very keen about Mitzi transferring from Summit to Central her senior year, but she seems to be enjoying it very much."

"I'm glad she did, otherwise I wouldn't have ever met her."

"I think she's getting a good education, but I was disappointed that she wouldn't graduate from Summit."

"Central has pretty high standards. We have some good teachers and our English department is as tough as any. Kids that go to the university are moved right up to sophomore English when they find out they've graduated from Saint Paul Central."

"That's good to hear. Say, how's your father doing?" he said.

"My father?" What did he know about my father? Darn, did he have spies? Did he know Dad was a drunk?

"Yes, Mitzi said he had been very sick."

"Oh, yeah, he was sick the night of the homecoming dance. He's fine now. Just a little flu or something."

Jeez, did Mitzi tell him everything?

"Did you drive tonight?"

"No, ah . . . Reggie, my buddy, is driving."

I didn't want to get into talking about *driving* with him.

Thankfully, Mitzi bounced into the room in a pink sweater with a matching ribbon in her hair, a plaid pleated skirt, and saddle shoes. She was so pretty I swallowed.

"Hi, Donny, I'm all set," she said.

My mouth went dry and I was afraid I was looking at his daughter as if I were planning on ruining her.

I jumped off the huge sofa. "Great . . . let's go."

Mr. Fitzsimmons stood. He crushed my hand again. I almost said *uncle.*

"Nice to meet you, Donald. You two have fun tonight."

"Yes . . . very nice to meet you."

"What time are you bringing my daughter home?" he said with a smile.

"Oh, around eleven . . . we'll probably get something to eat after the movie."

"That's good. I'll be up."

Gad, I could see him sitting by the front door with a stop watch and a shotgun. What if we were ten minutes late?

The maid handed Mitzi a white nylon jacket with a fur collar. I helped her slip it on and we were out the door.

"How do you like my father?" she said on the way to the car.

"He's swell, but what's with all this Donald stuff?"

She laughed. "My dad doesn't believe in nicknames."

"Where was your mother?" I said as I held the back door for her.

"She passed away."

I couldn't believe it. I didn't know what to say. She lost her mother too?

"I'm really sorry," I said and I wanted to tell her I knew what that was like.

We went to see *Roseanna McCoy* at the Uptown and I told Mitzi we had a dog named McCoy. The movie was about two sweethearts whose families hated each other and tried to keep them apart. I wondered what Mr. Fitzsimmons thought of me, he being so rich and all. Afterwards we ate at the St. Clair Broiler. We were all acting goofy and laughing at each other. Reggie was a born clown and he told us the swimming team wiped out Monroe that afternoon. I hadn't managed to get my arm around Mitzi's shoulders during the movie but I came close. My arm, now petrified, ached from holding it over the back of her seat for an hour and a half.

It wasn't quite ten when we were done eating and Reggie drove around town for a while, taking turns as sharply as he could. I loved him for it. With a hard left he'd throw Mitzi into my lap and I'd catch her and hold onto her. With a hard right he'd throw me up against her and before long I was holding her in my arms and not letting go on the straightaways. The best part of it all was I could tell she was enjoying it, snuggling up to me and laughing at Reggie's driving.

"I just got my license this afternoon," Reggie said, swerving around a corner.

"Really?" Mitzi said.

"Naw, just kiddin'," Reggie said.

"What kind of a car does your family have?" Mitzi asked me while Virginia moved close to Reggie and worked the radio.

"We have a '40 Hudson. It's kind of a pet with my dad. We had a '48 Oldsmobile but he says the Hudson will be a classic some day." I wanted to change the subject.

"Does he let you drive it?" she said.

"Oh, not really. I don't drive, I don't have a license."

"My father just let me get mine last summer. I haven't driven a whole lot," she said. "He always has someone drive me or pick me up. He has car dealerships all over the Twin Cities, you've probably seen them. FITZSIMMONS PONTIAC and FITZSIMMONS CADILLAC and FITZSIMMONS YOU-NAME-IT."

"Holy cow, that's *your dad?* I see his ads in the paper and hear them on the radio all the time. Jeez, you could drive any car you wanted."

"He has ads on television, too. Do you have television?" she said.

"No, not yet. My dad says we're going to wait till they improve it. He's kinda old fashioned."

"My dad promised me a car when I graduate."

"My dad promised me a scooter." We both laughed.

I kept my arm around her as Reggie drove slowly up Summit.

"How old were you when your mother died?" she whispered.

"Fourteen," I said and I tried to duck it. "How old were you?"

"She died when I was a baby. I never knew her."

"I'm sorry," I said and I pulled her close.

"Golly, you knew your mom all those years. You must really miss her."

"Yeah, I do."

"How did she die?" Mitzi whispered.

"One day she just died."

"Was she sick?"

"No . . . she just died."

I wanted to kiss her to stop her questions but I didn't dare. I kept one arm around her until Reggie pulled up at the big house on Summit. It was ten-fifty. We stood on the stoop for a minute.

"I had loads of fun, Donny," she said.

"Me too."

"I liked the movie. I want to meet McCoy sometime."

"Oh, sure, you'd like him."

I was getting ready to kiss her, but there were bright lights on each side of the big door and I could see her dad kneeling behind the door with a stopwatch, peeking through the key hole.

"I'll see you in school," I said and I beat it to the car.

After Reggie took Virginia home, he dropped me off. When he stopped in front of my house, he got out of the car and came around like he wanted to talk. I should've known better. He jumped me and we wrestled on the lawn until he made me say *uncle*. I thanked Reggie for all the sharp turns and he drove away. When I went in the house, the world caved in.

Chapter 18

It was eleven-thirty and I found the house lit up like Lexington Ball Park. When I came in the front door, Clark and Reenie were sleeping on the davenport in the living room, the radio going. Shoot! I just about jumped out of my skin. McCoy was sleeping in the window bench with only his head showing as if he'd been beheaded. I turned off the radio and woke them.

Clark sprang up. "Is D-Dad home?" he said.

"Dad isn't home?" I said.

"He went out to help someone," Reenie said as she sat up.

"When?" I said.

"After supper, after you left," Reenie said, screwing her fists against her eyes.

"Where's Stewy?" I said and I raced up the stairs.

Stewy's room was dark but from the hall light I could see he wasn't in his bed.

"Stewy! Stewy!" I called with Clark and Reenie on my tail.

We searched all through the upstairs and finally found him under a blanket under his bed.

"I was hiding from Miss Doomsday," he said. "Will she get me now, Donny?"

"No, she won't get you."

I heard someone in the kitchen. When I raced down the stairs, I found Uncle Ellie-Ellie sitting at the table in his pajamas, playing solitaire. He had his helmet on as well as his gas mask. He sounded like a spook when he talked with his gas mask on.

"You have to be ready," he said. "You never know when they'll hit you."

"Have you seen Dad?" I said.

"No, but I'm guarding the fort, don't you worry."

We gathered around the kitchen table, slumping into the chairs.

114

"Why did Dad go out?" I said.

"Mr. An-Andrews called, you k-know, the guy who gives us a di-dime if we wash his win-windshield on the inside."

"What did he want?" I said.

"His car was stalled, that old Buick," Reenie said. "Dad went to get it started."

"And he never came back?" I said.

"He's AWOL," Uncle Ellie-Ellie said.

I went to the phone book and looked up the Andrews' number. His first name was Ralph. I dialed and let it ring—six, seven, eight times—until someone answered.

"Is Mr. Andrews there?"

"Yes . . . this is Mr. Andrews."

"Hi, Mr. Andrews, this is Donny Cunningham. Did my dad get your car going tonight?"

"Yes, yes he did. Something about the carburetor."

"What time did he finish with your car?"

"Oh, about eight o'clock. Is he all right?"

"We don't know, Mr. Andrews, he hasn't come home."

"Oh, my, I hope he's all right. Maybe he's fixing someone else's car. He's a whiz at it. Got my car going like nothing."

"Thanks, Mr. Andrews, sorry to bother you so late."

I hung up and got all the kids to bed. Stewy slept with me and Uncle Ellie-Ellie laid out on the davenport, on guard. I prayed Dad hadn't been drinking. I prayed he'd come home in the morning with a perfectly logical story. But I knew he would've called home if he hadn't been drinking and had some kind of trouble. I'd about lost my knack for fooling myself, and some place deep inside, I could see him drinking. The most I could hope for was that he did it quietly, out of the way, drunk somewhere where no one would notice. No police. No trouble. No ammunition for Miss Doomsday.

I could hear Stewy ask me quietly, "Will Miss Doomsday get me?" I had promised him she wouldn't. But who was I kidding?

As I lay in my bed, listening to every little sound, I

couldn't believe I had been out with Mitzi that night and held her in my arms. I lived in two different worlds.

The phone woke me a little before six. It had to be Dad. I scrambled to the phone in the kitchen, just about killing myself going down the stairs. It was the police. Dad had been arrested. They wanted to talk to his wife. I told him I was his oldest son. He paused for a minute.

"He keeps talking about his lovely wife, Helen."

"She's dead," I said.

"Well then, you'll have to come down and bail your father out."

"How much money will it take?"

"Forty dollars."

"Where do I go?"

"The city jail."

"Thank you."

I woke Clark and Irene. I collected whatever money they had down to the penny: piggy banks, hiding places, saved allowances, paper route money. It came to forty-three dollars and seven cents. I sent Clark to do the paper route. Reenie would make breakfast.

"Don't let Stewy out of the house," I told Irene.

"Dad was drinking all night, wasn't he?" she said.

"Yes, until they arrested him."

"Do you tell your friends that your dad's a drunk?" she said.

"No, he's not a drunk. He just drinks too much sometimes."

"Next thing it'll be Sterno," she said with a bitter voice.

"What do you know about Sterno?"

"I hear stuff, I know about winos and Sterno."

"Dad isn't a wino," I said.

"Well, he's on the way."

My little sister was growing up.

Uncle Ellie-Ellie marched for home across the alley, his duty done. I pulled on my clothes and ran over to Marshall to catch a Selby-Lake for downtown. Riding the streetcar, I remembered riding that day with my mother. She told me my whole life was an adventure. I didn't know what she meant. But I think I was catching on. I wondered if these were the best years of my life.

Downtown, I found the city jail over on 11th, paid the forty dollars to a desk sergeant, and they brought Dad out. He looked terrible, his clothes a mess, his hair uncombed, his unshaven face sick and pale, so ashamed he wouldn't look at me. We took the streetcar home like strangers.

"Where's the car?" I said as we sat side by side on the half-empty streetcar.

"I don't remember," he said. "The last I remember I was at the Three Pals . . . I think."

"Why did you do it, Dad, why? You were doing so good!" I tried to keep my voice down. "Now Miss Doomsday will find out, she'll have all the evidence she needs. Why did you DO it!"

My dad didn't answer. I could tell he was still woozy from the booze. He looked like a bum on the street who'd been drinking Sterno. I walked him home from the streetcar, got some coffee in him and got him to bed. I left Clark in charge, he'd finished the paper route. I ran down to the station to get it open. More than ever we needed every dollar we could make.

When I opened the safe and got the money tray for the cash register, it was almost empty. I didn't know how I'd make change. When I pumped gas, I'd watch it carefully and always stop on an exact dollar amount. Business was good and I got grease on my good pants. I called the drugstore and told Mr. Carpenter I wouldn't be able to work until afternoon. About an hour later, Irene came down with McCoy and brought me lunch. I didn't know I was hungry until I saw the grilled cheese sandwich she made me.

"Dad will be down in a little while," she said.

"How is he?" I said.

"As usual. He says he's sorry." She frowned at me. "You know who started all this, Donny."

"Yeah, I know."

Since our mother died, there had always been a shadow between me and Reenie. I could feel it. I hated it.

The next week we were holding our breath, walking on eggshells. I wanted to ask Mitzi to the Turkey Trot on Wednesday night but I didn't dare. I had relaxed too much with Dad, and look what happened. I told her I had to do stuff with my family and relatives. She was swell about it and I hated lying to her.

Thursday was Thanksgiving and we all helped with the dinner. We had a big turkey with all the trimmings. The station was closed and just in case we had a plan. One of us kids would answer the phone and tell whoever needed help with their car that Dad wasn't home.

With Thursday and Friday off from school, we kept close tabs on Dad over the weekend. We played games and went to Afton for ice cream on Sunday and tried not to think about tomorrow. But tomorrow came on Tuesday when the Friendly Visitor showed up after school and we had another *interview*. She had stopped at the station before she came to the house.

"I left a summons with your father," she said, spreading out on the window bench. "He will have a hearing before a judge next week. Then we shall see what must be done in this pitiful situation."

"What's a pitiful situation?" Stewy said.

"It's when your father is . . . well, shall we say, unreliable. He's not capable of raising and caring for you children."

"What will happen to us?" Reenie said.

"You'll be put under the protection of the county. You'll be placed in caring, dependable homes where you get the affection and proper upbringing you deserve."

"I want to stay here," Stewy said.

"Don't worry, sweetheart, you will be very happy when you get used to your new family."

I stood up. "We're not talking to you anymore! The judge will decide, not *you*. We're staying together and you can't break us apart. Please get out of our house!"

She narrowed her beady eyes and pursed her lips.

"Well," she said as she gathered her notebooks and files. "We'll just see about that."

She huffed and puffed out the front door and I wanted to sic McCoy on her. She had no right to come here and scare the wits out of Stewy. We'd already lost our mother and now she wanted to take our father. He loved us, he didn't hit us or hurt us or yell at us or any of that kind of stuff. Maybe the judge would understand.

On the following Monday, I stayed home from school for half a day so my dad could go to the hearing with the judge. He wouldn't let me go, said we had to keep the station open. When he came home that night, I knew it was bad. He wouldn't tell us what the judge said. We ate and then huddled around the Zenith console and listened to our favorite programs.

I saw the sadness in his eyes that I saw in the Coca-Cola bear. I felt like we were soldiers about to be separated and sent off to war. My dad sang to Stewy when he put him to bed. I fought back tears because I figured it was Dad's way of saying good-bye.

Chapter 19

The next week it felt like our ship was taking on water. Dad was quiet, not himself. I only smelled his aftershave once. He wore sadness like an overcoat. No more Glenn Miller on the phonograph, no more singing, no more dancing.

Clark got caught stealing a comic book from the five and dime across from the station. The owner, Mr. Simonovich, hauled him to the station by one ear. Dad put him to work cleaning out the oil pit, the hardest and dirtiest job there was, and the next day, after school, Clark had to apologize to Mr. Simonovich and offer to work for him on Saturday for free. Mr. Simonovich worked Clark's tail off hauling boxes out of and into the five and dime basement.

Irene got in trouble in school for fighting on the playground at recess. She had to write "I will not fight at school" on the blackboard with good penmanship one hundred times.

"Well, Nancy was yanking on my pigtails and it hurt and it takes so long to braid them. Mom could do it lickety-split," she said to my dad.

"Fighting is unladylike. You want to be known as a bully?" my dad said.

"Joe Miller is the bully. I socked him in the nose. They won't yank my pigtails again."

We could see fear in each other's faces. Dad had gone to two hearings, or whatever, with judges and lawyers and the welfare board and he wouldn't tell us anything. He'd just keep saying Everything will be all right.

On Thursday I had a note from my dad to let me out at noon because I had to run the station again. He had another court appearance with some judge. In homeroom I told Mitzi I was out after third period.

"If you have time, we could eat lunch together, out on the steps," she said. "I have first lunch."

"Yeah, I can do that. Dad's appointment isn't until two."

We sat on the huge steps in the sunshine while other kids did the same around us. We needed our jackets but the weather was still nice for late November. I ate my peanut butter sandwich and banana and Hostess cupcake while Mitzi nibbled at her little banquet.

"Jeez, how do you eat all that stuff?" I said.

"Oh, that's Mildred. She doesn't want me to go hungry."

"You don't make your own lunch?"

"No, they won't let me." She laughed.

"You're still a Summit girl when it comes to lunchtime. Are you going to eat all that?"

"No, please help yourself."

I polished off several shrimp, half a tuna salad sandwich and a piece of chocolate cake. There in the sunshine, I felt calm eating lunch with Mitzi, a timeout from my life. I wanted to tell her what was going on with my family, why I was acting so strange, why I didn't ask her out. I wanted to tell her about Dad and my mom, all of it, but I couldn't.

"Did you hear what Hugh Mayer and Phil Costello did a few weeks ago when the marching band was practicing?" Mitzi said.

"Oh, yeah, those goof-offs. Everyone heard about that."

I started laughing just thinking about it.

"Well, Virginia was in the band room when those two came in with their report cards," Mitzi said. "Mr. Hambull was sitting at his desk. They told him they had to have a double 'A' in band or they'd have to quit. They needed a double 'A' to keep their grade points up. Mr. Hambull had only given them an 'A'. They were the only clarinets in the band. Mr. Hambull just looked at them for a long time, like he was thinking. Then he took his pen and gave them both 'AA'." We both laughed.

"Those guys have more guts," I said.

Mitzi looked into my eyes. "Do you like me, Donny?"

Boy, she took me by surprise.

"Oh, gosh, yeah, I really like you, a lot."

"Don't you like to go out, on dates?"

"Yeah, I really do. It's just that right now I've got to help my dad out at the station, and with the kids, and then there's my other jobs."

"You work at the drugstore on Saturdays?"

"Yeah, and I set pins at Highland Bowling Center Friday or Saturday night sometimes and I share the paper route with my brother Clark and—"

"I'll come and see you at the drugstore on Saturday, if you don't mind."

"Oh, gosh, no, that'd be swell. I'll make you my super-duper chocolate malt."

I checked my watch and hightailed it over to Selby to catch a streetcar. Dad was waiting at the station. Business was slow. He put his hand on my shoulder and said, "What are we going to do, Donny, what are we going to do?" Then he drove off for the house to change into his Sunday suit.

I pumped gas and jotted down two grease jobs on Dad's calendar. I had to fix a lousy flat but I sold a tire doing it. I felt scared all afternoon, worried that Dad would lose Stewy in all those courtrooms and welfare offices.

Clark came by when he picked up our bundle of papers on the corner of Cleveland and Marshall.

"Have you seen Stewy?" Clark said.

"No, isn't he at home?"

"No. I w-walked up to Gordon but d-didn't see him."

"Did you look in the trees?"

"Yeah, ev-everywhere. I figured he w-walked home."

"Well, go home and get Irene looking for him too. Have her walk up to Gordon and back. He walks different ways. Tell her to check the alleys. He's always bringing home junk from trash cans. Look under his bed. Check with Uncle Ellie-Ellie, go on, hurry!"

I just about went nuts waiting for Dad to get back. He drove up alongside the station around five and just sat in the car. I finished with a customer, rang up the money, and opened the Hudson's passenger door.

"We can't find Stewy," I said.

My dad wouldn't look at me, but I knew instantly that he knew where Stewy was.

"Where's Stewy?" I shouted. "What have you done with him?"

"He's with the Ramsey County welfare people."

"What! You just gave him to them!"

Dad got out of the car and looked at me across the hood.

"It's just for a few days, a trial," he said.

"A trial! You let them take Stewy away! I *promised* him. He'll be scared and all alone. Didn't you fight them? Didn't you hang on to him when they tried to take him. Didn't they have to break your arms to get him? What kind of a father are you?"

My dad pounded the hood of the Hudson with his fist.

"Don't you go pointing the finger at me, boy! Remember how this all happened. Never forget, it was *you* who brought this down on us, *you* who tore my heart out, *you* who ruined all of our lives!"

My father's face turned red, veins bulged, hatred filled his eyes. He pounded the hood with both hands like he'd go nuts.

I slammed my fist on the hood.

"I know it! I know it!"

I started running. I didn't know where. My glasses were all smeared. I ran fast. I could see Stewy, scared and crying with strangers who didn't know him. I could see Irene with my mother on the tire swing, laughing and calling, Higher! Higher! I could see my mother teaching Clark how to fry an egg and hugging him when he got it right. I could see my mom and dad dancing in the living room and softly singing "I'll Be Seeing You."

I ran. Into the side door of St. Mark's and down the rows of pews. I was really bawling. I went in a confessional and pulled the door shut. I turned to the darkened screen.

"Bless me, Father, for I have sinned. It has been five days since my last confession." I caught my breath.

"I killed my mother."

Chapter 20

"I didn't just kill my mother. I *slaughtered* her."

When I was fourteen, my dad was teaching me how to drive. I couldn't wait. I'd get my driver's license when I was fifteen. One hot August day, after we'd been up on the North Shore and a week before school started, my mother planned to do some errands with the car. I grabbed the keys off the kitchen counter and ran to the garage. I'd back the car out, a chance to practice. She hated backing out of the garage.

I held down the clutch and started the engine. I shifted into reverse. Then I turned and watched over my right shoulder through the back window, the way my dad taught me. I let the clutch out slowly but my foot slipped off the pedal. The car lurched and I panicked. I jammed my foot for the brake but hit the gas pedal. The car came out of the garage like a roaring monster. Rocketing for the street, I fumbled for pedals with both feet. I found the brake and jammed it hard enough to kill the engine just short of the street. My face was covered with sweat. I looked around, no one had seen me. I was in the clear. I sighed with relief. No harm done.

Then my body forgot how to breathe. My mother's purse sprawled in the middle of the lawn as if someone had pitched it there. At once I remembered when the engine was roaring, a thump. A strange thump as though I'd hit something. I couldn't get out of the car. My blood pounded through the veins in my temples. It felt like I'd swallowed a rock and it got stuck in my chest and I was gagging. I knew what I'd find before I looked. My life as I had known it was over.

I couldn't move. I sat there like I was in a dream. I wanted to wake up but I couldn't. I wanted to start the day over, I wanted to start my life over. Somehow, I forced myself to open the door and push myself out of the DeSoto. I got down on my hands and knees and peered under the car.

"Mother! Mother! Oh God! Mother! Oh please God, no!"

I saw the horror of my life! My mother, mangled into a strange tangle of arms and legs. She was still moving, twitching. Was she alive? I grabbed her arm and pulled, but I couldn't move her. Her body was wedged tight. I jumped up.

"Help! Somebody! Help! Quick! Help!"

I ran to the other side of the car and crawled under. I could see part of her face twisted against her shoulder, her body tangled out of shape, a leg by her head. I kept screaming for help. I kept screaming at God. I scrambled up and took hold of the back bumper. I tried to lift the car. *God make me strong enough!* It rose off the shocks and springs but I couldn't lift it high enough. I wasn't Charles Atlas. A stronger son could have lifted the car off his mother. Then, like in a dream, there were people all around me. Two men grabbed the bumper with me, but we could only raise it a few inches.

A cop car had parked at the curb. An ambulance barreled up the street with siren blaring. Neighbors stood in groups with horror on their faces. A tow truck had backed up to our DeSoto and started to lift it. Men on their bellies reached under the car, talking fast and shouting instructions. But no one could get my mother out.

Then I saw my dad. He circled on the lawn like a man who'd gone insane, carrying Irene and howling! "Oh, no! Oh Jesus, Oh Jesus! No! No! It can't be! Don't let this happen, God, please, don't let this happen!"

Clark clung to his leg as they circled. I wanted to run to him and tell him I was sorry, that I knew he told me to stay away from the car unless he was with me, that it was that damned-to-hell clutch! But I couldn't take it back. I couldn't look into his eyes. I stumbled into the garage and threw up into a trash barrel.

They had to jack up the car and put it on blocks to get my mother out. I stayed in the garage until they took her away.

Uncle Ellie-Ellie washed away all evidence of the accident with a garden hose.

It had happened in five or six seconds. The world had changed, my life had changed, in five or six seconds.

Someone led me like the blind into the house. Neighbors hung around and tried to think of things to say. I sat on the window bench in the crowded living room and no one would sit next to me or even look at me. They weren't being mean or anything, it was so horrible they didn't know what to say or do. It was as if I wasn't there, no one came near me. I kept forgetting to breathe.

I wanted to run, fast, far away, but I couldn't make my body move. My dad, sitting across the room on the sofa, hadn't said a word to me. He was so shocked he didn't even look like himself. He couldn't talk and he hugged the kids and cried and then buried his face in his hands and sobbed. I knew how much he loved my mom and I figured my life had ended with hers.

Stewy came crawling in the front door in just a diaper and little shirt. He'd been lost in the uproar. He crawled over to where I sat.

"Nonny," he said.

He had something in his hand he wanted to show me. I pulled him onto my lap, thankful to be touching somebody, thankful to be talking to someone, still a part of the human race.

"Nonny."

He opened his little hand. It was my mother's small silver cross that she kept in her purse.

I didn't sleep that night. I lay awake in the dark bedroom. I could hear my dad moving around the house like a ghost. In the shadows of my room I vowed to God that I would take my mother's place. I promised that I would help raise my brothers and sister, that I would take care of the house so my dad could work. I'd work twenty hours a day if I had to. I'd raise them until they were out of high school.

Towards dawn, my bed drenched with sweat, I knelt beside it. I made my solemn vow to God.

At my mother's funeral no one spoke to me. As if I had a contagious disease, no one even stood by me. At the grave in Calvary Cemetery, Dad sat between Clark and Reenie with Stewy on his lap. I sat two chairs over, two empty chairs over. He never looked at me. I didn't blame him. Uncle Ellie-Ellie stood behind my chair. He wore his army uniform and had his helmet under one arm but he didn't put it on. Stewy looked up into the sky to see what Uncle Ellie-Ellie's lazy eye was gazing at.

The priest read some stuff out of the book and prayed and I don't remember a thing he said. But he forgot to tell them that I'd destroyed the most precious part of my life, that I'd cut out my own heart and had to go on living without it, without her. I wondered if Mom would be all knit back together in heaven.

They lowered her into the hole and some threw flowers in on top of her. I wanted to throw myself in the hole with her. I couldn't look anyone in the face. No one spoke to me. People started walking across the lawn toward the cars and I stood there alone for a minute.

"Good-bye, Mother. I'm . . ."

I started to cry. I used every ounce of strength to hold it back. Dad and the kids walked toward the long black Cadillac as if they'd forgotten I was there.

At the house I became the invisible boy again. Lots of people visited, ate, sat around. They wouldn't look at me. They knew I'd disobeyed my father and run over my mother. I left my family without a mother and wife. Uncle Ellie-Ellie leaned down and whispered in my ear. "You never know when they will hit." I went up and closed the door to my room and threw myself on the bed.

Lying there, it made a guy so sad I thought I'd break. It felt like a piece of me had been ripped out. I could feel the wind blowing through me. I wished I'd never been born. I could hear my mother saying, "Smile and the world smiles with you, cry and you cry alone." I *hated* that. I was sad, I wanted to cry. But I didn't want everyone to desert me when I cried, to only be there when I smiled, to only like me when I smiled. I wanted them to cry with me. Why did I have to cry alone? Even little kids, waiting for Santa Claus are warned. ". . . better watch out, better not *cry* . . ."

Over the years I'd learned to fake it. I'd cover the sadness by always fooling around, makin' jokes. I'd never let them catch me out in the open with my real feelings. I'd smile a lot.

Something in my closet moved and I almost jumped out of my skin. Stewy was there, in the corner, under my hanging clothes. McCoy lay beside him. Stewy crawled up on my bed.

"Is Mommy coming back, Nonny?"

"No."

"Not never?"

"Not never."

"Where did she go?"

"Heaven," I said and I reached over and hugged him.

"Can we go to heaven to see her?"

"No."

"Can we call her on the phone?"

"No, Stewy, they don't have phones in heaven."

"I want to go to heaven and see her," he said.

"So do I."

It rained for a week. The sun never showed its face, as if it were too sad to come out. It rained night and day and I knew it was God's tears for my mother. The whole world had a broken heart.

The Minnesota State Fair is a big deal. Hundreds of thousands of people come to it every year. It goes on for a week. Yet, the August my mother died, they called off the State Fair. They canceled it! They said it was because of the polio epidemic, but I knew better. The world changed because my mother was gone.

I started going out to my mother's grave the next spring. At first I couldn't do it. I turned around about twenty times. I didn't tell anyone, even after I'd made it. I'd sit next to her tombstone and talk to her. If anyone came by, they'd think I was nuts. I'd talk out loud, and as crazy as it sounds, I could tell my mother heard me, every word. And I could tell she was talking back. I'd listen real hard, not moving, hardly breathing. Once a robin landed on my leg I was sitting so still.

The nightmares started after she died. At first lots of them, once a week. Then they got further apart. I'd try to wake up but I couldn't. It was always the same. We're running down a country road through the woods, running *from* something. I could never see what. Dad and the kids scream and as they run their arms fall off and their legs and their faces. I try to catch them and put their arms back on, only I can't run fast enough and they fall apart until there is nothing left of them. They disappear down the road. I'd be screaming, trying to save them, but I never could. I'd wake in a cold sweat, like I'd been running miles.

Dad went out to the graveyard a lot. A whole lot more than we knew. Sometimes he'd tell us, but he never invited me to go with him. I didn't blame him. A locked door stood between us and he had the only key. It could only go back to the way it was between us if my mother came back from the dead. So far, only Jesus had done that.

Sometimes, when I'd go to the grave, there'd be fresh-cut flowers, in the dead of winter, and I'd know he'd been there just hours before. The snow would be tracked where he'd walked. He got her a nice tombstone of St. Cloud granite and had it engraved:

HELEN MARY CUNNINGHAM

1903–1946

"I'll Be Seeing You"

Chapter 21

After I left St. Mark's, I ran until dark. When I left my dad at the station, I wanted to kill *him*, too. And he looked like he wanted to kill me. He probably wished I'd never been born. He and my mother would be living happily with the other three kids. In a strange way, I guessed my hatred toward him was really toward myself. In the end, I was the one who got Stewy shanghaied. When I reached the streetcar barns up on Snelling, I turned around. I slowed to a walk, totally wrung out, my head spinning.

A half hour later, I cut through our lilac hedge from the alley and stumbled in the back door. I found my war-torn family sitting around the kitchen table with half-eaten food and dirty dishes.

"Where you been?" Reenie said.

"Walking, thinking," I said. I didn't look at Dad. "We've got to get Stewy back."

I pulled up a chair and joined the war council.

"Where is Stewy, what did they do with him?" I said.

"They're going to put him in a foster home," my dad said, without glancing at me. "A regular family with other kids. But it's only *temporary*. It's a trial. The court has to decide if it's going to be permanent."

"How did they get him?" I said and looked into my dad's eyes.

He just stared at the cluttered table.

"I packed his bag and picked him up at school. I brought him down there," my dad said. "Otherwise, they'd have come and got him. I knew that would scare him the most. And if you kids were here, it would've been a free-for-all."

"We have to get him back before they can keep him for good," Reenie said.

"Where is the foster home?" I said.

My dad buried his face in his hands.

"They won't tell us. It's secret. They don't want us messing around. They want Stewy to have a clean break, a whole new life."

"He b-belongs with us, his *r-real* family," Clark said.

"Can't we get him back?" Reenie said.

"We're going to. There has to be a way," I said.

Irene started crying.

"I'll h-help, Donny."

"It's no use," my dad said without looking up. "They'll just come and get him again. They could put me in jail. Then they'd farm all of you out."

"We'll hide him . . . everyone will help," I said. "Uncle Ellie-Ellie and Nana Riley and all the neighbors will help. They can't just take Stewy from us, that's kidnapping."

"Remember, Uncle Ellie-Ellie's son is a policeman," my dad said. "We'd have to be careful there."

"There's got to be a way," I said. "But first, we have to find out where Stewy is."

"How you going to do that?" my dad said.

"Miss Doomsday. She said she's coming out for an interview next week. If we play along, maybe we can find out from her," I said. "We've got to be little angels with her."

"Little a-angels? I'd like to b-beat the tar out of her," Clark said.

"No, if we're going to do it, we have to do it right," my dad said, "so they can't use the law against him. If we can get him back, we can tell Miss Doomsday that he's staying with your Aunt Ruth in Palo Alto. They couldn't do anything about that."

"All right," I said, "we'll show them a perfect family so they can find nothing wrong."

I glanced at my dad. Would he drink all the more now that we'd lost Stewy? No matter what he said to me, I knew he blamed himself for all of this now. I knew he was ashamed.

Fresh snow covered the city, and after school on Tuesday, Clark and I shoveled the walk and drive. We'd rest and snowball a car now and then, ready to run. A car I almost nailed pulled to the curb. Shoot, the Friendly Visitor, like the flu bug, came tipping up the walk. I dropped the snowball, wanting to impress her that I was old enough to run the house. Only a few weeks before Christmas, we all missed Stewy and worried about him. I knew he'd be miserable without us, and we were without him, and every day was agony for me. But we had devised a plan to find out where he was.

We cluttered the kitchen table with stuff so we'd have to use the dining room table. Miss Doomsday sat at the head and we sat around it as though we were eating. She had a leather folder with her records and notes. I knew Stewy's new address would be in there somewhere.

"Well, now, children, how have you been these past few weeks?" she said in her highfalutin tone.

We knew what was at stake.

"We've been just fine and dandy," Reenie said. I could see that she had her fingers crossed behind her chair.

"Has your father been . . . sober, lately?" she said as she looked into each of our faces.

"He's been very good," I said, "home at six, helps with the breakfast and supper, does laundry at night. We make a list of the groceries we need and order them Saturday."

"Excuse me a minute," Irene said and she went into the kitchen. We knew what she was doing. She was signaling with a dishtowel in the kitchen window to Uncle Ellie-Ellie. He was going to try to keep Miss Doomsday on the phone for as long as possible. Reenie hurried back into the dining room and sat down.

"Can we send C-Christmas presents to Stewy?" Clark said.

"No, no . . . we feel it's best for your little brother to make a clean break, so he'll forget about his early years," Miss Doomsday said. "He has new brothers and sisters now."

"They aren't his b-brothers and sisters. They're s-strangers," Clark said.

I gave him a slight shake of my head.

"He won't ever forget *us,*"Reenie said.

They weren't following the plan to agree with everything Miss Doomsday said. The phone rang. We all sat there. We knew it was Uncle Ellie-Ellie.

"One of you better answer the phone, I don't mind," Miss Doomsday said.

Irene got up and went into the kitchen. The phone stopped ringing. We all held our breath. Irene stepped back into the dining room.

"The phone's for you Miss Doom . . . Miss Boomray."

"For me? Who knows I'm here?"

"It's a man," Irene said.

Miss Doomsday laid aside her pencil and went into the kitchen. Irene stood in the doorway between the kitchen and the dining room as a lookout. When I heard Miss Doomsday on the phone, I jumped up and started scanning through her papers. I read frantically. Notes on when my father came home late, didn't come home at all, was seen drunk, didn't open his station, left the children unattended. Dates, times, comments, page after page like the FBI, but no address for Stewy.

Then I hit it. Youngest, Stewart, removed from home and placed in foster home, December 6, 1949. I scanned on: court's decisions, Judge John Baker, custody hearings, Frank Cunningham on probationary status, unfit father—

"She's done!" Irene whispered and slipped back into her chair. I stacked the papers the way they had been and dropped into my chair.

"That was a neighbor of yours, Mr. Riley," Miss Doomsday said as she almost crushed her chair. "He told me you were all doing quite well. But of course he can't know what's really going on in your family."

"He can. He's over here all the time," Irene said. "He practically lives here."

"You children must realize that I'm . . . the welfare board is concerned that you receive not only adequate food and shelter but the steady, trustworthy parenting and the affectionate care that you deserve in your most formative years."

"What do you mean?" Clark said.

"That you get the love you deserve," Miss Doomsday said. "I'm only doing my duty to see that you are loved."

"No one could love us more than our dad does," I said, "and now you've taken Stewy away from his father's love."

I wasn't sticking to the plan, either, and I was itching to bust Miss Doomsday in the chops.

Chapter 22

At school I'd walk down the hall like a zombie, thinking, planning. My friends had to grab me to wake me up. Mitzi sat by me in homeroom all the time now, talking about basketball games and dances and I could only think about Stewy, afraid and lonely, off in the world with strangers. Reggie and the swimming team were winning every meet. He wanted me to come and watch and I promised. I kept my jobs because we needed every dime. I still couldn't figure where all our money was going. Christmas came fast and I couldn't stand it if Stewy wouldn't be with us. We still tried to make the best of Christmas without my mother. Without Stewy it would feel like another funeral.

Without thinking, I stopped by Gordon after school to pick up Stewy. For a moment I forgot. It was snowing lightly and melting as it hit the ground. I hiked for home and as I came down Carroll, I could see the water shining off the driveway. Darn, the memory jumped up and caught me by surprise.

One day when I was a sophomore I hurried home from school to do my paper route. It had been raining, but by the time I hit our block, the sun was back out. When I got a few houses from home, I stopped in my tracks. For a second the light reflected that wet smear down the driveway, and I'd swear it was dark blood. Shoot, that same bloody streak exactly as it had been that day. I shut my eyes and looked away. I couldn't catch my breath. I'd never walked on our driveway since I killed my mother.

Step on a crack, you'll break your mother's back.

I'd walked around, avoided that bloody stretch for two years, afraid I'd be stepping on tiny shreds of my mother. The memory made me a little nuts.

I found a ten-pound sledgehammer in the garage. I peeled off my jacket and started pounding the concrete driveway

like a maniac. It was old concrete and had lots of cracks. I
kept pounding until a piece broke free. It was over three
inches thick and the size of a big piece of pie. I tossed it
on the lawn and kept on pounding, hammering one spot,
shouting at it, cussing it, over and over, until another piece
broke off.

Stewy came out of the house and asked what I was doing.
I told him I was fixing the driveway. He said Oh, but I could
tell by his face that he didn't think it needed fixing. I pounded until I couldn't lift the ten-pound sledgehammer above my
waist. Clark and Irene watched for a while. They thought I
was crazy. Uncle Ellie-Ellie offered to help. I'd broken out
four chunks.

Already worn out, I still had to do my paper route. After
dinner, I put the four pieces of concrete in the canvas bag I
used for newspapers and hiked down to the Lake Street
Bridge. I walked out to the middle of the bridge. When no
cars were close, I dropped the chunks of driveway over the
railing a hundred feet down into the Mississippi. There was a
splash like an explosion and they disappeared. I felt as
though I was burying my mother at sea. I was beat, but on
the way home I promised myself I'd bust up that whole stinking driveway and drop it in the river.

I kept my promise. I told my dad the driveway needed to
be replaced, like our neighbor Mr. Winfield's sidewalk the
year before. I told him I had to do it. He'd been drinking and
he happily said he understood. He said he could park in the
street. It took me most of the summer, in my spare time,
when I wasn't working at the station or drugstore or setting
pins. We never went back to the North Shore after my
mother died.

Sometimes when it was hot and muggy, I'd wait until dark
to carry a chunk of the concrete down to the bridge. The
bridge was a little more than ten blocks from the house and
luckily it was mostly downhill. It was better when the sun
was down. Once in a while my dad would sit on the porch

and watch me. He offered to help with the sledgehammer sometimes but I knew he'd come home bushed from working all day. He said he'd drive me with the concrete chunks, but I told him I had to do it my way. I told him I found a hole in a vacant lot not far away to toss it in because I didn't want him to know I was bombing the river from the bridge.

The driveway ran eighty-three feet to the street. Some of the concrete had weathered more and broke up easier and that helped a lot. I learned that if I dug the dirt out from under a section, it broke off easier. One evening in August I hauled the last load down to the river. I hardly realized it, but towards the end I could swing that ten-pound maul for most of an hour.

I hired the same guy who put in Mr. Winfield's sidewalk to do our driveway. It would take most of what I made that summer. I came home one night around seven-thirty and all of a sudden there it was. A brand-new driveway. I walked past the house so I could see it from all sides. It had McCoy's footprints across it as if he thought he was a movie star. From then on I no longer walked around it, afraid I'd step on a microscopic part of my mother. I had calluses as thick as a rubber tire on both hands and I wished I could grow callus that thick on my heart . . . on my memory.

When I got the bill from the concrete man, my dad really surprised me. He said we needed a new driveway, and it added to the value of our house. He wanted to pay for it. I thanked him but told him I had to. I figured Dad gave the concrete guy some money because he only charged me half of what he said it would cost.

I don't know why I did it. Punishment? I'd always heard that convicts in the penitentiary broke rocks all day with sledgehammers. Or was it *something to do* that took away the horror, that made me feel like I was fixing it? Was I trying to dump my memory into the Mississippi? Was I trying to get the weight off my back? Whatever it was, it didn't work.

We had another interview with Miss Doomsday the day before school was out for Christmas vacation. My dad was going to be there by four-thirty with Irene and Clark. I told Dad to tell Miss Doomsday that I had to work at the drugstore after school. For our plan to work, I had to know where Miss Doomsday would be.

When I got out of school, I caught a streetcar and headed downtown. I hiked over to the welfare office in the Ramsey County Court House and went up to the second floor. A skinny lady, who looked as though she hadn't eaten since the Fourth of July, hunched over a desk behind a counter. A handful of people sat waiting on furniture that looked like *it* was on welfare. None of them appeared very happy and I figured they were dealing with one of the Friendly Visitors. I told the lady I was Donny Cunningham and I was supposed to see Miss Boomray. She looked at me over the top of her little round glasses.

"I'm sorry, but she's out of the office this afternoon," she said. She had black curly hair and she looked like she'd just been jilted.

"Oh, she can't be, she can't be, I have to see her." I went into my act. "She *promised,* she *promised!*"

"What did she promise?"

"She promised she'd send this Christmas card to my brother. He's in a foster home and we don't know where and she said it would be all right to send him a card. And if I don't send it today, it won't get there for Christmas and he'll be lonesome and think we forgot him and he'll have a miserable Christmas."

I tried to sound as if I'd start bawling. The lady pushed herself up and dragged over to the counter.

"Miss Boomray said it was okay?" she said.

"Oh yeah, just ask her, call her or something."

"I can't do that, I don't know where she is. She may not be back this afternoon."

"Please, my little brother will be broken-hearted. He's really lonesome. P-l-e-a-s-e. Can't *you* send it?"

She hesitated and looked into my eyes, which I hoped were as sappy as a puppy's.

"Well . . . if Miss Boomray said it was all right . . ."

"Gosh, thanks, thanks a million. Here's the card."

I pulled the large brown envelope from inside my jacket. I'd drawn a curlicue design around the edges so it would be easy to spot. I'd written Stewy's name on it with room for the address. I had a three-cent stamp on it.

She took it and looked at the name.

"You can address it, can't you?"

"Yes, I suppose I can," she said with a slight note of suspicion. "You're the Frank Cunningham case."

"Yes, that's us. Please do it right away, so it can get in the mail this afternoon. Otherwise—"

"All right, I will."

"Promise?" I said, pushing as hard as I dared.

"Yes, *I promise.*"

"Gee, thanks, and I hope you have a wonderful Christmas with your family. Do you have any kids?"

"Yes, I have three," she said as though they were a millstone around her neck.

I couldn't imagine how this broom handle of a woman ever gave birth to three kids.

"Well just think how they'd feel if they thought you *forgot* them on Christmas, if they were away from their family and feeling all alone."

"I will see that it's mailed."

The mailbox sat on the corner of Fourth and Wabasha. I waited across the street and watched everyone who mailed anything. After about fifteen minutes, another woman, younger, came out of the court house without a coat or scarf and hurried over to the mail box in the cold. She put something in and scurried back into the building. I prayed that that was it.

Cripes, I waited another hour, until after five. My feet were freezing and mobs of people were streaming out of buildings and heading for home. Then, at last, a mail truck pulled up. I scrambled across the street just as the guy was opening the box with a big brass key on a chain.

"Hello, I'm Donny Cunningham and I'm in big trouble."

The guy had a basket and he kneeled down and pulled all the mail into the basket. I think he thought I was looking for a handout.

"How can I help you?" he said and his friendly voice gave me hope.

"I just mailed a Christmas card to my dad who is in a hospital. He's dying from the wounds he got in the war and in my hurry I don't think I remembered to put a stamp on it. I have one right here if you could check and see," I said as fast as I could until I was out of breath.

"Well . . . I'm not supposed to let anyone touch the mail once it's in the box." He hesitated. His large sad eyes looked me over. Then he pulled the rest of the mail into the basket and locked the box. People were shuffling by and Christmas lights were coming on all over the place.

"Please, I don't need to touch it. It might be the last thing my father will get before . . ." I started to cry, or at least tried to sound like it.

He signaled me to kneel beside him. He was about five foot seven and wore a post office cap with ear flaps and I figured he played football when he was in high school.

"Take a look here, do you see it?"

He rifled through the mail and my brown envelope jumped out of the bunch with my designs around its edges.

"That's it!" I shouted. "Right there."

He picked out the envelope and turned it over.

"This one?" He held it out.

I took it from him and memorized it with one glance.

Stewart Cunningham
c/o Mr. & Mrs. Albert Erickson
P.O. Box 37
Boyd, Minnesota

"Looks like you remembered to stamp it after all," the guy said.

"Yeah, but I'm going to put another one on for good luck."

I licked the three-cent purple stamp and stuck it next to the other. Then I handed it back.

"I didn't know there were any vet hospitals out that way," he said.

"There's a new one near there. He gets his mail sent to my uncle." I didn't give him time to think. "Thanks a million, mister. You've just made a happy Christmas for our whole family."

"That's okay, kid. I'm sure sorry about your old man."

"My old man? Oh . . . yeah, he's a very brave soldier. He's braver than most people know. Merry Christmas."

I walked and skipped down Wabasha to catch a Selby-Lake home. I couldn't wait to look at a map. Now that I knew where Stewy was I could rescue him. I said it over and over on the ride home.

Albert Erickson, Box 37, Boyd, Minnesota
Albert Erickson, Box 37, Boyd, Minnesota
Albert Erickson, Box 37, Boyd, Minnesota

I hoped that right at that moment, like the Christmas spirit, Stewy could feel rescue in the air.

Chapter 23

Christmas without Stewy was hard. Still trying to make it a happy day without Mother, spending it without Stewy seemed too much. We tried, but our sadness stuck to everything like wet snow. Dad brought home a small tree as if we didn't want to overdo it or act very excited the way things were. We decorated it together on Little Yule Loften, the night before Christmas Eve. Like one of Miss Lornberg's drama classes, we spoke our parts. We knew we were faking it but no one caved in. We carried on with our family act. I always wanted to be in one of the school plays but I never had time. Christmas Eve I got to play my part, speak my lines, make them up as I went along, keep a smile on while I gritted my teeth and tried to forget.

We had each bought a gift for Stewy and when we were done opening presents Christmas Eve, his lay unopened under the tree which only made it worse. Dad spent more than we could afford and I hoped he hadn't charged things that would be hard to pay for. I knew he was trying to buy us some happiness with lots of presents and candy.

Mother had made us Christmas stockings to hang above the mantle and we hung them all, Stewy's and Mother's with the rest. We always stuck stuff in each other's socks, sometimes candy or gum and sometimes funny stuff like a piece of coal or a potato. Stewy was about to cross the line about Santa Claus, but we still played along. We left a sandwich and a glass of milk for Santa for Stewy's sake. The treat we left Santa became the first thing Stewy checked Christmas morning, and he always found one giant bite out of the sandwich and an empty glass.

Before we went to bed, we sat around our little tree and talked about where Stewy was and hoped he had a good Christmas. I hadn't told Dad I knew where Stewy was or about my plan because I was afraid he'd forbid me to try it. I told Clark and Reenie because they'd have to cover for me. The three of us couldn't wait for the day after Christmas. We glanced into each other's eyes and let the hope in us smile.

When the kids were in bed, I found Dad sitting in the living room with only the Christmas tree lights on. I smelled booze; he'd been nipping. I sat on the window seat and before I could speak he started in a low, quiet voice I'd never heard.

"You ruined my life, you know."

His face looked tortured. I turned my eyes to the floor.

"You tore my heart out, boy, you killed the one person I loved most in the world." His voice broke and he caught a sob. "The sun rose and set on your mother, she was my reason for living. She made me feel like a man, she made me feel like a king!"

I couldn't look at him. He groaned as if he were in terrible, unbearable pain.

"I *told* you to stay away from that car unless I was with you! I *told* you and you disobeyed me, and you killed her! And we can never get her back, Donny, do you understand? We can *never* get her back. And for that, I can never forgive you. If I live to be a hundred, I can never forgive you for killing my sweetheart."

I sat there and didn't say anything. To say I was sorry didn't count for spit. He sighed.

"You ruined your brothers' and sister's lives, too. You took away their wonderful mother, the mother they loved with all their hearts."

What he said wasn't so bad, it wasn't so bad. In my heart I said the same things to myself all the time, every day, every night I lay down to sleep.

Christmas Day I sat out on our back stoop thinking about rescuing Stewy. The snow had shrunk back and mild weather had returned. Uncle Ellie-Ellie came through the hedge in his long khaki overcoat and helmet and sat next to me.

"Well, how are you holding up, lad?" he said.

"Holding up? What do you mean?"

"With all you've bitten off here, running this home."

"Oh . . . I'm all right."

"You look worn-out, lad. Tell me, are ye feeling bad about yourself for what you did to your mother?"

No one had ever asked me that. It knocked me off balance.

"I try not to think about it," I said.

"I know what you mean, lad. There's times I feel bad about myself and I try not to think about it."

"What do you feel bad about?"

"I should have died in the war, in the trenches with my dear friends. We went into the Army together, three of us. We ended up in the same battalion, same company, ended up fighting side by side in the trenches. Both killed, right beside me. Buried in France, heroes in Duluth, our hometown, honored in parades and stories in the paper and pictures hung in government buildings."

"You can't help it if you weren't killed."

"I should've died with them, and sometimes I can't get over that. I came home unscratched, except for a small piece of shrapnel in my leg. I was just another soldier coming home and I never got to be a hero."

"You were a hero, Uncle Ellie-Ellie. You fought in the war, you got gassed, you *could have been* killed."

"I should have been. And sometimes I get to feeling bad about myself, because I didn't get killed. And I know how you must feel about yourself with that terrible accident. You're a tough lad. I've learned, feeling bad about yourself doesn't do a bit of good. My advice to you is just try to forget."

"How were your friends killed?"

"We were in the forest, got cut off from our main body. Germans all around us. We fought 'em off for four days and nights before our boys got through to us. No food, no water.

Five hundred and fifty of us went in. One hundred and nine-ty-four walked out, bombarded by the Germans and for a spell by our own guns. My two buddies died beside me, fighting with their bayonets. They were heroes. I should have died and been a hero with them. I found out a long time after that a pigeon had saved us, called off our guns that were shelling us."

"A pigeon?" I said.

"Yep, carrier pigeon with the message tied to its leg. That's how we sent messages."

"Why were your own guns shelling you?"

"They didn't know where we were in the forest."

Uncle Ellie-Ellie stood with a groan.

"Better get home. Grace will be looking for me. You remember what I said, Donny. Feeling bad about yourself won't do anybody any good. Your whole life is ahead of you. You'll have your chance to be a hero. It's too late for me."

I watched him crunch through the snow and push through the lilac hedge, an old man who thought he'd missed his chance to be a hero.

The day after Christmas I set out. Clark and Irene promised they'd not only do their chores around the house, keeping it sparkling, do the paper route, but also keep a sharp eye on Dad and work at the station with him as much as they could. Go down to work around five and walk him home or ride home with him if he had the Hudson. I told them I didn't know how long it would take, but I figured I'd be back the next day. They could only tell Dad late the first night if he noticed I didn't come home, or the next morning. But he'd most likely go to bed before I got home. Often I was working at the drugstore and setting pins and doing the morning paper route, and lots of times we didn't meet up for a day or two.

I took a streetcar downtown with the morning rush hour and got off on St. Peter, right in front of the Union Bus

Depot. I had a road map I got at the station. Montevideo was the closest the bus came to Boyd. I bought a one-way ticket. Boyd sat straight west of St. Paul, not far from the South Dakota border. The guy selling tickets said it would take about five hours with the stops.

When they called my bus, I found a seat way at the back. I wanted to be invisible on the trip but it felt as if everyone who looked at me was spying for the Ramsey County Welfare Board. I slept part of the way and pretended sleep most of the rest. The bus stopped at a cafe on the main drag in Montevideo. The town sat along a river and it had a movie theater. I walked south a few blocks, figuring the highway from the west would come in that way. I stopped at a gas station on a corner where Highway 212 came from the west. They told me the turnoff to Boyd was about six miles west, then another six miles south on County 275. Boyd was on the way to nowhere, a great place to hide a kid.

I walked along the highway at the edge of town and stuck out my thumb. About a foot of snow covered the ground but it had shrunk down some. The temperature must have been close to thirty degrees but the wind made it colder. The highway climbed a hill, moving away from the river bottom, and when I'd hiked to the top, I was sweating under my coat and wool shirt. The country rolled out flat and I could see silos and barns and wooded groves in all directions. I pulled up my collar and pushed into the wind. Little traffic passed, but my excitement mounted with every step, getting closer and closer to Stewy. Could he feel me coming?

A scrawny old woman in a rattle-trap pickup stopped and I shoved in beside her and three dogs. Mutts of every size and color, they darn near licked my face off. When we finally got settled, with tails wagging, and dogs frosting up the windows, and one big brown dog in my lap, she asked where I was headed.

"I'm going to Boyd," I said.

On the twenty-sixth of December, her face held its suntan

as if it were July. I had trouble understanding her because she didn't have any teeth and her tongue popped in and out like a puppet when she talked.

"Well, I can just as well go through Boyd to git to my place," she said and then giggled. "You live in Boyd?"

"No, no . . . just visiting some friends." I needed to change the subject fast. "How old are your dogs?"

"Betsy there is eleven. Maud, the black 'un, is fourteen, and Ralph, the one in your lap, is only around ten."

She slowed and then turned south.

"How old is your truck?"

"'Tis a '36 Ferd. The only vehicle I ever bought new. Right in the middle of the Depression. Saved up the cash and bought her. Brand new. Paid seven hundred and sixty-three dollars for her. We've been best friends ever since."

I said good-bye to Betsy and Maud and Ralph and the old woman. I never asked her her name because I didn't want to give mine.

"Thanks for the lift," I said.

"Anytime, little fella, anytime."

I could feel my heart beating under my coat. I stood on a corner in Boyd, Minnesota, the very town where they held Stewy prisoner. The town only had about two blocks of businesses: a cafe, Eckhart's Grocery Store, two bars, post office, Knutson's Hardware, town hall. At the south end a Texaco station sat on one side and a lumberyard on the other, with a big grain elevator along a railroad track just beyond. I wondered how often the train came through here and if it ever stopped. The size of the town made a guy figure the train only stopped when it derailed.

It was almost three in the afternoon, still cold, with people coming and going about their business. Before I could step away, a squad car coasted down the street towards me. Holy smoke, the '48 Mercury sedan had SHERIFF painted across the door over a big gold shield and enough lights to land an airplane. The sheriff, a big son of a gun, looked at me as if I'd just led a jailbreak out of Stillwater. He stopped. I broke out in a sweat. Could they be on to me? Only Reenie and Clark knew where I was going. Had Doomsday made them talk, tricked them into telling?

I stood on the corner, unable to move. The sheriff stared at me through the windshield. The time had come to run!

Chapter 24

The sheriff smiled and waved at me to cross. Jeez, only being polite. I was seeing bogeymen. I crossed the street and realized that neither Irene nor Clark would ever spill the beans. I kicked myself. A four-foot-eleven kid who weighs one hundred and thirteen pounds, has no facial hair, and can't grow a pimple to save his life, is not a suspicious character. The sheriff probably thought *grade-schooler.*

But I didn't want to stick out like a sore thumb so I started hiking around the town as if I lived there, hoping I might get lucky and spot Stewy. I walked the whole town in about a half hour. No sign of Stewy. Some people stared as if they were trying to figure out where I fit in, but others didn't give me a second glance. I went back and hung around the grocery store for a while in hopes Stewy would show up with his foster mother.

By four-thirty I tried to hang onto my fading hope. I didn't want to give myself away, but I had to ask. I walked down to the gas station and found the guy greasing a Chevy on the lift.

"Hi, can you tell me how to find the Albert Ericksons?"

The young, stocky man was about five six and he looked strong.

"Sure, you're just about there." He wiped his hands with a rag and stepped out from under the car. "Just keep going down this street another block and when the town ends you're on Ericksons' drive. It's about a quarter mile from town. You can see the grove from here." He pointed south through the leafless trees.

"Thanks." I turned quickly and started hoofing it.

"You know the Ericksons?" he said but I pretended I didn't hear him and I kept chugging.

The guy hit the nail on the head, one step you're in town and the next you're out in the country. I could see the grove

ahead and beyond it a large barn and silo. The farm buildings sat on a little rise. I didn't know what to do next, and I
shivered with excitement. Gosh, Stewy was right up there in
that big white farm house. When I got about halfway, I could
faintly hear kids playing, shouting, screaming, laughing, but I
couldn't see anyone. It sounded like a playground at recess.

I cut off the road into the snow and tramped in behind the
grove. There were six or seven rows of trees and the snow
had drifted deeper around them. Several pieces of farm
machinery stuck out of the snow, buried alive. I plowed
through the grove and sneaked in the barn door which stood
open. I could hear the kids' voices much clearer and I
listened for Stewy's. I'd know his voice anywhere.

Suddenly a large collie came barreling into the barn and
barked at me like mad. I turned and talked to him.

"Good boy, good boy, it's all right."

He stopped barking and held his ground. I kneeled down
and sucked my lips together, the sound I use to make up to
all dogs. He hesitated. Then his tail started wagging and he
came over to me slowly.

"Good boy, that's a good boy."

I reached out and stroked his head and he became a
pussycat, all bluff and huff. He must have smelled Betsy and
Maud and Ralph on me because he darn near licked my face
off. His barking brought no one to investigate. After we
became friends, I coaxed him out of the barn and closed the
bottom half of the split door.

Not much daylight made it into the dark and shadowed
barn. No animals, but lots of stalls and those iron things that
hold cows while you milk them filled the bottom floor. The
barn had a nice smell: hay and gunnysacks and rope and
leather. I walked up the center to the far door which stood
half open. I peeked out into the farmyard. A bunch of kids,
bundled in their winter clothes, ran and chased and shouted.

I found a ladder along the wall and climbed into the loft.
There I could lie on my stomach on bales of hay and peer

through the loft door without them spotting me. I watched for a while, counting kids. There were six, then seven, and then I spotted *Stewy*. My heart danced and a few tears trickled down my cheeks. I had to figure out what I'd do. Could these all be Ericksons or were there some neighbor kids and other foster kids in the bunch?

They were playing Washington Poke, a game we played a lot. The person who was it had to stand facing a wall or a tree and close his eyes. With a finger, someone would draw a large circle on his back. Then, with all the kids gathered around him, one of them would poke him in the back. If he guessed who poked him, that kid was it. If he didn't guess right, he had to count to a hundred with his eyes closed and everyone would run and hide. The first one he caught would be it for the next round. If you ran in and touched goal before he said One-two-three on you, you were home free. When we played, Stewy would hide so well we could never find him. We'd have to call olley-olley-oxen-free. But I could tell, the way he was playing now, his heart wasn't in it.

For a minute I thought about what it would be like for Stewy here, after he got over his homesickness. Was it possible it would be better for him to live with this family? He'd have a reliable father who wasn't a drunk. He'd have a loving woman for a mother, a good life in the country, maybe his own horse. I was mixed up. And what about the Ericksons? Would they be badly hurt to lose Stewy now? But that didn't work. The Ericksons had only known him a few weeks. They had kids of their own. It wouldn't be painful, yet, for them to give Stewy back. Stewy belonged with us, his real family, for better or worse, and I knew he felt terribly lonesome. I wouldn't waver; I'd go on with my plan to kidnap Stewy back into the family who loved him.

I counted at least eight kids besides Stewy, and they began a new game. One of the older girls came to the barn wall just below me and closed her eyes. One of the boys chanted, "I will draw a frying pan and who will put a wiener in." They all hesitated. Then one of the younger girls poked the older girl.

"Tom?" the girl guessed.

"No, it was Darlene," they yelled and went running off in every direction.

Could I catch Stewy alone? I bombed down the ladder and headed for the other end of the barn. But when I was only half way there, a boy opened the far door. Out in the open, I desperately turned to find a place to hide. Several wood bins with hinged covers sat along the stalls. Like a shot-gunned whooping crane I crash landed into the one with the lid up as my only chance. I'd barely been able to pull the cover shut when the boy reached the row of bins. From the sound of it, I figured *he climbed into the bin next to me!*

I couldn't move. My arms and legs were tangled but I didn't dare untangle them for the noise it would make. If they found me, I was a goner. And what if Stewy saw me before I could warn him? We hid side by side in the wood bins, and it felt like a priest and a parishioner at confession. I almost started confessing. *"Bless me, Father, for I have sinned."*

Crammed in the bin, no bigger than our clothes hamper, I didn't dare breathe. It smelled like a big box of oatmeal. Through cracks in the lid I could tell it was getting dark. The December cold bit through my winter coat and settled in my feet and hands. I waited like a guy about to be hung. When I tried to fix things for my family, I kept screwing up, making them worse.

Then I heard her, coming through the barn, shouting, trying to flush someone. She dashed back out, probably to protect the goal and catch someone trying to get in free. Afraid the kid next to me could hear my breathing, I wanted to swallow; I sweat, my glasses fogged up. I couldn't stand it any longer. My head kept telling me to jump out and run. I lifted the cover slowly. By the time I had it high enough to peek, she nailed me. She'd crept back into the barn and was only a few feet away.

"I see you, Eric, in the oat bin!" she shouted and ran screaming.

Shoot! I was dead! I was caught. My plan to rescue Stewy was over. They'd call the sheriff, they'd call Miss Doomsday! They'd ship Stewy away to where we'd never find him.

Chapter 25

Before I could think or untangle myself, the kid next to me exploded from the bin and raced after her, thinking she had seen *him*. I lifted my lid enough to see him go out the door. His cap was a lot like mine: tan with ear flaps and a visor. Holy Moses, she'd seen my cap and thought she'd seen him.

I piled out of my bin and hightailed it for the other end of the barn. I could hear her shouting, "One-two-three on Eric!"

I'd lucked out. I crouched in the dark corner along the back wall and tried to figure out what to do. Part of me wanted to get out of there and try again later. Then, with the collie ahead of him, Stewy walked slowly into the barn as if he didn't care if he got caught or not. I stepped out and grabbed him.

"*Donn—*"

"Shhh, be quiet, c'mon," I said and I dragged him into a stall.

"Donny, Donny, how did you find me?" he whispered.

I wrapped my arms around him and hugged him hard and my eyes blurred.

"How are you?" I managed to say.

"I want to go home, I runned away three times."

"I'm going to take you home, I'm going to take you."

I held him by the shoulders and shook him gently.

"Listen, we don't have much time. You do everything normal tonight. But after everyone's asleep, get up, put on all your warm clothes, sneak out of the house, come to the barn. Can you do that, is there a clock in your bedroom, do you sleep alone?"

"There's a clock. I sleep in the room with Roger but he never wakes up."

"Good. I'll be out here in the barn, up in the loft. Drink a lot of water before you go to bed, that will help you wake up if you fall asleep."

"I won't go to sleep," Stewy whispered. "I'll just wait. I can get under the covers with most of my clothes still on."

"Will the dog bark?"

"Naw, Skipper's a good old dog."

"Okay, go play the game. I'll see you tonight."

"I'm glad you found me, Donny."

"I am too."

"You won't go without me, will you?" Stewy said.

The fear in his face was pitiful.

"I'll never go without you again, I promise."

I hugged him, something in me unable to let him go. Then I pushed him towards the door. He took off running the way he did when *we* played the game. Skipper bounced off with him.

I snuck out the backside of the barn, alongside a dilapidated chicken coop, and then hightailed it into the grove and down the road. I sprinted. Daylight had faded fast and I wouldn't come back until pitch dark. I sauntered into the cafe and ordered dinner, hoping I wouldn't run into the sheriff. My stomach growled. A few families ate there, two men alone, and three high school kids. They served roast beef and gravy on bread with mashed potatoes and beans and corn and raspberry Jell-O. I cleaned my plate. It cost seventy-five cents. I had over nineteen dollars with me so I figured we'd be okay. I left a nickel for a tip.

I hung around, taking my time finishing my Jell-O because I knew the barn would be cold. I drank three glasses of water besides the glass of milk. I reread the note I'd mail to the Ericksons once I knew I'd gotten clear with Stewy. It thanked them for taking care of him and told them he would now be happy with relatives in California. I knew Miss Doomsday wouldn't believe that for a minute, but I hoped it would make the Ericksons feel good.

When I came out of the cafe, the only buildings with lights were the two stinking bars. The wind cut with cold. As I walked out the gravel road to the barn, I could see a million stars, just like I could on the North Shore. My heart pumped with excitement and I worried that Stewy would get caught sneaking out of the house. I wondered if my mother could see me, if she rooted me on. It seemed like I'd been trying to get things right for a long time.

A yard light made the barnyard spooky. The night felt a lot colder. I crept inside the barn and listened. Not a sound. I felt jumpy and I thought about all that could go wrong. I hoped the collie slept in the house. Climbing into the loft, I winced at every sound I made. After I checked the empty barnyard, peering through the half-open loft door, I pulled the wires off a bale and spread the hay, fluffing it until I had a deep bed. I crawled into it and kept pulling it over me until the weight of it felt like a gigantic quilt. After I lay still for a few minutes, I warmed up. I started to sneeze and I muffled it with my mittens. The yard light came through cracks in the barn wall and I could read my watch. It was nine-ten. I had a long wait.

Lying in that barn somewhere out in the farm country of western Minnesota, my real life seemed far away. Was this a dream? Were these the best years of my life? Mitzi had invited me to the Deb-Soko Dinner Dance and I had to turn her down with more family excuses. I heard she invited Jack Woods. He was a good guy, about five foot ten. But I wished I was going with her. I figured she'd fall in love with some other guy. Why shouldn't she? I never had time for her.

I woke suddenly. I'd been sleeping and something moved under the hay beside me. Two of them. I froze. Spooky. Thankful I had my leather mittens on, I figured that whatever crept under the hay might bite. A skunk? Raccoon? Porcupine? I moved slowly, rolling away from the critters and keeping my mittens between them and me. They kept coming, closer, silently stalking me. Then one moved up by my face, touched my cap. I counted three of them. I took a deep breath and got set to bolt when I heard the *Meow*.

Holy moly, I started to breathe again. Three cats were snuggling up to me, purring, adopting me for the night. Under all my clothes and the pile of hay, I was sweating.

I could see that one of the cats looked like Patches, a cat I knew a long time ago. I scratched his head and he purred so loudly I thought they'd hear him in the house. I pulled the hay over us, me and the three cats, and I tried to go back to sleep, knowing that if Stewy made it out of the house, he'd wake me. Try as I might, I couldn't quit thinking about that cat some ten years ago. I had tried to forget. The memory still haunted me.

I was seven that summer at Wood Lake in Wisconsin. Clark was three, Irene two, and my mom sat around the beach and watched them play in the sand. I'd go off and find things to do, fish off the dock, row the old wooden boat around, swim, dig worms. There for three weeks in July, my dad would drive over on Saturday night and go back early Monday morning.

One day, while I roamed around, I found a friendly cat. Or it found me. Probably one of the cats from the nearby farm that were half-wild. He took to me as though I had "cat" in my blood. I played with him for hours, we became chums. I'd hide on him and he'd find me; I'd pounce out from hiding and he'd do the same to me. I'd watch him hunt for mice when I'd roll over a bale of hay in the field behind the cabins. I'd climb a tree and he'd go zipping above me. I'd sneak food for him and I built him a little house next to our cabin with some old boards. He was gray with some white and black patches. I called him Patches.

One day I hunted along the shore for frogs when I came to a house where two boys were shouting and laughing.

"Hey, come here," a boy with red hair called. The other one had a crew cut and was taller. They acted friendly. I'd guess they were thirteen or fourteen, like grownups in my seven-year-old eyes.

The redhead had Patches in his hands. "Watch this," he said. Then, with all his might, he threw Patches at the wall of the house like a baseball. Somehow Patches was able to twist around in midair and hit the wall with his four feet.

"Look at that," the redhead said.

He did it again, and then again, and I had a bad feeling in my stomach.

He picked up Patches and said, "Watch this." He disappeared into the house and the tall kid and I waited. The boy opened a window on the second floor. With both hands, he threw Patches as high as he could. I was so scared I couldn't breathe. Somehow Patches turned in midair and again landed on his paws. I never understood why Patches didn't run away.

The kid with the flattop picked up the cat and said, "C'mon."

I was scared and all mixed up. These big kids were including me, befriending me, as if I were one of their buddies. So, somewhat proudly, I tagged along. They hiked down to the shore and the redhead picked up a gunnysack. He put two large rocks in it. Suddenly, I realized what they were going to do. My throat went dry.

Run, Patches, run cat, run for your life!

"C'mon," they said, and they got into a wooden rowboat. I got in with them and sat on the backseat. The taller kid had the cat, the redhead rowed.

They must have seen the horror in my face.

"You don't want him, *do you?*" the redhead said.

In that split second, that tormenting moment, I was a seven year old being accepted by teenagers. "You don't want him, do you?" It was what he implied: You're not some little sissy who wants the stray cat. You're a big kid like us. You're tough like us. We're having some fun together and we're letting you in on it! You're not some little snot-nose Mama's boy, are you?

Then a word came from someplace in me I didn't know. A word that will haunt me until the day I die. I've thought so many times of Patches, how he'd relax when he heard them ask me if *I wanted* him. Of course I'd say yes, we were pals, we play together every day, we really like each other.

"You don't want him, do you?"

"Naw."

Not me. I'm no sissy, I'm tough like you guys. I'm big. I'm not some little girl!

The redhead rowed out in the lake until it was fairly deep. The cat was becoming hard to hang on to, uneasy out in the boat. The kid with the crew cut took him by the back of the neck and dropped him, scratching, into the gunnysack. The cat wailed as if now he too knew what they were doing. The kid tied the top. Then he picked up the heavy sack and dropped it over the side.

I sat there, stunned, shocked, silently screaming. The boy inside me wanted to dive into the lake and grab the bag and bring it quickly to the surface where Patches could find a breath of air. But I just sat there, tough like my new friends. We watched until the last bubble came to the surface. They laughed and talked but I didn't hear a word they said. I couldn't take my eyes from the still, deep water.

The redhead rowed to shore. I walked away from the dock unable to speak. I wandered in the woods, alone, with no one I could tell. I cried for hours. I hated myself. I was ashamed of who I was, what I'd done. I'd sold out my heart to be the kid I was expected to be.

I relived the scene at the bottom of the lake in my mind over and over. The gunnysack drifting down through the lake weeds to settle on the sandy bottom, the burlap thrashing for a few seconds as the frenzied cat tried to find an opening and a breath of air. Then the sack settling quietly, motionless, as though all it held were dead stones. Each time I relived that cruel and heart-ripping scene, my stomach went queasy, my chest ached, my breathing came in gasps as if *I* were drowning. Sweat broke out all over my body. And I thought of Patches, betrayed by his good friend, wondering why I would do this to him.

It wasn't only the cat who died in that lake. A part of that small boy died, also. I'd become a coward; my cowardliness killed the cat. That night I couldn't sleep. I kept thinking I heard Patches outside my cabin window. I kept getting up, looking for him, tiptoeing out of our cabin and walking barefoot down to the edge of the lake to listen. A loon cried over the lake for Patches, a million stars bowed their heads. And in my mind I could hear him scream seconds before the lake silenced him forever.

I can never go back and save the cat. But that horror warned me, even at seven, that life is unforgiving. Now, sometimes when I'm tempted to sell out my heart, that suntanned kid tugs at my shirt sleeve and says, "Are ya gonna drown the cat again?"

In that barn, he was tugging at my sleeve again. And I swore that I'd speak up for Stewy, that I'd never let the welfare people take him away. "You don't want him, do you?"

"Yes! We want him, so keep your dirty hands off him!"

I had fallen asleep without dreaming. When Stewy shook me, I sat up with a start.

"Are you awake, Donny?"

"Yeah. Good, you got out okay?"

"Yep. Roger didn't wake up. Nobody did."

I checked my watch, almost five-thirty.

"Did you fall asleep?" I said.

"Yeah . . . I tried to stay awake, Donny."

The cats showed themselves in the shadows.

"Did you sleep with the cats?" Stewy said.

"Yeah, c'mon, we gotta get outta here. Where's the dog?"

"Skipper? He's in the house. They keep him in at night 'cause he's always gettin' into skunks and porcupine."

We went out the back of the barn, through the snow-drifted grove of trees, and out onto the icy road. I was wide awake in the cold night air and so excited I scrambled, dragging Stewy like a dog on a leash. I *had* him! Jeepers, it was working, I could hardly believe it.

"Not so fast, Donny, I can't keep up," my little brother said.

"Sorry." I slowed. "Were you scared when Dad took you down to the welfare office?"

"Yeah. Dad kept saying he was sorry. Boy, he got really mad. He punched a guy in the nose."

"He did?" I looked at my little brother chugging along beside me. "That's good. Good for Dad."

"Yeah, three guys had to hold him. They said they'd toss him in jail if he didn't calm down."

I felt my chest swell with pride. I loved my dad.

We got to town a little after six, not much going on, only a car now and then. Out in front of the grocery store one of those boxy bread trucks parked at the curb. TAYSTEE BREAD. We walked by and saw the bread guy in the store, talking to the grocery clerk. The truck idled roughly and it looked as if the guy had made his delivery. TAYSTEE BREAD looked like our only chance that early in the morning. I led Stewy around to the back and opened the door. I hoisted him in. The truck had racks and racks of bread, but still room to sit on the floor.

"Just sit quietly and I'll be right back," I said.

I closed the door and hoofed it down to the corner on the other side of the street. I found the little post office already open and I stepped in. I wanted the Ericksons to be sure to get the note right away, maybe before they called the police or the welfare people. A white-haired elfish-looking man with a pot belly stood behind the counter sticking mail in little cubbyholes. About five foot three, he reminded me of Santa Claus.

"Will they get this mail today if I mail it here?"

"Is it for someone close by?" he said.

"Yeah, they live just out of town."

"I'll put it in their box myself," he said. "They'll get it this morning."

"Thanks a lot," I said and I slipped it into the mail slot.

I dashed out of the post office and down the sidewalk. Morning light came slowly in a thick gray overcast. When I looked up the street, I caught a glimpse of the bread truck. It turned the corner and drove out of sight.

"*Stewy!*"

I took off in a sprint.

Chapter 26

My heart jumped into my throat and I flew around the corner. The truck chugged a block ahead. Ripping over the ice and snow-packed road, I gained on it. The truck went two blocks and turned right. I almost went down on an icy spot when I cut the corner, past a big church. The truck slowed, crossing railroad tracks. The driver didn't want to dump his bread. I nearly caught them when he turned left onto a highway.

I gasped for air and poured it on, but the truck left me behind, going east into the gray winter morning. Stewy would feel lost and afraid and think I ditched him. I kept running until I could only see the taillights a long way down the road, growing smaller and smaller.

I prayed like crazy. No matter how hard I tried, I kept making things worse. How could I tell Dad and the kids that I lost Stewy in a *bread truck?* And what would happen to him now? He'd be kidnapped and sold as a slave to some king in Arabia or something. In English class last year my teacher quoted some guy who said *What doesn't kill you makes you stronger.* I wasn't dead yet but I didn't think I was any stronger.

I couldn't keep up the pace and I fell back into a jog. I heard a strange noise coming behind me, clackity-clackity-clackity. I glanced back as I ran and a pickup with tire chains on the back wheels clicked along, slowly gaining on me. When the guy pulled alongside, I stopped and bent over with my hands on my knees. My chest heaved, sweat poured off me.

The man rolled down his frosted window.

"Do you always run along here in the morning or would you like a lift?"

"Yeah," I said, puffing, "I'd really like a ride."

I pulled open the door on the prewar Ford and hopped in. The whiskered man looked as if he'd been plowing fields and milking cows for a hundred years. He had several layers of coats and shirts and his face had several layers of work and sun. His sweat-stained red cap had its ear flaps tied tightly. Made a guy think refugee.

"Where ya headed in such a hurry?"

"Ah . . . to the next town." I wiped off my glasses.

"You mean Clarkfield?"

"Yeah, Clarkfield. Does Clarkfield have a grocery store?"

By then we hit about fifteen miles an hour and I felt I could've gotten there faster on foot.

"All that runnin' make you hungry, huh?"

"Yeah . . . how far is Clarkfield?"

"Oh, 'bout eight miles."

What would the bread man do with Stewy? Turn him over to the sheriff?

The cab was cold, wind coming through the floorboards. I'd sweat pretty good under my winter clothes and now I felt the chills. The heater made a lot of noise but that's all it did. The pickup smelled like a barn. He drove so slow I wanted to reach over and push my foot on the gas pedal. But I'd learned all about pedals. He seemed to read my mind.

"Can't drive 'er too fast with the chains. What's the big hurry?"

"I have to meet a friend."

"You sure run fast for a little fella."

When we finally pulled into the town, I tried to spot the grocery store through the frosted windows.

"Grocery store's right over there," he said and came to a stop.

"Thanks for the ride, mister."

I jumped out and slammed the rusty door, expecting it to come off at the hinges. I saw no bread truck anywhere. Stewy would be really scared.

I rushed into the grocery store. A wrinkled old woman with sunken eyes stood by the front counter in a long apron.

"Hi, ma'am, do you have a bread truck stop here today?"

"Like clockwork, sonny."

"When will he be here?"

"Oh, 'bout now Tom's over at the cafe having a cinnamon roll and coffee. He'll be along in a spell. Looking for fresh bread?"

"No . . . thanks, which way is the cafe?"

"Down the main drag about two blocks." She pointed.

"Thanks."

I sprinted the two blocks, and sure enough, the TAYSTEE BREAD truck sat alongside the cafe. When I opened the back door, Stewy got a great big smile on his face and scrambled into my arms. I could tell he'd been crying. I hugged him till his tongue stuck out.

"Oh gosh, Stewy, I'm so glad to find you. The truck left without me."

He wiped tears from his face. They had soaked the front of his coat.

"I didn't know where you were," he said. "I didn't know what to do."

"I'm sorry, Stewy, I ran my tail off to catch you."

"I did like you said. I sat quiet and didn't make any noise."

"Good for you. You done good, you done real good. You're a tough cookie, Stewy, a tough cookie."

"You sure run fast," he said as he stood up.

"I didn't run all the way, I got a ride with a farmer. C'mon."

I helped him out of the truck and closed the door.

"You smell like a bakery," I said as I pulled his cap down on his head.

"I was getting hungry."

"Hey, let's have breakfast," I said and we went into the cafe.

We passed the bread man in his brown uniform and sure enough, he had a cinnamon roll and coffee. While we stuffed ourselves with pancakes and eggs and bacon, I felt pretty good. I'd lost my little brother and I got him back, like Jesus finding the one lost sheep. But I had to find a way to get back to Saint Paul. If we took the bus, I figured the police might catch us. Hitchhiking would be dangerous if the cops were looking for us.

Outside the cafe, we walked along railroad tracks that ran through the middle of town. Ahead about a block I spotted a hobo with a gimpy leg limping beside the boxcars. Then, slick as a whistle, he swung himself up into one and disappeared. The cops would never catch us in there.

"C'mon," I said to Stewy and we ran across the tracks and down to that boxcar. I pulled myself up enough to see in and the guy was crouching in the front. He had a large backpack and bedroll and wore a long khaki overcoat and dark blue watch cap.

"Hey, mister, can we ride in here with you?"

Tall and skinny, he had a nose birds could perch on.

"You're sure welcome, there's plenty of room."

"Does this train go to St. Paul?"

"Yep, Minneapolis, St. Paul."

I boosted Stewy in just as the train lurched and started moving. I thought I was cracking up. Every time I got Stewy in something with wheels the dang thing took off. Jeez, I tried to climb in but I was too short. The train picked up speed. I ran alongside, trying to keep up. Stewy hollered bloody murder. The hobo reached down and grabbed my hand and jerked me in like a mail bag. He was strong.

"You don't do this much, do you?" the guy said.

"First time," I said, puffing. "Thanks a lot."

The hobo sat with his back against the front wall of the box car and we crawled over to him.

"You boys a little young to be riding the rails, aren't ya?"

"Yeah, I guess so," I said. "We're going home."

"Where's home?" he said as he unrolled a heavy khaki blanket and spread it along the wall.

"St. Paul," I said.

"Here," he said and patted the blanket. "Sit on this and it won't be so blame cold."

We sat beside him on the doubled-over blanket with our backs to the front wall, riding backwards.

"Are you going home?" Stewy said to the man.

"No . . . no, I haven't been home since the war."

"Were you in the war?" I said as the train roared down the tracks.

"We're riding the train!" Stewy shouted like a kid at the State Fair. "We're riding the train!"

The man gimped over and slid the door all but shut. Then he sat down and dug in his pack.

"You look too old to have been in the war," I said.

"The First World War, fought in France."

"You haven't been home since *then?*" I said. "Why not?"

"It's a long story," the hobo said.

"You were in Uncle Ellie-Ellie's war," I said. "Tell us about it."

The guy looked at me for a minute, pausing.

"Yeah, tell us," Stewy said.

"We was in the trenches, one of the first American units to get in the fighting. They called it the Argonne Forest. The trenches was a nightmare. You either went deaf from the bombardment or you went crazy waiting to go over the top and charge the German lines."

"Were you scared?" Stewy said.

"Yeah, I was plenty scared. One day they were zeroed in on our trenches, big guns that shook the earth, blowing us into ashes. I looked to my right and the trench was gone, all my buddies were gone. I couldn't hear, I was deaf and the whole world was blowing up. The air was full of dirt and bone and flesh and wood and metal, like it was raining. I turned to move to my left, and the trench was obliterated."

The hobo paused.

"It looked like graves. Arms and legs and heads sticking out as if the workers in a cemetery quit early. I couldn't find no one alive, nothing left in one piece, and the shells were sailing in every few seconds. I jumped out of what was left of our trench and started running. It's funny, but just three or four seconds can change your whole life."

"Yeah," I said, "I know about that."

"I wasn't running *at* the Germans, I was running *away*."

The train rocked and the wheels clicked beneath us. It wasn't real cold, sitting on the blanket. The man took an empty coffee can from his pack with a small can of Sterno in it.

"I ran all that night, until I could hardly hear the big guns behind me, found my way out of the woods, kept off roads, hid behind hedge rows. I found a dead French farmer beside his dead horse. I put on his clothes. The pants were short but his boots fit. I headed west and south, staying out of sight, sleeping in barns or ditches during the day. And then, all of a sudden, the war was over. The craziest thing. Just like that they stopped killing each other."

"Why didn't you go home?" I said. "The war was over and you were safe."

"I was too ashamed. I ran away. I was a coward, a deserter. If they'd caught me, they'd shoot me. How could I go home when my family and friends would know I was a deserter, that I was yellow? I made my way back to America on a freighter out of Portugal and I've been riding the rails ever since."

"Did you ever go near your home?" I said.

"Once, two years after the war, I called the hardware store I was working in before I went in the Army. I told them I was an Army buddy and wondered if they knew what happened. They put me on with my old boss, old Mr. Jenson. He said I had been killed in action, that I was a hero, that my folks was mighty proud, that they had my picture up in the front of the store, that everyone in town knew what a sacrifice I'd made and young boys wanted to grow up and be like me."

"Gosh, that would be spooky. But then you could go home, no one knew you ran away," I said.

"Where could I tell them I'd been for two years? Why

wasn't I at the front with my outfit? Why wasn't I discharged from the Army like other men? I was more ashamed than ever. I'd run away from the battle and my hometown was proud of me."

"Are you ever going to go home?" I said.

"Guess not. My home is long gone now, I have no home."

We rode for a few hours without talking. Stewy fell asleep with his head in my lap and I dozed off a few times. Close to noon, the guy spread some things in front of him on the blanket.

"You boys must be hungry."

He opened a little box of Ry Krisp and he had a can of Spam. He twisted the key around the can and opened it. With a large pocketknife he cut the Spam into three pieces. He lit the can of Sterno.

"Our soldiers won the war eating Spam," Stewy said.

"You each take a piece. You can warm it over the Sterno if you like."

I held the piece of Spam over the faint Sterno flame for a minute and it did seem to warm it some. He shared everything he had with us: a jar of peanut butter, raisins, a slice of cheese, water, and a few squares of Baker's chocolate.

Stewy and I ate every morsel and food never tasted better.

"What's your name, mister?" I said.

"My Christian name is Michael, but when I was growing up I was skinny and short and I got the nickname 'Runt.'"

"Golly, you must be over six feet," I said.

"Yep, six one. I didn't grow much in school, but when I was around nineteen I started growing to beat the band. The nickname just stuck. To my friends I was always 'Runt.'"

"That's keen. Maybe I'll grow like that," I said.

"Maybe you will."

"Where are you going when you get to Minneapolis?" I said.

"Oh . . . I'm going to head south for a few months, get out of the cold."

"Is it hard, not having a home to go to?" I said.

"I guess this boxcar is my home . . . wherever I'm at is home."

"Don't you miss having a family, a wife and kids and everything?" I said.

"Yeah . . . I think on it sometimes. But this way, none of the people I meet know I'm a deserter."

"Well, when you come back this way, come and stay a night with us, have a good meal, a roof over your head. We live at 1763 Carroll in St. Paul and you're welcome anytime."

"That's mighty good of you. What's your name?"

"Donny Cunningham. My mother called me Donald but everyone else calls me Donny. She named Stewy after James Stewart, the movie actor, and Clark after Clark Gable and Irene after Irene Dunne. My dad thinks she named me after one of her old boyfriends but she never would say. My mother died four years ago."

When we slowed coming into the freight yards of Minneapolis, I woke Stewy. Runt slid the door open a ways on the right side of the train and watched. When the train stopped, he told us we'd have to run across the mess of tracks and up a snow bank. The fence at the top was full of holes that we could squeeze through.

"I'll watch for bulls," he said.

"Are there bulls walking around on the tracks?" Stewy said.

"Railroad cops. Got to watch out for 'em, they can be mean. That's how I got this bad leg. In Colorado Springs one of 'em busted my knee with a lead pipe."

We waited until he gave us the okay. Stewy gave Runt a big hug and I thanked him and told him he could come home with us any day.

"I think you're a real hero, just for being in that trench," I said. Then we climbed out of the boxcar and ran for it.

We climbed through the fence and found ourselves on a street lined with warehouses and big semis unloading. We walked several blocks until we hit Hennepin Avenue and I got my bearings. We hiked over to Washington to catch a University streetcar. It was getting dark and I was glad, hoping no one would notice us in the rush of people heading home from work.

We got off the streetcar at Finn, a few blocks from home. I knew they'd be watching for us, the cops and Miss Doomsday. Stewy could hardly keep up and I took him the rest of the way piggyback. We made our way home using alleys. At our backyard, I stopped in the dark along the lilac hedge and checked out the neighborhood. No strange cars in front of the house, the Hudson parked in the driveway, Dad home. Everything looked normal but I didn't dare take any chances. Stewy and I snuck along Uncle Ellie-Ellie's wood fence and up onto his back stoop. I knocked. Nana Riley opened the door.

"Well, heavens to Betsy, where you been?"

"Bringing Stewy home," I said.

"George is over at your house," she said. "They've been looking for you." She patted Stewy's cap.

"Can he stay here for a while? I'll be back for him as soon as I can. He's pretty hungry and tired."

"Of course, of course, come on in here, Stewy."

"If anyone asks, please tell them you haven't seen him. They'll try to steal him back."

"I think they've already been trying," she said.

I snuck into our house through the backdoor and found everyone eating around the kitchen table. When they saw me, they all jumped up and fired questions.

"Where's Stewy?" Reenie said, and she took me by surprise by hugging me.

"Where have you been?" Dad said. "Did you see Stewy, he's missing."

"Did you g-get him?" Clark said.

"Yeah, I got him. He's over with Nana right now. I didn't think it was safe to bring him home."

Reenie and Clark raced for the back door.

"Whoa! You stay put!" I said. "They might be watching the house."

Irene and Clark looked at Dad. Dad shook his head and they dropped back into their chairs with their lower lips sticking out.

"Aw, shucks," Irene said, "I want to see Stewy."

"Yeah," Clark said, "w-when can we s-see him?"

"Did you really *get him*, Donny?" my dad said. "Did you really *get him?*"

"I got him, and I told the people who had him that he's with our aunt in California."

"Good for you, lad," Uncle Ellie-Ellie said and he clapped.

"Miss Doomsday was here, with a cop," Dad said. "She said I could go to jail if I had anything to do with it."

"That's why I didn't tell you anything about it."

"How did you do it? How did you ever find him?" Reenie said.

"I was lucky."

Then I told them about the Christmas card and the farm and the bread truck and the freight train and Runt. They were laughing and cheering and ooing and aahing like they were at a ball game.

"But how are we g-going to keep him, h-hide him?" Clark said.

"I don't know," I said and I almost fell out of my chair.

I shuffled into the living room, eating a waffle on the way, and when I stretched out on the davenport I fell asleep like a rock.

Chapter 27

Later that night, after a lot of celebrating that just about wore Stewy out, we got together around the kitchen table to figure out what we could do. Stewy, after opening his Christmas presents, slept in Dad's bed just in case. The big oak came right up to Dad's bedroom window, and if the cops broke our door down, Stewy could go out the window like one of Clark's squirrels and disappear into the night. McCoy slept beside Stewy with one ear cocked.

"Maybe we should turn him over to the county welfare," Dad said. "They'll have to give him back soon if I quit drinking and have a clean slate. I'm only on probation."

I didn't know if Dad was testing us. I figured Clark and Irene didn't think Dad could quit drinking. But we all hollered together, "No!"

"They'll ship him further away this time," I said, "and maybe we'll *never* find him."

"If we tell them he's with a relative in California, what can they do?" Reenie said.

"Yeah, that's f-family," Clark said.

"Okay, then, what do we do with him until I'm off probation?" Dad said.

"The *Dutch* families!" Reenie shouted. "They hid the Jews in their houses. We can hide Stewy. Winfields will help. Uncle Ellie-Ellie and Nana will help. We can save him from the Nazis!"

"And if they find him?" Dad said. "We might never see him again."

"They won't catch him," I said, coming fully awake. "But we have to tell Stewy we're playing a game with Miss Doomsday. Like hide-and-seek. We don't want him to be scared all the time. We can move him around to different houses."

"Yeah, and we can h-hide him in the car and t-take him to

playgrounds over in M-Minneapolis and go sledding and skating."

"He'll have to miss out on school for a while," Dad said.

"No . . . he can still go to school," I said. "Miss Doomsday knows he goes to Longfellow in the morning. Maybe he could keep going to Gordon in the afternoon. She'll never suspect that."

We talked late into the night. Dad kept pointing out the flaws in our ideas, kept knocking holes in our schemes, but I think he wanted to see how tough we were. Finally he came over to our side. We'd hide Stewy from the welfare people and keep our family together.

"We have to have a hiding place in the house they can't find," Dad said. "In case they surprise us and make a search."

"Can they do that?" Reenie said, "just like the Nazis?"

"I don't know," Dad said. "I think the judge made Stewy a ward of Ramsey County, but we have to stay ahead of them whatever they try. They might surprise us someday with a search warrant and go over the house with a fine-toothed comb. Or maybe they'll give up on it all, not worth the time and trouble."

"If you quit . . ." I caught myself.

"If I quit drinking," Dad said. "And maybe they'll believe Stewy is with Aunt Ruth in California."

The next day, with school out for the rest of the week, we went to work in our deadly serious game with Miss Doomsday and the welfare board. Clark and I ran the station while Dad worked in the house. About ten years ago we switched from burning coal in our worn-out furnace to putting in a new, smaller oil-burning boiler. The big old furnace sat in its own doorless room in a corner of our dusty, dingy basement. Dad planned to dismantle it and haul it piece by piece to the dump. But after my mother died, he never worked up the ambition.

He came up with the idea and he worked on the old furnace all day. He tore out the iron innards, turning it into a large empty barrel. It looked like a big iron octopus with water pipes coming out of it in all directions. When he'd hauled all the inner parts out behind the garage, he cleaned and scrubbed the inside until you could eat off it. He left the outside sooty and black.

He cut an old rug to fit the floor, ran a wire down one of the pipes, and fixed a light inside. He pasted some of Stewy's coloring pictures on the inside walls, brought in some of Stewy's favorite books and toys, and tossed in a blanket and pillow. He didn't forget a small potty. Last of all, he took the handle off the outside of the furnace door and bolted a latch on the inside so the door could be locked from the inside only. Stewy could duck into the furnace, lock the door, and be perfectly safe from anyone searching for him. From the outside, the furnace looked as though it was still heating the water in our radiators.

When I got home after closing the station with Clark—and we did lock the front door—Dad showed us Stewy's hideout.

"What do you think?" Dad said as we took turns looking into the spacious hideout.

"It's perfect," I said.

"They'll n-never find him in t-there," Clark said.

"We're a *Dutch* family, Daddy," Reenie said. "I feel just like a Dutch girl. We'll hide the Jews from the Nazis."

I went across the alley to the Rileys to see if Nana would help us. I'd be asking her to lie. Uncle Ellie-Ellie was standing guard by their front door and I hollered from the kitchen to him. When I told Nana what we were going to do, she jumped right on the bandwagon.

"Why, land sakes, that little lamb belongs with his family," she said. "Your father's a good man. Of course I'll help. But we better not let Michael see him." Michael was their son,

Sergeant Riley, the cop who brought Dad home drunk. "When Michael's around, I'll put Stewy up in the attic. He likes to play with George's war souvenirs."

"Thanks, Nana, thanks a million. We're afraid if they get a hold of Stewy this time, we'll never see him again."

We got through the week looking over our shoulders like bank robbers. Stewy loved his furnace hideout and wanted to sleep there every night with McCoy. He had to lift McCoy's rump and shove the dog through the high furnace door. We got back into our routines, the station, the paper route, working at the drugstore. On Friday afternoon Mitzi showed up at the drugstore with Virginia and Joan Quinlivin. I was so glad to see her I couldn't think of anything to say. The girls climbed up on stools at the soda fountain.

"Hi," I said. "What can I get for you?"

Mitzi kept smiling at me as if I'd just hiked in from Siberia. I had to laugh. Boyd seemed to be halfway to Siberia.

"I would like the best chocolate malted milk in Saint Paul," Mitzi said.

I tossed the scoops of ice cream into the air and caught them in the malt can. I wanted to show off and I nearly missed while making Virginia's strawberry malt.

"Did you and your family have a nice Christmas?" Mitzi said as the other two girls gabbed with each other and left Mitzi and me to talk.

"Yeah, swell, we were all together. How about you?"

"It was okay. My dad and I went over to Wisconsin where I have an uncle and his family."

I wanted to tell Mitzi about our plan with Stewy and my crazy adventures in Boyd, but I knew I couldn't. Secrets get spread around, I'd learned. She stayed after she'd finished the malt and I waited on other people. I didn't want to ask her about the dinner dance, and my legs were killing me from standing on my toes. I'd noticed lately that my calves bulged like biceps from all the time I spent on tiptoe. I figured someday I could be a ballet dancer if nothing else came along.

"Virginia's having a party at her house New Year's Eve," Mitzi said. "Do you think you could come? She's invited Reggie and a whole bunch of kids."

"Oh, well . . . maybe I could come. I'll have to check with my dad, to see if he has any family plans."

"I hope you can," she said with her pretty smile.

"I'll try."

Criminy, Mitzi came to the drugstore and invited me to a New Year's Eve party. I wondered if she invited Jack Woods, too? He was about five ten. I really wanted to go. I'd have to work it out with the kids. One of us would have to be with Dad from the time he closed the station until he fell asleep. I knew a lot of people used New Year's Eve for an excuse to drink. It was Saturday night and I worried. The hairs on the back of my neck told me Miss Doomsday, with binoculars and notebook, recorded every step we took.

I went to confession when I was done at the drugstore.

"Bless me, Father, for I have sinned. It's been a week since my last confession."

I paused. The priest shifted his weight, I could see the shadow of his head.

"I killed my mother."

The small window slammed shut. I could hear him get up, leave the confessional, and open the door where I sat.

"Come out of there, Donald, I will have no more of this!"

I stumbled out, stunned. What had I done? What had I said?

He walked me up the side aisle and nodded for me to sit in the front pew. He stood in front of me, looking down at me.

"Donald, I can't think of anything on God's earth more devastating than a boy accidentally killing the mother he loves. I can think of nothing that would torment a soul more. But you have confessed that sin for *four years*, and you have refused to accept God's forgiveness. Your Heavenly Father has forgiven you, lad. You must believe that."

"How can I when my own father hasn't forgiven me?"

"Has he told you that?" the priest said.

"Yes, and I can tell by the way he's different with me ever since it happened."

"You confess this sin over and over and refuse the forgiveness God offers you. Donny, you must believe you are forgiven."

"Could you, if you killed *your* mother?"

He didn't answer. He took several steps towards the altar and turned back to me, his face weary with sadness.

"If you don't accept God's forgiveness, Donald, you'll wander in the desert of despair all your life, lost, consumed by guilt, burned up with it until there's nothing left of you or your life."

"But I—"

"Therefore, I forbid you to come to confession until you accept the forgiveness God offers you. Until you quit confessing something you've been forgiven for, until you forgive *yourself.* Do you understand?"

"Yes," I said with my throat filling. "I gotta go."

I ran from Saint Mark's. I didn't know how a guy could forgive *himself.*

I didn't have to worry about New Year's Eve. None of us did. I walked Dad home after I helped him close. He washed up and changed his clothes and we ate supper together. With both doors locked, Stewy ate with us in the kitchen. While I worked up the nerve to announce I'd been invited to a New Year's Eve party, someone knocked on the front door. Reenie and Stewy hustled down the basement stairs. My dad opened the front door and there stood Bob and Doc. They'd stopped by the station earlier and invited themselves over to spend the evening. We called down to Reenie and Dad locked the front door.

Dopey showed up in the kitchen, giving away the fact that he'd be sleeping in our bedroom all night. Clark and Dopey put on a show for Bob and Doc that they watched with their mouths hanging open. Clark hid a peanut in his right rear pocket and had Dopey hunt for it. The squirrel went through each of his pockets methodically until he came up with the prize. Clark put Dopey on the icebox and moved about eight feet away. At Clark's signal, the squirrel leaped the distance and landed on Clark's shoulder. Bob and Doc applauded each trick and almost fell out of their chairs when Dopey went up one leg of Clark's pants and came out the other.

"You say there's seven of them?" Bob said.

"Eight," Clark said. "There's an albino, Snow White. She's curled up somewhere out there. She's pretty wild."

"We have a squirrel with your name," Stewy said to Doc.

"Well, I sure want to meet him sometime," Doc said.

Dopey rode on Clark's shoulder when he took him back to the bedroom. Doc and Bob shook their heads in amazement. I noticed that Clark never stuttered once when he'd do his act with one of his squirrels. McCoy tolerated the squirrels, barely.

A half hour later when Reggie honked, I left them playing cards at the kitchen table, cooling A&W root beer in the icebox and making popcorn. Stewy and Clark and Reenie played Old Maid on the living room rug. Stewy laughed and tried to avoid the Old Maid without a thought about Miss Doomsday. They planned to get him to sleep by listening to New Year's Eve in New York on the radio and banging on some pots and pans. Satisfied he'd been up until 1950, the New Year and half century, he'd willingly go to bed.

Stewy was home safely and so was Dad. I didn't know who Bob and Doc were, or where they came from, but I started to believe in angels.

Chapter 28

Virginia threw a swell party. Mitzi stuck to me like a wood tick. Taller boys came around but she let them know she was "with" me. We danced a lot. Virginia had stacks of good records and I, short as I was, had the advantage for once. My mom had taught me how to dance from the time I was in third grade. Most of the boys really didn't know how, other than the one-step. Virginia's parents had rolled up the carpet in their large living room and most of the songs were for slow dancers.

But Mitzi and I did the lindy hop and boogie-woogie and left the taller boys watching. I tossed her and twirled her and pulled her through my legs. Shoot, she felt light compared to a truck wheel and tire. Everyone did the hokey-pokey. When we slow danced, Mitzi cuddled up to me cheek to cheek. Her big blue eyes made a guy warm all over. Up on my toes, I could feel my calves bulging. That wasn't all.

Virginia's parents kicked us out around twelve-thirty and Reggie and I gave Mitzi a ride home. I'd worked up the nerve to kiss her at twelve midnight and I kind of botched it. So at her door, when I took her in my arms like Bogart, bright lights blinked on and the door swung open.

"Oh, I thought I heard someone," the fabulous John Fitzsimmons said. "Did you kids have a good time?"

We did until now.

As I turned Mitzi loose and took a step back, I heard her whisper, "Oh, darn."

"Yes, we had fun, Daddy. Donny is a wonderful dancer."

"Happy New Year, Donald," he said.

"Oh, thanks. Happy New Year to you, sir."

He offered his hand to shake but I retreated to the car, going down in flames like the Hindenburg.

"Jeez, did you see that?" I said to Reggie.

"Yeah, bad luck," Reggie said. "You hope all week for a good-night kiss, and you end up in a police lineup, for cryin' out loud. Her old man must be using radar."

We stayed as alert as sparrows the first few weeks in January. I started to believe that Dad would overcome his drinking. With Miss Doomsday always on the prowl, we kept Stewy out of sight. It completely changed our way of living. We'd never locked a door, except when we traveled to the North Shore for vacation. We kept the doors locked, the shades and curtains closed at night. Each of us kept an eye peeled along the street and around the neighborhood. We noticed everyone coming and going.

Stewy would put on his Halloween getup at Nana Riley's, the Shirley Temple wig, a girl's scarf, and the wraparound skirt. With his pants rolled up to the knees, he passed for a cute little girl. We taught him how to go up the alleys and come out behind Gordon. He'd stash the wig and stuff in a garage and join the kindergarten kids for the afternoon. Once, so excited to get to school, he walked into his class with the outfit on. Thinking fast, he told his teacher it was for show and tell. His classmates thought it such a good idea, they started wearing costumes to school.

Miss Doomsday didn't believe that Stewy was with our aunt in California anymore than she could rollerskate backwards, but she couldn't prove otherwise unless she caught him. She knew we had him, she said, and it drove her nuts. I think she lay awake nights plotting how she'd catch him. She might drive right past him on his way to school and only see a little blonde girl.

Dad was going out one or two nights a week for an hour or so with Doc and Bob, to some kind of meeting for people who drank too much.

I had two dates with Mitzi, and the night we went to *Father Was A Fullback* at the Paramount downtown, I didn't take any chances at running into her father at the door. I kissed her in the car when Reggie pulled up in front of her house. Sure enough, we no more than planted a foot on the top stone step when the door opened like magic. John Fitzsimmons appeared as if he wanted to sell me a car. I hoped, in the faint light, that Mitzi's luscious lipstick wouldn't show on my lips.

In the car I thought how nice it would be to have a dad who was reliable, a dad you could count on, someone who people admired. I knew my dad could be that. He had been, once.

January slammed in cold with several blizzards, one after the other, and Dad worked hard keeping customers' cars running and full of gas. We sold a lot of Heet. When it snowed, Alfred Olson plowed out the station with his truck for ten bucks, but there were still hours of shoveling to get it all. Doing the paper route got tougher and tougher. Clark and I divided it up and both went out into the storms. Every two weeks we had to go around collecting after supper when people were home, good weather or bad. A dollar twenty. We kept half, sixty cents, and we made just over a hundred and sixteen dollars a month, good money.

I could roll a paper with my gloves on and toss it to the doorstep with sharpshooting accuracy, except for the time I put it through Townsleys' storm window at six in the morning. On the last leg of the route, I'd stop at the station to warm up. On Wednesday, when I came down the block toward the station, a black Buick pulled out and spun wheels on the ice as it pulled away. I found Dad inside, howling in pain.

He'd smashed his finger. He'd bled a lot and he tried to wrap it in a clean rag. His finger made a guy think of a mashed worm, flat and wide as a piece of bacon. The bone must have been crushed. His wedding ring was flattened like a gold money clip, both knuckles pulverized. I helped him bind it up but I had to keep looking away. He held his hand in the other and paced around in the station, as if he could walk away from the pain.

"You have to get to the hospital," I said.

"No . . . no, they can't do anything. It's smashed."

"How did you do it?"

I sat on the edge of his small desk.

"The jack slipped, putting on chains for the Allens. Just slipped off and caught my finger."

My dad didn't look at me, the way he wouldn't when he'd lie. Had he been drinking again and gotten careless? When sober, my dad was a very careful mechanic, never took short-cuts or chances.

"Let me see it," I said, standing and blocking his pacing.

He laid his hand gingerly in his other and I got close to him and sniffed. No alcohol. Grease, oil, sweat, but no booze. Still he was acting the way he did when he was lying.

"You can't work anymore. I'll close for you. We have to get you to a hospital."

He started closing as best he could and I went out and filled a tank on a '47 Mercury.

"Want me to check the oil?" I shouted in the blowing snow.

"Not tonight." The man laughed. "You can let the wind-shield go, too."

When we finished closing, I noticed Allens' Chevy sitting there in the garage and all the chains *were on*. It made a guy wonder. Could he have finished putting chains on with a smashed finger?

I wished I could drive for him, but Dad managed to make it home. His ruined finger bled a lot but he wouldn't go to the hospital. He swallowed a handful of aspirin and we did what we could to comfort him. Stewy offered to kiss it and make it better. Reenie couldn't look at it.

The blizzard outside made us feel safe and hidden inside, but we all ached with my dad. I knew he probably wanted a drink in the worst way, to numb the pain. We listened to the

radio, a Lakers' basketball game, and we worried about him.
When I was falling asleep, I tried to figure how you could get
only your ring finger smashed, caught under the tonnage of
the car, without scratching your middle finger or little finger?
Why hadn't he smashed several fingers, his whole hand? And
who finished putting the chains on Allens' car? The unanswered questions seemed to point to the conclusion that Dad
had been drinking, getting more cunning. He knew how mad
we'd be if he risked losing Stewy again.

In the morning the blizzard still roared and my dad didn't
open the station. We stayed home from school. Clark and
Irene and I did the paper route around nine because the
papers hadn't arrived until then. The milkman didn't show up
at all. With traffic snarled all over town, my dad agreed to go
to Anchor Hospital around noon. I went with him and he
came out without his finger. He only spoke once on the
stormy ride home.

"Sure glad it's my left hand."

He had his flattened wedding ring in his pocket, and I
thought, Did fate have to smash his wedding ring, too?

Saturday morning we did our household chores. Cal Gant
delivered groceries a little after ten, banging through drifts.
Central lost to Murray Friday night and Cal was down about
that. "We should've beat them by twenty points," Cal said.
When Clark worked on his room, he'd let Happy and Bashful
in to get out of the weather. I asked him where the others
were and he said they hadn't showed up. He worried about
them like a mother hen. Irene, with a load in the wash
machine, was playing Sorry with Stewy on the living room
floor.

In the middle of scrubbing the kitchen floor, I heard the
front door burst open and strange voices. Clark had come

downstairs and opened the door too quickly. Without hesitating, Miss Doomsday shoved her way into the house. She had a cop with her. She handed her coat to the cop and marched into the living room. I about swallowed my Adam's apple. I followed her. There sat Irene, cross-legged, playing Sorry with *herself.* I quickly glanced around the room. No sign of Stewy!

"I know that boy is here, I've seen him!" Miss Doomsday shouted.

I looked at Irene but she didn't give a hint. Where was Stewy? Miss Doomsday made a quick search of the living room while the cop stood inside the front entryway. A guy could tell he felt embarrassed with this duty, hunting down a five year old. Miss Doomsday headed for the front closet.

"D-don't open the c-closet!" Clark hollered.

His words only egged her on. She grabbed the handle and jerked the closet door open. In a horrendous noise, out came an avalanche of pots and pans and toys and silverware and roller skates and empty hangers and a hubcap and books and shoes and cans of Spam, scaring the wits out of Doomsday, making her jump backwards and fall on her pratt. Fibber McGee's closet. Clark and Irene had booby-trapped the closet, imitating the closet on *Fibber McGee & Molly* that they heard every week on the radio.

The cop had a smirk on his face when he helped Miss Doomsday grunt back on her feet. She plowed through the house, high and low, basement included. Ahead of her upstairs, I opened Stewy's closet and pulled down the folding stairs to the attic. Up there we had boxes and trunks and all kinds of junk. I hoped Miss Doomsday would waste a lot of time scratching around in that unheated storeroom. Licking her chops as if she knew she had him, she started up the narrow stairs. Near the top, Happy and Bashful flew out of the attic and bounded off her head onto Stewy's bed.

"Oh! Help! Get them off me, get them off me!"

She backed out of the closet in a panic. She gathered herself and then she made the poor cop crawl around up there, sure he'd come down with Stewy. After banging around up there for a while, he climbed down wrapped in cobwebs lousy with dead flies and hornets.

When she searched the room Clark and I share, Happy and Bashful scared the wits out of her again. They exploded from under the bed and shot across her feet on the way to the closet. She reared back and nearly fell.

"Those filthy squirrels. It's time we get rid of them!" she said, catching her balance. Clark, watching from the hall, looked scared.

I was plenty scared. Where was Stewy? After searching the house, she came back to the living room and plopped down on the window seat. She made us sit, Clark and I on the sofa, Irene on the floor where she had been playing with Stewy.

"Now you children listen to me. I know your brother is here somewhere, and if you don't tell me right now, you'll be breaking the law, harboring a fugitive. You can all be sent to an orphanage or worse, to jail."

She huffed and puffed from her search and she threw daggers at us with her eyes.

"I'll give you one more chance!" She made a fist and pounded on the window bench with each word. "Where [pound] is [smash] your [whack] little [thud] brother?"

I noticed Irene, doing her best to keep a smile off her face. Didn't she realize the danger here?

"I know he's here!" she screamed. "Tell me where he is or . . . or . . . or I'll have this officer haul you all off to jail!"

Then it hit me. She was *sitting* on Stewy. He hid inches away from her in the window bench. Like a prank at school with a scary teacher, you bit your lip and did everything in your power to keep from laughing and, at the same time, you were scared sideways. She could stand up, flip up the seat, and grab Stewy by the scruff of his neck like a helpless kitten. She glared at Irene.

"What do you find so amusing, young lady?"

"That you think Stewy is here when he's in California. We got a card from him today."

"Let me see it," Doomsday said.

Irene hurried to the small table in the entryway, stepping over the contents of Fibber McGee's closet. The cop stood like a drugstore Indian. Reenie delivered the postcard. Aunt Ruth had penciled out a message that looked like Stewy's big printing. Bad spelling, letters backwards. It said Hi to all the kids and Dad and had a picture of an orange grove. The postmark wasn't from Aunt Ruth's town.

"Humph," Doomsday said, "this doesn't prove anything. I've *seen* him, I tell you, I know he's here."

Had she really *seen* him, coming or going between houses?

"Your aunt is going to be in a lot of trouble as well. We'll sic the California authorities on her."

She heaved herself up to standing and leaned one hand on the window bench. I held my breath. Would she realize that the padded bench had a seat that opened? She looked into the entryway.

"Your little closet trick wasn't funny, either. I'll speak to your father about your behavior. This is all going down in my report. Especially those filthy squirrels."

Winded and beaten, she got her coat from the cop, pulled it on with his help, and stormed out without a word. The poor cop followed like a dog who didn't like his owner. I locked the door and we stood watching until they drove away. Then we ran to the living room and opened the window bench. Out popped Stewy.

"Olley-olley-oxen-free!" Irene shouted.

We clapped and danced and laughed until we'd all fallen down in a heap on the living room rug.

"She couldn't find me," Stewy said. "I thought I was going to cough."

"Lucky you didn't—"

Someone banged on the front door. It was *her!* Trying to trick us.

"When we go to the door," I said, "Stewy get through the kitchen and down into the furnace!"

We went to the front door, stepping over the stuff from the closet. We stood three abreast so Stewy could get by without being seen from outside. I deliberately fumbled with the lock opening the door.

Without a word, Doomsday shoved past us and rushed into the living room like she was about to wet her pants. She took hold of the bench seat and flipped it open. Empty! except for games and books and pillows. She reached in and put her hand on a pillow. Could she, like a hunter, tell that her quarry had been lying there minutes before?

"Did you forget something, Miss Boomray?" Reenie said.

"Oh, damn it! Damn it!" she said as if she'd just hit her thumb with a hammer.

"Miss *Boomray*," Reenie said with raised eyebrows and one hand over her mouth.

It had occurred to Miss Doomsday a minute too late. With a dangerously close call, we'd been lucky. We stood there with satisfied expressions. She could probably read it in our faces. *She'd had him.* She'd missed Stewy by inches. It made a guy wanna cheer.

Chapter 29

We drove Miss Doomsday nuts with the little boy who wasn't there. We had more close calls. Stewy cried when Clark and Reenie wouldn't take him tobogganing in Merriam Park on Saturday. So they made him wear his Halloween outfit and Shirley Temple wig and they took him along with the Winfield and Cooper kids, nine in all. They explained to the neighbor kids that a mean woman was trying to take Stewy away to an orphanage. That they couldn't tell anyone, not even their parents. That they should call him Sally if anyone else was around. The Coopers had a little girl, Carol, who was six, about the same size as Stewy. We were the only ones on the block with a toboggan. So off they went with Stewy, now a little girl, one of the neighborhood bunch.

Once, when they hiked back to the top of the hill, Miss Doomsday stood there in the snow like the mother of doom.

"Are you children having fun?" she said.

Irene said she just about wet her pants. The kids turned the toboggan around and Stewy hopped in front, his curly locks sticking out from his snugly tied head scarf. Clark, scared silly, quickly lined them up to give them a running push. Irene stood petrified. Miss Doomsday, like a cat in the canary cage, checked out the kids in the gang. Not ten feet from Stewy, she didn't bat an eye. All the kids couldn't ride each time and Irene waited at the top of the hill with Willie Winfield and Laura Cooper. Clark ran and jumped on the back and they hollered all the way down.

Without knowing what to do, Irene played it by ear.

"Do they make you work on Saturday?" Irene said.

"No . . . no, I'm on my own time."

"Well then, you can take a ride."

"Oh . . . no, I just wanted to see if Stewart has come back from California," she said with sarcasm.

"No, he hasn't. We'll tell you when he does. We got another card from him. Are you sure you wouldn't like a ride. It's lots of fun."

"Well . . . I've actually never done that, ride a toboggan."

"Not even when you were a *kid?*" Irene said, coloring her words with amazement.

"No, never, we lived in Arizona."

The kids had pulled the toboggan back to the top of the hill and they piled on.

"Wait! Wait!" Irene shouted. "Miss Boomray wants to ride."

The kids looked flabbergasted.

"Well, I don't know . . ." Doomsday said.

"Aw, c'mon, you'll like it," Irene said.

Clark climbed off and left the back of the toboggan empty. Miss Doomsday wrapped her dress around her legs, kneeled on the back, and grabbed a hold of the side ropes. At the last second, while Clark was giving them a push, Stewy ran and jumped on and wedged himself in front of Miss Doomsday. Down the hill they ripped, screaming, snow flying, Miss Doomsday and the little boy who wasn't there. They banked to the left, swerved back and rolled over at the bottom of the hill, all of them somersaulting in the snow.

Stewy's scarf and wig came off in the tumble. He was sitting in the snow, back to back with Miss Doomsday. While she straightened her skirt, Stewy pulled on the wig, wrapped the scarf around it, and Laura Cooper tied it tightly.

By the time Miss Doomsday got to her feet, brushed off the snow, and puffed her way to the top, Stewy was on the loaded toboggan flying down the hill again.

"Did you like it?" Irene said.

"Yes, I did, but I know what you're up to, young lady," she said as she watched the kids roll off the toboggan at the bottom. "I know that kid's right here somewhere. You think you're so smart. You won't be so smart when I catch him."

For a second Irene panicked, thinking Miss Doomsday had spotted Stewy, about to stomp down the hill and grab him by

the ear. Irene decided to shout to Stewy to run, when Doomsday trudged over to her car. She hollered back at Irene.

"You don't fool me for a minute, little girl!"

Then she drove away.

"Oh yes we do," Irene said out loud.

When she told me about it, even though I knew how
deadly serious it could have been, I couldn't help laughing.

When he heard about it, my dad didn't laugh. We were all at
the supper table when Stewy spilled the beans. Dad hit the
ceiling.

"You took him *sliding!* He rode on the toboggan *with Miss
Doomsday!* Are you completely out of your mind! Don't you
realize how dangerous this is!" he shouted. "I could go to jail
and all of you would end up in an institution! Is that what
you want? We don't break our rules because Stewy wants to
go sliding or because Stewy cries when he doesn't get his
way. We're in a war here. Uncle Ellie-Ellie's right. You never
know when they'll hit you."

I still caught a whiff of Dad's aftershave sometimes and I
wanted to shout at him and punch him in the mouth. He yelled
at the kids for taking Stewy tobogganing while he still drank!

Saturday night I got ready to take Mitzi to the Jalop-Hop.
Clark tore through the house with Irene's diary and Irene
right on his tail.

"Irene's in l-love with Brandon Vandyken!" he shouted.
"She says he's her d-dream, forever."

They almost knocked me down as they passed me on the
stairs.

"You gimmy that, Clark, right now!"

Around the dining room table they ran, shouting.

"Reenie's in l-love with Brandon, she s-says she wants to
marry him."

"I hate you! I'm taking you out of my will!" Reenie shouted.

Ever since mother died, Reenie made out her will and took people out and put people in. It became her biggest threat; she'd take us out of her will.

Then my dad came in the front door.

"Daddy, Clark has my diary and he won't give it back!"

"Reenie's in love with B-Brandon, Reenie's in love—"

"Give it back," my dad said and pointed a finger at Clark. "And don't you touch it again. That's private."

"Aw, Dad, she's in l-love with a d-different guy every week."

"Not anymore," she said.

Clark handed her the diary. Dad opened Fibber McGee's closet carefully and hung up his coat.

"You let her be," Dad said. "She's supposed to have boyfriends. Don't you have girlfriends?"

"Yeah, Clark," Reenie said. "Besides, Brandon's a Dutch boy. His grandparents came to America on a boat from Holland. They'd hide the Jews in his house. Maybe someday, if we get married, we'll hide the Jews in our house."

"Maybe y-you won't have to h-hide anybody," Clark said.

"There'll always be someone who needs hiding," Dad said.

"You should have a girlfriend, Dad," Reenie said.

We stopped in our tracks. No one said anything, like Reenie had just committed the unforgivable sin. I'd thought, lots of times, that some day Dad ought to find another woman he could love. He needed someone to love. We stood there like mannequins in a store window. Then Dad shrugged it off.

"Where's Stewy?" he said.

"He's at Uncle Ellie-Ellie's," I said. "Nana's making chicken pot pie for him and she's bringing a big one over for us."

A squirrel ran into the kitchen.

"Clark! Get that critter out of here," Dad said. "You know the rules."

"Out!" Clark said and he clapped his hands. The squirrel bolted up the stairs.

"Was that Grumpy?" Irene said. She wanted to learn to recognize them.

"No, Sneezy," Clark said.

"Oh, darn," Irene said.

I lived in a zoo.

Reggie picked me up for the dance. The Minute Men and Sigs put it on at the Mac Lodge with Gary Berg's band. Reggie, all excited, told me he'd actually talked to his secret girlfriend on Friday. She had a new boyfriend, and he promised himself that the very next time he hears she's broken up with a guy, he's going to ask her out immediately. He was feeling pretty good about himself. The swimming team had just won its eighth straight meet by drowning Johnson 54 to 12. Reggie swam the backstroke and was on a relay team. They were a cinch to take the city title.

I'd figured out how to quit worrying about Mr. Fitzsimmons at the door. I'd start kissing Mitzi before we came anywhere near her house and she seemed to like necking. So sweet and warm, she made a guy excited all over. Sometimes we'd kiss so long we'd both have to come up for air.

After we'd eaten at the Flat Top Drive-In on Lake Street, Reggie dared to park on the River Boulevard. He and Virginia gabbed and listened to the radio. When Mitzi and I were necking, Frank Sinatra started singing "I'll Be Seeing You." I stopped kissing Mitzi and sat there, thinking of my mom, thinking about how much my dad missed her. Mitzi kissed me on the cheek and nuzzled my ear and it made a guy wonder if he'd ever dare love someone that much? When the song ended, I tried to forget about it. I wrapped my arms around Mitzi and held her close all the way home. Neither of us said a word.

When I walked Mitzi to the door, I had turned back to the car before Mr. Fitzsimmons could come out. I didn't want to leave her, and all of a sudden I felt awfully lonesome. When

I slid in the front seat, Reggie got me in a hammerlock. It didn't help.

I couldn't sleep. I didn't know if the song set me thinking about Mom or if Mitzi stirred me up. I remembered lying in bed like that before, after we'd come home from the North Shore.

"You can buy them that way, or you can file them off like this," Mr. Jackson said, as he filed down several hooks for me. August had finally come in my thirteenth summer, bringing us from the sticky, humid heat of the city into the air-conditioned world of Lake Superior. The war had just ended with Japan's surrender and everyone felt happy about that and awfully relieved. Excited to be back, I knew I'd never get enough of the crashing waves and wild wind and screaming gulls. But my curiosity was killing me. I wanted to catch Splendid more than anything in the world, only to know he was there, alive and well. To reduce the chance of hurting him again, I'd use barbless hooks.

"Shows you're growing up to be quite a fisherman when you're willing to give them a bigger edge," Mr. Jackson said. I didn't try to explain. I hot-footed it to Sunnydale Cabins' garden plot to dig for worms. Sarah wanted to know if I'd be back in time for an evening powwow. I told her that I would and I felt pretty good about her interest in me.

Even though it was the summer Buzzy and I freed the Coca-Cola bear, I never lost sight of the goal that had grown daily through the long winter: to find out if Splendid was alive and to see him again.

I fished the pool several times during the day without a smell, afraid that I'd killed Splendid a summer ago. In the back of my mind, I'd suspected that I had from the first. That evening all the kids played capture-the-flag for hours and Dad played with us for a while. He had the flag once and ran full throttle for a win when Buzzy cut him off and tagged him. We had a bonfire on the rocks when it got dark, and even though I had a lot of fun, I couldn't stop wondering about Splendid, couldn't get over that heavy feeling of helplessness.

Raymond had turned fourteen and he took the lead with the gang, a loudmouth and braggart in my opinion. But we had great fun playing together for those quickly passing days each summer. With the local kids, usually around fifteen showed up. More and more our play took up the day as well as the evening, leaving me less and less time to fish the Onion River with my willow pole.

I attempted to rid my mind of Splendid's nagging memory. It would be stupid to let that one trout ruin my precious days on the Shore. My folks saved and scrimped all year to make that trip, and I knew we might not be able to come again. Shaking off my sadness, I played happily with the summer gang on the wonderful rugged shore of that great lake.

But as the days ran away, I headed for Splendid's pool. A quiet rain had started to fall late in the afternoon, and dark clouds were moving lower and lower. With raindrops dancing on the pool's glass-like surface, I had little hope of catching him.

He took the worm on the second pass, and by the force of the attack, I felt sure it was Splendid. I shouted my joy into the gloomy world around me. Unwilling to even set the hook for fear I would gouge an eye, I played the fish lightly. All I hoped for was to see him clearly, before he slipped off the hook and broke free. With my pole dipping to the water, I felt his weight. Since I had no intention of landing him, I stayed at the deep end of the pool.

Then, suddenly, he broke water, fully airborne, flinging his mouth from side to side as he soared above the pool. Holy cow, it was Splendid! I remember the tears in my eyes as I watched him spit out the barbless hook and fling a laugh in my direction on his way to the safety of deep water. I hooted!

"Hello, Splendid! I'm glad you're still here!"

Then, just like that, he vanished. I stood frozen and listened. Only the cry of a distant crow and the sound of the cascading water. But there was no doubt. It was Splendid. I guessed he weighed close to three pounds, bigger than any trout I'd seen caught out of those tributaries. I itched to tell someone about the fish I'd befriended, but I knew I never would.

I hiked down to the cabin through the drizzling rain with a song in my heart. I wondered how that fish could make such a difference in the way I felt. I knew it was cuckoo, but I couldn't deny my light-hearted step and soaring spirit. It had occurred to me from time to time that someone else might luck upon the pool and catch Splendid. But I believed the long, hard climb from the highway through underbrush and insects would keep other fishermen from ever stumbling onto it. I told myself that my wild friend lived safely in his hidden pool.

Labor Day came quickly, the Jacksons were packed, and Raymond had already left with his family. The usual sadness came on as Dad and I carried suitcases to the car. A mist drifted inland off Lake Superior, the clouds hung low, and the wind carried a sharpness that reminded me of winter.

I gazed up the hill into the thickening weather, over the steeple pines, and I imagined Splendid moving about his pool in that beautiful place. I wondered if he ever got lonely. Knowing he lived there made me feel good. I would leave with the hope that Splendid would be there when I returned.

Chapter 30

I remember thinking that things would work out. I could tell that Miss Doomsday was in the process of blowing her cork. She kept claiming she'd actually *seen* him, like a drunk with pink elephants. She started showing up on weekends and at night, making a guy figure it'd become personal with her. She stalked Stewy on her own time, trying to find his track, showing up at all times of the day or night, haunting the neighborhood, peeking in windows.

Dad went to three meetings a week and made it home by eight-thirty so he could spend time with us. He hadn't been drunk for weeks. I could tell he still nipped sometimes and that made me furious inside. Another month or so and he'd be off probation if he didn't blow it. Stewy would no longer be a ward of the county. He could come out in the open again and live normally.

But Stewy didn't seem really scared, even with the close calls. He seemed to be enjoying the game with Miss Doomsday. Sometimes he'd want hobo food and eat it in the furnace, like on the freight train with Runt. I went out with Mitzi almost every weekend, having fun at school, and Reggie and the Central Swim Team won the city championship.

I was half asleep in my bed when I heard Clark whimpering, crying.

"What's the matter?" I whispered.

He didn't answer. He sobbed quietly. I could make out his shape from the streetlights casting shadows in our bedroom.

"What's the matter, Clark?" I rose up on one elbow. He was staring at the ceiling.

"I wish y-you hadn't killed Mom," he said. "I w-wish so much that you h-hadn't killed her." His voice choked on anger.

"I wish I hadn't too," I said. "I wish it every day, every hour."

"I hated y-you for k-killing her."

Clark hadn't moved. He stared at the ceiling, softly weeping.

"I know," I said. "I hated me, too."

Clark got out of bed and went over to the window. He looked out into the shadowed yard. He tried to get control of his crying.

"Are there any squirrels in here tonight?" I said, wanting to steer away from his sorrow.

"No," he said with a sob. He sighed deeply. He wiped his face on his pajama sleeve. "Donny, I'm afraid to die."

He floored me. I sat up and swung my feet onto the floor.

"You're young, Clark, you won't die for a long, long time."

"But I'm going to die, someday, like Mom."

"That's far away, something you don't have to think about. You'll probably live to be fifty or sixty. Just enjoy life now, while you're young. Don't worry about something that's so far off."

He'd stopped crying. I stood up and walked over to the window beside him. I could see his face. The sadness etched there broke my heart. I put my arms around him and held him.

"Go to sleep, now, Clark. You've got your whole life ahead of you. Don't worry about it."

"I'm still afraid," he said. "I don't want to die."

I let him go, he crawled into his bed, and I got into mine.

"Good-night," I said. He didn't answer. I knew I'd lied to my brother. He could die tomorrow. I told myself I'd never lie to the kids while I helped bring them up. I couldn't tell him the truth. I'd blown it. I left his question unanswered. What do you tell your little brother who is afraid to die?

Wednesday Irene and I made spaghetti and got dinner ready. She told me all about Brandon, the Dutch kid she planned on marrying, though she wouldn't admit it when Clark was around.

"Just think," she said, "his relatives might have been one of the families who hid the Jews."

I thought she might fall down in a swoon.

"Have you asked him about it?" I said.

"No. He's sweet on Marsha Wilson."

"You mean he isn't even your *boyfriend?*" I said as I moved the noodles off the burner.

"No, but he'll see the light. He's very smart. He'll see what a perfect wife I will be for him."

I didn't know what to say. Should I tell my little sister that life might not be quite that simple? I left her in her swoon.

We had everything ready: the kitchen table set, the food ready, Clark home from the paper route, Stewy eating hobo food in the furnace with McCoy, and Uncle Ellie-Ellie sitting at the table with his helmet on.

And then Dad came home limping.

He didn't say anything about it until I asked. He said he dropped a wheel rim on his toe and it was a little sore. Two days later it was my turn to empty the hamper and do the washing. I found a sock half-soaked with dried blood. Dad's sock. Was he lying to me again? Was he drinking at work and found a new way to hide it? And what about his steel-toed work boots? It made a guy wonder. When the other kids went to bed, I found him sitting at the kitchen table drinking warm milk.

"Let me see your sore toe?"

"Aw, it's nothing, Donny."

"Let me see it."

"Why?"

"Have you been drinking again?"

I pulled up a chair and sat across from him.

"You want some milk?" he said.

"I'm not going to bed until you show me your toe."

He looked at me for minutes without moving, thinking. Then he gingerly pulled off his boot and his bloody sock. The toe next to the little one had been mashed, exactly like his ring finger. Just that one toe, snuggled next to the others, now a foul mess. It turned my stomach. That couldn't happen by accident.

"What's going on, Dad? How did it happen?"

"They're out to get me, Donny. I don't know what to do."

"Who's out to get you?"

"Gangsters. Hoodlums."

"What do they want?"

"Money. I owe them lots of money. Back when I was drinking, I'd get to gambling a little. Penny-ante stuff, I'd win a few bucks. They egged me on. Then they asked if I wanted to play for higher stakes, said I was a born winner, make some big money, roulette, craps. I was a fool, falling for their bull."

He glanced into my eyes.

"They saw I was an easy mark, I suppose. The games moved around, different places, back rooms, basements. I'd call a number and they'd tell me where the action was that night. Pretty soon I owed them almost three hundred dollars."

"Three hundred dollars!" I said.

"I kept thinking I'd win it back."

He gingerly moved his bare foot under the table where I didn't have to look at it.

"That's where the money's been going?"

"Yeah. A while back they gave me the chance to go double or nothing with the debt. I owed them over a thousand dollars."

"A thousand dollars!"

I jumped up and walked in circles around the table.

"Yeah. I cut the cards, double or nothing. I know they cheated, Donny. They didn't give me a fair shake. I lost. Now, I owe them over three thousand dollars, and I can't hardly keep up with the daily interest they charge."

"And *that's why* they smashed your finger? and your toe?"

"Yeah, they say they have a reputation to protect."

I dropped into a kitchen chair, plenty scared. "How did they do it, your toe?"

"Three of them held me, standing up. They took off my boot and sock. The fourth thug pulled my little toe to the side. With my foot flat on the concrete floor, he smashed the next toe with my ballpeen hammer."

"Oh, criminy! Oh, cripes! Oh, Dad!" I felt like throwing up.

"He hammered my toe two or three times. I buckled and they let me slump to the floor. I howled. I was sure I'd faint."

The guy with the hammer said, "We only want to do one at a time, nice and neat. Give you something to think about."

"Those dirty rats. I wanna kill 'em! I wanna take the sledgehammer and *kill* 'em!"

"I'm scared, Donny, I don't know what to do."

"Go to the police. Tell Sergeant Riley. He'll get those goons and throw 'em in jail."

"I can't. They warned me. If I go to the police, they'll hurt you."

"Me?"

"You or the other kids. I can't go to the police and I don't know where I can get the money. I can get some of it by taking out another mortgage on the house. But it won't be near enough."

"I can work more, get another job," I said, "get another paper route."

"They're going to break my legs, Donny." My dad reached over and took hold of my arm. "If I don't pay them soon, they're going to break my legs."

I sat at the kitchen table with my brutally mangled father. When would it stop? I felt helpless and I was thinking like crazy. The only time I ever heard of Dad gambling, I was a little kid, and he was jumping up and down because he won forty dollars betting on a racehorse named Seabiscuit. Like a family of gypsies, we hid Stewy from the law and kept an eye out for gangsters who wanted to break my dad's legs. Circus people, walking a high wire while doing a juggling act. And the lions were getting loose just below.

Dad had his smashed toe removed in the emergency room at Anchor Hospital. I wanted to go to the police, to tell Uncle Ellie-Ellie's son, Sergeant Riley. But Dad said no, we didn't dare do that. I knew what happened when I disobeyed him about the car, so I promised. We tried to have someone with Dad all the time. But when we went to school, we couldn't. I told him he needed to get a gun. He said he'd think about it. He could use Uncle Ellie-Ellie's rifle but we used up all the bullets that Fourth of July. The rifle was useless.

I did talk to Sergeant Riley one night when he came over looking for his dad. Dad and the kids were eating supper at the dining room table and I stood at the back door where they couldn't hear me.

"We're having a tight time with money right now, Sergeant Riley," I half whispered, "and I wondered if there was any chance that you could get your squad car serviced at my dad's station. It would really help, and gas, too."

I figured a cop car around the station now and then would keep the legbreakers away.

"We have a designated garage downtown that takes care of our cars, Donny, but we have some leeway if we're low on gas. I'll see what I can do."

"Gosh, thanks, Sergeant Riley. It would sure help."

I led him through the kitchen into the dining room. When Dad saw him, he offered Sergeant Riley a cup of coffee and the policeman pulled up a chair. I figured Dad felt a little safer with Sergeant Riley hanging around.

"Say," Dad said, "did you get involved with that nut who held up a drugstore over on University with a bow and arrow?"

"No, no, but we have some crazy ones. I had a kid call me just the other night and tell me he had a dead body he was going to bring me."

"What did you do?" Dad said.

"I told him not to touch it, that he'd destroy clues. I tried to get the kid to tell me where the body was."

"What did he say?" I said.

"He hung up on me," the sergeant said. "Probably just a crank call, anyway."

Just then, Uncle Ellie-Ellie came up from the basement with his gas mask on.

"Where's Stewy?" Uncle Ellie-Ellie said.

Clark said, "He's w-with the squirrels—"

Irene said, "He's in the furnace—"

"He's in California," I said, cutting off Irene and giving both of them a dirty look.

We lived in a nut house and we'd gotten dangerously care-less around Sergeant Riley.

From then on Dad drove to work. He tried to stay alert when he worked alone, watch his back. After school I jumped on a streetcar, if I didn't catch a quick ride hitchhiking, and I stayed with him from around three-thirty until closing. I always liked working on cars before my mother died. Dad taught me how to change points, clean and set plugs, change oil, oil filter, carburetor, distributor. But after Mom died I didn't want anything to do with cars. To me, every DeSoto grill made me wince, every DeSoto grill sneered at me like the toothed jaws of a shark.

I'd ride home with Dad and we'd keep a sharp eye out dur-ing the night. For a while, Uncle Ellie-Ellie marched up and down in front of the house with his Army stuff on: helmet, rifle, browning belt with bayonet in its scabbard. It was like our neighborhood had gone bananas.

Uncle Ellie-Ellie was marching back and forth on the side-walk when Miss Doomsday showed up and wrestled herself out of her car. I hurried from the house to intercept her. Uncle Ellie-Ellie held his rifle out and shouted, "Who goes there?"

He wouldn't let her pass without a password. I stopped beside him, holding my breath.

"You know me, Mr. Riley," she said with a chuckle. "Have you seen Stewart today. Sweet little Stewart? I know he's here."

"You mean Stewy?" he said, still standing at a challenge.

His lazy eye drifted up and Doomsday looked into the sky to see what he was looking at. I held onto Uncle Ellie-Ellie's arm and said to her, "You want to come in?"

She ignored me and bore in on Uncle Ellie-Ellie.

"Yes, Stewy. Have you seen Stewy today?"

He brought his rifle down to parade rest. Thinking.

"Ask me no questions and I'll tell you no lies," he said.

Standing slightly behind Uncle Ellie-Ellie I circled my ear with my finger and stuck out my tongue, accusing Uncle Ellie-Ellie of being crazy.

I didn't know if she bought it, but sometimes I figured our whole family was crazy.

Chapter 31

I met Mitzi after school Monday by the parking lot door. We stayed inside because of the cold outside. The school emptied fast with kids streaming past us.

"I'm going to have to work Friday and Saturday nights for a little while," I said. "I have to help my dad."

"Oh, I'm sorry, Donny. You work so hard."

"Yeah, well it'll only be for a couple of weeks. But I don't want you to miss out on stuff. This is your senior year, so I want you to go out with other boys for a while."

"I just want to go out with you."

"Me too," I said, "but you shouldn't be sitting home on the weekends and miss the dances and games and movies."

"That's awful nice of you, Donny. If I did go, it would just be to have fun with other kids."

"Yeah, that's what I mean, just to be with your friends and have some fun."

"Maybe I'll come to the bowling alley some night when you're working," she said.

"That would be swell. I could get you and your friends a free line or two."

The halls emptied fast, the school seemed deserted. Mitzi leaned over and kissed me, warm and sweet. Holy cow, she caught me off my tiptoes.

"You let your friends know you haven't got a date for the Valentine's Dance," I said, catching my breath. "There'll be lots of guys who'd like to go with you. Okay?"

"Okay."

"I gotta run. See you in school tomorrow."

I shoved through the door and ran over to Marshall to catch a ride. I could taste her lipstick. It was one of the hardest things I'd had to do, looking into her pretty face and seeing the sadness in her eyes. But our senior year poured through the hourglass and I didn't want to mess up more than one life at a time. I didn't want to be responsible for anyone else's happiness.

I came out of school on Wednesday with my mind muddled. Mitzi had given me a Valentine yesterday, Valentine's Day, that said *I love you.* I gave her a funny one with a Teddy bear saying *Be my Valentine.* My dad said I should've given her a box of candy but that sounded scary to get that serious. I'd seen how Dad had hurt the last four years and I figured a guy ought to learn from that. Right after lunch I'd stopped to see Nurse Armstrong with high hopes. Mitzi's Valentine made me feel taller. No luck. Four foot eleven, one hundred and thirteen pounds.

Along the curb on Marshall two cars sat waiting. *Both* looked familiar, a black Plymouth and a black '46 Ford. When I thought about it, that Plymouth parked there every day. I caught a ride quickly and didn't give it another thought. The decrepit old guy who picked me up told me he went to Central and I found it hard to believe. I thought he might die with his next breath, like a few of my teachers. He brightened up when he talked about Central, like all he had now in life was his memories. He turned right on Snelling and I hopped out. When I started down Marshall, I looked back to make sure a car wasn't turning. There the black '46 Ford idled at the intersection, Miss Doomsday, the Friendly Visitor, following me.

It made me laugh. Did she think I had Stewy stashed somewhere? I planned to hike right home, change clothes, and get down to the station to be with Dad. But then an idea popped into my head. She'd pulled over to the curb, watching me hustle down Marshall. A friend of mine at Central lived right there, Tom Yarusso. I turned in at his house, walked up to the door and rang the doorbell. As I waited, I glanced over my shoulder. Down three doors, Doomsday crawled out of her car and sauntered toward me. Mrs. Yarusso opened the door.

"Hi, is Tom home from school yet?"

"No, no, not yet," she said, looking me over.

"I'm Donny Cunningham, Mrs. Yarusso. I'm a friend of Tom's at Central. Can I come in for a minute?"

"Surely, come in, Donny."

She let me in and closed the door. Perfect.

"I've heard Tom mention you, Donny. You're the shortest boy in Tom's class, aren't you?"

She said it so kindly it didn't hurt.

"Yep, that's me."

She was the kind of mother, in her apron and slippers, that reminded a guy how much he missed having a mother. I wanted to hug her.

"And aren't you the one who hid in the girl's lavatory and—"

"Yeah, yeah, that was me. I wasn't too smart as a sopho-more."

"Well, we all got a good laugh over it," she said.

I figured I'd better get going. She offered to feed me and have me wait for Tom.

"I gotta go. We're playing a game, almost like a treasure hunt. There's some kids trying to follow me. Would it be okay if I go out your back door?"

"Why of course. That sounds like fun. I'll tell Tom you were here."

She led me to the back door.

"Thanks, Mrs. Yarusso," I said and headed for the alley.

I followed a wood fence, cut behind a garage, and crossed the neighbor's lawn on the other side of the alley, coming out on Iglehart. I ran all the way home, laughing. I found the back door locked and I had to knock to get in. We weren't used to locking our house and we started banging our heads and knees when we'd try to swing right through.

Stewy and Irene were home from school. I changed clothes and headed for the station. Clark would do the paper route and then join us at the station. I couldn't help but wonder how long Miss Doomsday would spy on Tom Yarusso's house before she'd go home. Or before she'd get a cop and search the place. I hoped she wouldn't bother Tom and his family.

I pumped gas so Dad, limping around like an old cowboy, could catch up on grease jobs and oil changes. I kept my eye peeled at every car that came by, taking a good look at their faces. I wondered if we could get Uncle Ellie-Ellie to march back and forth in front of the station like the Coca-Cola bear. Trouble was he wouldn't scare a school kid. He'd only make people laugh.

Word got out like stomach flu and Mitzi went to the Valentine's Dance with Bud Jorgensen. He stood about five foot ten. Reggie told me all about it when he stopped at the drugstore on Saturday. I made over seven dollars between the drugstore and setting pins.

The following week, when I finished the afternoon paper route, I hiked down Cleveland to the corner, on the way to help Dad and keep watch. I'd worked up a big thirst and I stopped at Mattocks Drugstore to get a green river. I felt guilty spending the nickel. We were trying to save every cent we could lay our hands on to pay off Dad's debt with the gangsters.

Marilyn made me a green river at the soda fountain. She was a senior at Central and we'd known each other since grade school. I always liked her but she stood around five foot five. She was working her tail off making peanut butter and jelly sandwiches for a mob of Saint Thomas cadets who wanted to take them back to the dorm. The cadets lined up at the pay phone to call home long distance. They pumped coins into the phone the way you'd play a slot machine.

When I came out of the drugstore, the stoplight changed and the cars on Marshall started moving. I waited before crossing and I saw them. The legbreakers! Four of them in a big black '49 Packard, slowing as they approached the station across the street. My mouth went dry. I watched as they passed the station, drove up a block and turned left on Moore. They planned to come around behind the station on Wilder where they wouldn't be seen by Dad until too late.

I ran back into the drugstore and shouted at the owner.

"Mr. Mattocks! Help! Some guys are going to beat up my dad!"

I did the same at the grocery store with Mr. Swenson and the five and dime with Mr. Simonovich and the bakery with Mr. Nordquist.

Then I dashed across the street to the station. I could see Dad in the garage when the Packard crawled to a stop in the street beside the station.

"Dad! Dad! The legbreakers are here!"

I picked up a tire iron and my dad hurried to the front door. Out in front the local men came running. Gordy Simonovich, the size of an icebox, once played for the Chicago Bears. He had a baseball bat in his meaty hand. Tall, skinny Sigrud Swenson had a meat cleaver. Pot-bellied Mr. Nordquist had a rolling pin. And Mr. Mattocks had a cane. Dad and I joined them by the front pumps. I got up on my toes.

The four men in the Packard sat there for a moment, as if they were trying to decide what to do next. We looked like the volunteer fire department from Stillwater. The Packard moved off, turned sharply on Marshall and gunned away.

We stood there like we didn't know what to do with ourselves. The emergency had passed. A guy in a green DeSoto started to pull in for gas, took a look at the armed gang standing there, and drove away. We laughed. Dad eyeballed these men we'd known all our lives. Us kids grew up coming to their counters with pennies or a nickel in our grubby little hands. We got the Shirley Temple wig that Stewy wore at the five and dime years ago. It must've been a hundred times we got a sugar doughnut at the bakery when we could come up with three cents, licorice Snaps at the grocery store for two pennies, an ice cream cone at the drugstore for a nickel.

I called for help and they came like gangbusters. I could tell, as he looked into their faces, that my dad was choking up.

"Thanks, men, I appreciate it," he said and he ducked into the station.

"What did those goons want?" Gordy Simonovich said tapping the baseball bat in his open hand.

"They're gangsters. They're trying to make Dad sell the station so they can run it," I said, thinking fast. "Dad told them he never would sell so they're trying to scare him or hurt him."

"You just holler if they come back," Mr. Swenson said. "This is America and we don't have to sell if we don't want to."

They crossed Marshall, telling each other what they'd do to those thugs if they ever showed their faces again on that corner. Friends like that made a guy proud. But I had a weight in the pit of my stomach that told me the legbreakers would be back.

We didn't see a sign of the legbreakers for over two weeks. Dad made contact with them and, as instructed, left one hundred and twenty dollars at a bar in Mendota to show he meant to pay them. We tried to cover Dad as best we could. The local proprietors of the business places on our corner seemed to take turns, walking over and having coffee with Dad, standing where they could be seen from the street, always one at a time. Sometimes it was hard for Dad to do any work. Gordy Simonovich even pumped gas once in a while, said he'd always wanted to do that.

Mitzi took my advice and went out with other guys. But she always told me about the date during homeroom, as if she wanted me to know it was only having fun with other kids. She'd gone to the basketball game on a Friday night when Central beat Monroe and stopped them from winning the city championship outright. I set pins that night but I read about the game in the morning paper. It was a swell ending to our basketball season. Mitzi had gone out twice with Larry Turner, he stood about five foot eleven, and the hackles were up on the back of my neck.

There'd been no sighting of the legbreakers, but one night Irene had us holding our sides and rolling on the floor at supper. She'd come out of school and hung around for a few minutes with some of her friends. Then she spotted Miss Doomsday, sitting in her car, spying on her.

"She scared me for a minute," Irene said, "but then I decided I'd have some fun. Miss Doomsday was the Nazis and I would be a Dutch girl who would lead the Nazis astray."

"What did y-you do?" Clark said.

"I did what you did, Donny. I started looking around with squinty eyes, looking suspicious, as if I didn't want anyone to see me. Then I took off walking fast along Prior. I glanced over my shoulder without letting her know I'd seen her. She followed in her car."

"Where were you going?" Dad said.

"I didn't know. But after three blocks I saw the railroad tracks. They would get her out of her car. I cut across a vacant lot and crossed the tracks."

"Did she follow you?" I said.

"Yep. Sometimes I thought she'd given up, but then I'd spot her, puffing away and still coming. I made sure she saw me go into an apartment building. I snuck down the hall and went out into the alley. I slowed up until she came out."

"Did you wave at her?" Stewy said.

"No, I didn't want her to know I knew she was following me."

"I wave at her sometimes," Stewy said.

"What do you *mean?*" Dad said.

"When she's looking around and I'm a long way away, I wave at her," Stewy said.

"You better not, young man. Are you crazy!" Dad said. "If she finds you, she'll take you away again."

Was Stewy kidding!

"I stopped a man on the sidewalk," Reenie said, "and cupped my hand when I talked to him, like spies."

"What did you s-say to him?" Clark said.

"Oh, I just asked him what time it was. When he told me, I cupped one hand to my mouth and thanked him. Then I scooted off, over to Snelling. I didn't have any money so I looked for transfers in the dirty snow. I picked up three and found the one punched to the nearest time. Miss Doomsday was a half a block away when the streetcar came. There were a bunch of people so I knew she'd make it. I got on the streetcar."

"You got on the streetcar!" we chorused.

"Yeah. I gave the conductor the transfer and I went way to the back platform where the men stood smoking. Miss Doomsday got on last and kept an eye on me. She sat on the bench seat right behind the motorman. I got off at Selby and hurried by the Park Theater. When I glanced back, she came huffing but I could tell I'd about wore her out."

"Good for you, Reenie," I said.

"How did you d-ditch her?" Clark said.

"That was easy. I cut through to the alley and found an apartment building that had a fire escape. I hurried back to the front and went in and climbed to the third floor. I leaned out over the banister and made sure she could see me. She was really puffing. When she got to the third floor, I lurked at the end of the dark hall for a second and then I pretended to ring the doorbell on the back apartment. She hung back, watching, catching her breath.

"Did she say anything?" I said.

"No, she still didn't think I knew she was tailing me."

"What did you do?" Dad said.

"I went over to the fire escape door, opened it, and climbed out. I figured that would be the end of it. But when

I was halfway down, here she came, out the door and down the iron steps above me. I couldn't believe it. Then I heard her grunting, real loud. She had wedged herself between the iron railings. She was too fat. She couldn't go down and she couldn't go up. She wrestled and grunted and it felt like the whole fire escape would rip off the building and crash to the ground. She got stuck like a mouse in a trap."

We laughed until it hurt, picturing Miss Doomsday hung up on the fire escape.

"I waited on the ground, a little ways down the alley, until the police and firemen showed up. They worked with ladders and ropes and Doomsday was hootin' and hollering. They had to saw away some of the iron railing and haul her back in the third floor door. Then I beat it for home."

"What about her car?" Dad said.

"What if she couldn't find it?" Stewy said.

Then we went on laughing in the teeth of Stewy's monster. After the humiliation of being caught like a fat mouse in the fire escape, we could all imagine Miss Doomsday hiking around the neighborhoods of Saint Paul in the dark, trying to find her car.

"Can you see her taking a streetcar home," Dad said, "and having to explain to her boss how she *lost her car?*"

"And trying to tell her boss what in heck she thought she'd find?" I said.

"I was a good Dutch girl," Irene said. "I led the Nazis away from the Jews."

She beamed with pride.

"You did a swell job, Reenie. Brandon would be proud of you," I said.

Chapter 32

Springlike weather had blown in, when I hustled along Dunlap with hundreds of kids after school. I'd been riding the streetcar to the station without taking a chance on losing time hitchhiking. I wished we had a Coca-Cola bear to attract crowds. That would keep the legbreakers away. I didn't know if I'd stop their attempt by being there, all four foot eleven and one hundred and thirteen pounds. But like before, they probably didn't want witnesses. When I thought of Dad's finger and toe, I wanted to smash somebody. I wished I was big and powerful so I could grab one of those thugs and beat the living daylights out of him.

At Selby a gang of kids waited for the next streetcar. I wedged in along the curb and looked toward downtown. A streetcar at Lexington headed up the hill. I'd be with Dad in no time. The streetcar got halfway up the hill and stopped. No, it didn't stop, it was spinning its wheels but not moving. There it sat, slowly sliding back and then lurching forward. Someone had greased the tracks!

I looked around. Across the street in front of the drugstore I spotted Jim Kinsey and Mike Birt and Howie Simon with some other seniors, laughing their heads off. I thought of enlisting those crazy guys to help us against the legbreakers. They could keep those thugs befuddled with their pranks.

The motorman gave up and went into a house, probably to call for help. They'd have to clean and sand the tracks before the streetcar could get up the hill. By the time the cops arrived, my buddies would be long gone. I wanted to laugh, but Dad was alone and I had to get there. I raced back to Marshall and caught a ride in about five minutes. A good-looking guy in a creme-colored '46 Dodge coupe dropped me right in front of the station. The coupe had a bad muffler.

Dad still had two good legs, working on a Chevy's water

pump. I took care of the customers and Mr. Simonovich came over to visit. I kept him there a half hour asking him about when he played professional football. Clark came by after finishing the paper route and reminded me that we had to collect after supper.

We helped Dad close and rode home with him. When we pulled in our driveway, we noticed a commotion up on our porch. There were three cars in front of the house. That terrible heart-stopping feeling grabbed me. *They'd caught Stewy!*

We bombed out of the car and hustled over as three men half-dragged, half-shoved Miss Doomsday off our porch.

"I've *seen* him! He's in there, I tell you!" she shouted, dragging her heels.

A fourth man in a suit and overcoat rushed over to us.

"Are you Frank Cunningham?" he said, looking at Dad.

"Yes. What's going on?"

"I can't apologize enough. I'm John Reynolds with the Ramsey County Welfare Board. One of our workers, Miss Boomray, I'm sure you know her, has gone far beyond our procedures and rules of conduct. We think she's had a serious nervous breakdown."

"He's in there, I tell you! Go, look! I *saw him!*" she shouted as the men wrestled her down the walk and proceeded to cram her into the backseat of a car.

"She's been removed from the case," the man said. "She'll probably be up for review and in all likelihood be fired. Let me apologize for the Ramsey County Welfare Board. This is not how we operate and we won't stand for any of our people acting in this manner."

"Does this mean you're not looking for my little brother anymore?" I said.

"I'm not familiar with your case, but a new welfare worker will be assigned after a review. You will be informed in a few weeks."

The man thanked us again for our understanding and the three cars pulled away like a funeral procession. I wanted to cheer. We could see Miss Doomsday's face pressed up against the side window and she was shouting and pointing. All three of us looked back to see what she was pointing at. Stewy was standing by the corner of the garage, waving at her!

All along Stewy had been playing hide-and-*peek* with Miss Doomsday, rather than hide-and-*seek*.

The kids laughed so hard at supper I was afraid they'd choke.

"You said to play hide-and-*peek* with Miss Doomsday, Donny," Stewy said with a frown. "I heard ya!"

"No, no, Stewy, I said it would be like playing hide-and-*seek*."

"No you never," Stewy said. He was really teed off. "You told me hide-and-*peek!*"

"Did you let her see you other times?" Reenie said, almost gagging on her food.

"Yeah. I waved at her a lot when she was far away," Stewy said.

We all looked at each other, shook our heads, and went on laughing, realizing little Stewy, the boy who wasn't there, had brought down Doomsday all by himself.

That night I floundered in my bed, wide awake. At times like that, when I couldn't sleep, I'd go back to the North Shore in my memory.

When I was fourteen we made it back to the North Shore for our August vacation. I was out of the car before Dad stopped beside our cabin. I dashed down to the shore and leaped onto the rocks and hooted to that wonderful world. Spray from the crashing waves showered me and the gulls screamed back at me. And I was as happy as I'd ever been.

The Sunnydale bunch gathered again and kept me busy with games in the woods, wave-jumping on the rocks, and bonfires at night. I didn't fish nearly as often. Much of it had to do with Sarah Jackson, who, without warning, had turned into a really cute girl.

Without having seen her for a year, I was immediately smitten, young love howling at the moon. The trouble was, she affected Raymond in the same way, and that big mouth show-off, a year older than I, seemed to impress Sarah more than I did. I couldn't believe that anyone so pretty could at the same time be so naive and blind. Sarah treated me like one of the gang, as if she didn't notice the sappy look in my eyes and the way I stammered when I'd talk to her. Only a summer ago I'd have thought nothing of knocking her flat trying to beat her to the flag or reaching a goal safely.

Raymond held her hand at the first bonfire, and I worried that the rat might have kissed her when he walked her to her cabin in the pitch darkness. I was a happy-go-lucky kid that summer, while Raymond was always challenging, boasting, the leader of the Sunnydale gang. Anyone could see that he and I were in an unspoken competition, trying to outdo each other to get Sarah's attention, to win her love.

That August, life centered more around the gang than on stuff we'd do with our families. Sarah probably enjoyed it the most with two cow-eyed boys chasing after her. Every day it looked as if one of us had the inside track until the following day when the other would. On the days when I was running second, I would go to bed downhearted. And as our storybook days flew by, I was no longer winning every other day.

Then I heard about the contest at the resort store. The village of Tofte announced a celebration to wind up the season and bid farewell to its summer guests. There would be a dinner with a smorgasbord of special foods, followed by a dance for all ages, and the night would be topped off with a fireworks display over the lake. But the event that caught my imagination was the *fishing contest*. With an adult division and a kids', sixteen and under, prizes would be awarded. With Raymond already bragging how he'd bring in the biggest fish, I knew that the real prize would be Sarah Jackson.

As it rushed in on me, I began gloating, knowing that no
fish around, except in the big lake, could hold a candle to
Splendid. All I had to do was catch him. My secret was like
holding onto a hot potato. I couldn't wait for the day to
come. Though I'd intended to, I hadn't made it up to the pool
that summer, always waylaid by the plans the kids kept making. But I never doubted that Splendid was there and that I
could catch him when I wanted to. With that huge trout, I'd
not only win Sarah's affection and the admiration of the
gang, but I'd be the hero of the whole Tofte wing-ding. Holy
cow! Giddy with my stroke of good luck, I muffled my happiness and confidence. Gritting my teeth, I good-naturedly
listened to Raymond boast of his coming triumph.

My dad drove me to the sign-in. Raymond and a lot of kids
I'd never seen before showed up. I gave the man my fifty
cents and got the rules. It was money in the bank. Raymond's
confidence seemed thin at the sight of so much competition
while mine only snowballed.

Dad dropped me at the Onion River, and I scrambled
uphill, ignoring all the other water as I made a headlong dash
for the pool. Quickly tiring, I sweat and gasped in the climb
that had no give for boys who hurry, forcing me to stop and
rest and catch my breath. Straight out, the distance seemed a
lot further than I'd remembered, and my patience grew thin
as time whittled away. Then I recognized the familiar ground.
I was there!

With the excitement of the fishing contest driving me, I
crept through the brush toward the cascading water and
stood thunderstruck. A tree had fallen across the middle of
the pool, making it really tough, if not impossible, to play a
large fish and land it. I crouched for a minute, collecting my
wits and figuring what I'd have to do if I hooked him. I
planned to let my worm come from the upper end with the
current, yet if I wanted to beach the fish on the shallow ledge
at the end of the pool, I would have to cross the log with
Splendid on the line. If the trout snagged my line on the tree

for only a second, he could break free and be gone. I didn't dare try to land the fish at the deep end without a net. I knew there'd be no second chance.

I flicked the worm into the white water under the falls. This hook was armed with a barb. The line floated with the current, under the log, and the worm showed up at the far end of the pool, intact, untouched. Trying to control my impatience, I reeled the worm back as close to the edge as possible, hesitating several times so as not to alert the fish if he was casting a wary eye at that obviously phony worm doing the backstroke upstream.

When I had retrieved the worm, I waited for more than ten minutes, attempting to do nothing that would give the fish a suspicion of anything unnatural. The evaporating time urged me to throw caution to the wind, but for the moment, I fished carefully.

It was afternoon when Splendid took the worm and raced under the log to the other end of the pool. I set the hook, trying to keep the line from fouling on the snag. I hadn't seen him and I was scared out of my wits. I worked my way toward the fallen pine and slid my left leg over the trunk. While lying on my stomach on the tree, with branches poking me in the stomach and nearly knocking my glasses off, I passed my pole from one hand to the other, under the water, to the other side of the trunk. When I'd pulled off the switch, Splendid still tugged on the line. Holy smoke, I'd done it!

I tired Splendid with a steady give and take, coaxing him into the shallow water near the lip of the pool. When I caught a glimpse of him, it startled me. Gigantic! He turned back into deep water, and the line went slack, sending me into a cold sweat. Carefully I gathered the line and the fish hung heavy at the other end, worn out. I dry-docked him on the slippery shelf and eased him away from the water. I had him!

I let out a whoop that broke out over the wilderness like the call of a wild animal. I slid two fingers under his gills and lifted him. I couldn't believe his heft, guessing he had more than doubled in size since I first caught him. My head spun with the promise of glory. I couldn't lose.

I laid him on dry ground and watched him puffing, fighting for his life as he had the time I hooked him in the throat. This time, I looked away, unable to duck the question any longer. I could see myself parading in with this prize-winning trout at my side, soundly shutting Raymond's mouth while at the same time turning Sarah's eye and winning everyone's applause. Without a doubt, Splendid would be the biggest fish of the tournament, men or boys, and all I had to do was cash him in.

I paused. He heaved and flipped, coating himself with pine needles and sand, trying to hurl himself back into the pool. I realized that each moment I hesitated, trying to decide, I was deciding. Splendid fought it, whacking the ground with his tail. I kicked myself for standing around, knowing I had to be back at the booth by six o'clock and that I had a long hike ahead of me. It had been that same hesitation that kept me from bringing him home in the first place. That seemed so long ago.

I refused to allow my mind another thought. I snapped a forked willow branch and numbly strung the fish on it. With a catch in my throat, I marched blindly away from the pool, forcing myself, down the hill, scrambling, refusing to look at him. As I moved toward the glory to come, Splendid banged against my leg, whacking me, refusing to give up, asking for his life.

Go back, go back, it's not too late! get him into the water quickly, save him!

I pushed myself, almost running, my arm aching from the weight of the fish, nothing compared to the ache in my heart. Commanding my legs to march, I slammed the door of my shouting heart and tried to ignore Splendid's pleading at my side. I cut away from the river and bushwhacked cross-country on a beeline for the village, removing any final temptation to rescue Splendid at the last minute.

I never noticed Splendid's last breath, never returned the final glance from that pleading eye.

Checking in under the deadline, bedraggled after bush-whacking my way through the timber, I drew unbelieving "oohs" and "aahs" from the people milling around the judges' booth. Their gaping mouths and wide eyes mimicked my dead fish. My arms ached from lugging him so far, and if it hadn't been for my parents, I might have had trouble con-vincing the authorities I caught that trout in the Onion River. The fish weighed in at 3 pounds, 11 ounces, knocking the socks off every fisherman who saw it banked in ice and on display all through the evening.

Raymond didn't place, and the winner of the men's divi-sion had a trout that weighed one pound, two ounces, an excellent fish for these tributaries.

The whole fantasy came true. I was the celebrity at the dinner, and Sarah stuck to me like oatmeal.

My mother took a picture of me with the fish and Sarah, and when they awarded the prizes—ten dollars and a Parker fountain pen to me, twenty-five dollars and an Elgin watch to the man—I could see the pride in my dad's eyes. I became a big spender during the dance, buying the gang bottle after bottle of Hires root beer and 7UP, as though, like Judas, I didn't want to go home with any of the money. I even bought Raymond several rounds of root beer, proving I was a good sport as well as a great fisherman.

I basked in the limelight, having one bad moment when my father asked if that wasn't the fish I'd told them about several summers before. My dad, calling it a humdinger, had noticed the damaged dorsal fin, and it saddened me. I felt like a traitor, betraying and killing a friend.

But in the excitement and romance of the celebration, that was swept away. Sarah and I danced more than once, and I was glad my mother had taught me how. Fireworks cannon-aded out over the crashing waves to end the evening, and I felt brave enough to put my arm around Sarah's shoulders as we snuggled together and watched.

But the last rocket flared out, the night ended, the prize money was spent, and vacation was over. By noon the next day, Sarah was gone, and Raymond, the local kids had started school, and I had a final hour to spend before we left.

I walked along the shore, and I couldn't keep Splendid from my thoughts. I'd struggled with the choices beside the pool and made mine, and everything promised came true. But I had a new perspective now. I never saw Sarah again, nor Raymond. No one else would remember much about the big day. It had all blown away like smoke, and Splendid was no longer in his pool. I'd made the wrong choice, and I ached to go back and make the other. He had tried to tell me that the prize wasn't worth the cost, and I had ignored his warning. I had betrayed a friend, and the regret seemed unbearable.

As I rode away, crammed in the backseat of the '39 DeSoto, my heart ached. For the first time in my life I thought about my own existence, and I realized that nothing had changed: The water tumbled into Splendid's pool, paused for a moment, and continued its journey to the sea as always. The rocks stood silent, ignoring the waves that pounded summer and winter. The forest went through its never-ending stages, and none of it with any notice that Splendid had ever been there. I understood, with a young boy's anguish, that it would be the same for me. That creation would continue, like it did this day, on and on, after I was gone.

I hid my sadness in a pretense of sleep, ignoring my brothers and sister. With my face pressed against the window, I watched the trees and creeks and rock outcrops, the seagulls and whitecaps on the lake, and silently, I cried. For Splendid, for all of it, for all those who were no more. With my new understanding of how brief life was in the scheme of things, I cried for myself.

Whenever I think back to those unforgettable summer days, I still remember best that fish, that lionhearted, courageous fish, and all he had taught me. He had been calling out to me on the journey down the hill, and I hadn't listened. But

I have heard him since, at times when I would least expect, bringing a sad smile and private satisfaction to my heart. Sometimes when I'm trying to make a tough decision, I can feel him thumping against my leg. It was my good luck to have had that trout as a friend for a while, and as a teacher. Like some unseen hand, Splendid led me from one ledge of life to another.

That was the twenty-third of August, 1946. Had I known what was coming, I would've run away, never gone home, and saved my mother's life.

Chapter 33

Like a black cloud over our lives, the shadow of Miss Dooms-day had blown away. Dad hoped to get off probation soon, though I was skeptical. I still caught a whiff of his aftershave now and then.

Tuesday night daylight had faded and I expected Dad any minute. Clark was in Irene's bedroom, teaching her tricks with one of the squirrels. More and more she could tell them apart, although she still got it wrong sometimes. I was changing clothes in my room when I saw Dad's headlights swing into the drive. Though the garage door was open, he parked on the driveway. Dark figures came swiftly from a car across the street and grabbed him when he stepped out of the Hudson. They dragged him kicking into the garage. In my stocking feet, I took the stairs three at a time, shouting at Clark and Irene.

"Clark, run to the Rileys', tell them to call the police! Tell them some thugs are beating up Dad! Go! Go! Go!"

Clark almost tore the back door off its hinges going out.

"Reenie! Call the police, give them our address, tell them someone's being murdered!"

I flew out the front door and sprinted to the garage. What could I do?

Without thinking, I slipped into the Hudson and locked the doors. Then I pulled on the headlights. The men were momentarily blinded. They struggled with Dad and shouted at each other. For a second they hesitated. They had pulled a flour sack over Dad's head. Dressed in black, they wore dark blue watch caps pulled almost over their eyes. Two men had Dad's arms and shoulders pinned. A third guy was stretching Dad's legs out on the concrete floor. The fourth man had the ten-pound maul in his hands.

They recovered from the surprise of the headlights and

ignored them as if they'd get the job done quickly and get out of there. The man raised the sledgehammer over his head when Uncle Ellie-Ellie stepped through the side door. He had on his gas mask and helmet and he held his Springfield rifle with the bayonet fixed. I knew he didn't have any bullets, that he was bluffing.

"So it's bashing ye want, huh boys?" he said and he thrust the bayonet into the back of the thug with the sledgehammer. The point of the bayonet came out the man's chest. The sledgehammer dropped to the floor. The man dropped beside it, as Uncle Ellie-Ellie pulled the bayonet from his body.

One of the guys holding Dad's arms jumped up and pulled a pistol from inside his coat. He shot Uncle Ellie-Ellie in the chest, point-blank, twice. Uncle Ellie-Ellie dropped the rifle and sunk to his knees. Then he toppled over backwards. Oh, God! I didn't know what to do. I started flicking the lights from high beam to low beam and honking the horn. The men looked at each other.

"Let's go!" the one holding Dad's feet shouted and they ran. The man who shot Uncle Ellie-Ellie stopped for a second and glared through the windshield. I was so low, behind the wheel, I didn't think he could recognize me. But I saw his face clear as a bell, a face I'd never forget. The man with only one nostril. Then he ran with the others.

I slipped out of the Hudson and hurried to Uncle Ellie-Ellie. Dad had pulled the sack off his head and the gas mask off Uncle Ellie-Ellie. He held Uncle Ellie-Ellie's head in his lap. A bloody foam oozed out of Uncle Ellie-Ellie's nose and mouth.

"Hang on," my dad said, "hang on, help's coming."

I knelt beside Uncle Ellie-Ellie and leaned close to his face.

"You're a hero, Uncle Ellie-Ellie!" I shouted, "you're a *hero!*"

He looked up at me. A faint smile came to his face.

"I am?" he said weakly.

"Yes! yes! you're a hero! You'll be in the newspaper and newsreels and on the radio. You saved my dad, you're a hero!"

He gazed at me for a second. Then his lazy eye rolled up toward his forehead. The other eye followed. He was dead!

Just like when I killed my mother, it happened in seconds. Seconds we could never take back. All of a sudden there were cops and ambulance drivers and neighbors all over the place. The rat Uncle Ellie-Ellie bayoneted was dead. I was glad. I wanted to go in the garage and piss on him. Sergeant Riley came roaring up in a patrol car with siren blazing, tires squealing. He pushed through the crowd and knelt beside his father. He lifted his father's head and shoulders off the floor and held him. No one said a word. Sergeant Riley was sobbing. Rocking his father in his arms and sobbing.

The police went over the gangsters' car, a black Packard, that they left behind. They'd jumped in and tried to drive away but the car wouldn't start. In desperation, they took off on foot, running in all directions. Reenie had opened the Packard's hood and removed the distributor cap. Cops were spreading out through the neighborhood hoping to luck into one of them.

The cops asked lots of questions and impounded the black Packard. My dad came out of it unhurt, but I knew this would only make the mobsters meaner and madder. Around nine Sergeant Riley came to the house and we sat in the living room. The other three kids were in bed after a lot of coaxing and threats. Riley looked like he'd been run over. One part of him seethed for revenge, the other choked on sadness. It was hard to find words.

"I'll get that sonofabitch if it's the last thing I do!" Sergeant Riley said. "Did you get a good look at him, Donny?"

"Yeah. I'll never forget his face."

"Can you identify him from mug shots?"

"I think so, I'll try."

"We'll keep it under our hats that we have an eye witness," Riley said. "We don't want the rat to know you can finger him."

My dad told Sergeant Riley about the money, that he

wanted to pay it back but he owed them over three thousand dollars, as much as he made in a good year.

"We've been after this outfit for years, but we can't get anyone to testify," Sergeant Riley said. "We had an undercover cop work for them for over a year, starting with run-of-the-mill work in a legitimate business. Then, when they trusted him, he got involved in the gambling and prostitution. We were close to nailing them when someone found him floating face down in the Minnesota River."

"Will they come back?" I said.

"The guy who shot my dad might, if he saw you," Riley said.

"I don't think he did," I said, trying to ignore my fear.

"How about the money?" Dad said.

"They'll collect. They can't let you get away with stiffing them, bad for their reputation. We'll tag this as a robbery-murder for the public. Won't let on that it had anything to do with gambling." The sergeant looked at Dad. "They'll figure you didn't rat on them. We'll say the robbers thought you had the day's receipts with you when they jumped you. A neighbor gave his life saving you."

Riley's voice broke, he paused, getting a grip on himself.

Stewy called from upstairs. My dad started to get up.

"I'll get it," I said and I went upstairs. Stewy wanted to sleep with me and I told him okay. My little brother had been around too much death. He climbed into my bed, across from Clark.

"Any squirrels in here tonight?" I asked Clark.

"Dopey and Doc are sleeping on the closet shelf," Clark said.

"Good," I said, "and McCoy can sleep with you and me, Stewy, okay?"

"Yeah. Okay . . ."

I turned to go.

"Donny?" Stewy said.

"Yeah."

"When I grow up I want to be a hobo like Runt."

"Okay, Stew, I'll come ride the trains with you."

As I came through the dining room I could hear Dad and Sergeant Riley talking quietly. I was still in my stocking feet. They hadn't heard me, and I don't know why, but I paused near the kitchen door and listened.

"Can't you clean out these rats?" Dad said.

"We're doing all we can. We're pretty sure we know who's behind it all, the kingpin, but he has too many fronts, legitimate businesses to hide behind. We're sure that most of the thugs who work for him don't even know they're working for him, never hear his name. And if they do, they're afraid if they snitch on him they'd end up taking a winter dip in the Minnesota River."

"Who do you think it is?" my dad said.

"Well, this is highly confidential. You can tell no one, Frank."

"Don't worry, I want you to nail that rat as much as anyone," Dad said.

"He's one of the biggest businessmen in the Twin Cities, new and used car lots all over the place. You've seen his billboards and advertising plastered all over the city. He has a perfect cover, pays his taxes, and is looked up to as one of our outstanding citizens." Sergeant Riley lowered his voice.

"Mr. John Fitzsimmons."

My mouth went dry and I caught my breath.

"John Fitzsimmons, the car dealer?" my dad said.

"Yep, I'd bet my pension on it."

I couldn't think. I might be in love with the girl whose father was going to break my father's legs, in love with the girl whose father murdered Uncle Ellie-Ellie! I went numb. I *knew* John Fitzsimmons. Could the man who waited up to see that his daughter got home safe be the top gangster in Saint Paul?

And more than that, did Mitzi know her father was a gangster?

At the funeral, the priest said that George Riley was fondly known by many as Uncle Ellie-Ellie. There must have been a hundred cops at the funeral. I'd hate to be in that murderer's shoes. Those guys were mad. Uncle Ellie-Ellie was in an open casket. In his old Army uniform he looked pale, as if he was sleeping. The city of Saint Paul had awarded him a medal for bravery. It was pinned on his uniform. My mother didn't have an open casket. I always wondered if they fit her back together. I didn't let on, but I cried when I said good-bye to Uncle Ellie-Ellie at the grave. I never thought about how much he was part of our family until he was gone. He was the best uncle I ever had.

At the Rileys' house after the funeral, Irene and I were sitting with Nana Riley in their breakfast nook. There were crowds of people filling every room but for a moment we had her to ourselves.

"Don't you *hate* the man who killed Uncle Ellie-Ellie, Nana, don't you just *hate him?*" Irene said with venom.

Nana looked at us for a moment.

"We have to learn how to forgive," she said softly. "In this cruel world we have to forgive."

"I'm never forgiving him," Irene said. "Never."

The *Minneapolis Star* and *Saint Paul Pioneer Press,* along with Cedric Adams on WCCO, described the shocking robbery-murder in our Saint Paul neighborhood. It told how Frank Cunningham was held up bringing home the day's receipts from his gas station. His neighbor, George Riley, the father of police sergeant Michael Riley, came to the rescue and was murdered. They reported that the police had no leads as to the identity of the robbers. The article made no mention of an eye witness. My name didn't appear, which helped me sleep a little sounder.

Most of the kids at school didn't pick up on my father's name or tie me into the news story if they read or heard about it. I told Reggie all about it, but I didn't mention John Fitzsimmons. I knew that Reggie might slip to Virginia and so on until Mitzi would hear about it. I felt strange at school, like someone was stalking me. I walked through my classes in a daze, avoided Mitzi whenever I could, and tried to pay attention in class. I couldn't shake the face of the scum who killed Uncle Ellie-Ellie. And I couldn't shake the questions I had about John Fitzsimmons.

Sergeant Riley took me downtown in a squad car to look at mug shots, pictures of criminals the cops knew about. I told him it was a guy with only one nostril. It was tiring, page after page, book after book of faces of criminals you'd never want to meet in a dark alley. After three hours, they ran out of books. Sergeant Riley was disappointed when he drove me back to Central. I missed my first three classes. Registered to someone who died three years ago, the Packard was a dead-end, but they did get lots of fingerprints off it. Riley wanted to give Irene a medal for her fast thinking and bravery. She said any good Dutch girl would've done the same.

Chapter 34

The following Friday I didn't know what to do. I had a movie date with Mitzi but I didn't feel like going. I missed Uncle Ellie-Ellie so bad it hurt. But I'd had lots of practice with missing people. Going to a movie seemed disrespectful with him just buried. But I really wanted to be with Mitzi. I wanted to hold her in my arms and have her hold me in hers and never let go.

It seemed preposterous. Could Mitzi's dad be behind the gambling and the leg breaking? Crazy. Mitzi was such a swell girl. But I figured she could think the same thing if she knew about my dad. *How could Donny be such a nice kid when his father is a drunk?* Sergeant Riley said they couldn't prove anything. Maybe her father wasn't behind the gambling ring after all.

We went downtown to the Paramount. I told Reggie not to bring up the subject of the murder unless Mitzi or Virginia did. We saw *Twelve O'clock High*, the story of our pilots who flew bombing missions over Germany. The whole time Gregory Peck was trying to figure out what to do as their commander, I sat there trying to figure out how I should feel and act around Mitzi.

I was really sweet on Mitzi but all mixed up. How could I kiss the girl whose father killed Uncle Ellie-Ellie? How could I find out the truth? Then, near the end of the movie, an idea popped into my head. I'd go and talk to John Fitzsimmons, but never let on that I suspected he was a criminal and murderer! It would be my chance to be on the stage. I'd tell him he's the only one I could go to, which was true. He's the only one who could lend us that much money. And I'd notice every blink of his eyes, the sound of his voice, any hesitation.

I'd learned from Mitzi that her dad liked to walk to one of his dealerships on Victoria and Grand. I could find him there without her knowing.

I figured Mitzi knew something was different between us. I took a long time eating at the drive-in so Reggie wouldn't have time to park. Still really confused, I didn't neck with Mitzi in the backseat. I kept yakking about the movie and goofing around so we didn't get mushy. I waited until we stood at her front door to kiss her, and as I hoped, John Fitzsimmons appeared. He stood there to see that I didn't make out with his daughter, when he could be the one who had my father dismembered and murdered Uncle Ellie-Ellie.

In the shadowed light I tried to look into his eyes. They were blue. I didn't know what I was looking for.

"Did you kids have fun tonight?" he said.

"Yes, Daddy, we saw a terrific movie."

Yes, Daddy, we watched your thugs break a man's legs while we ate popcorn.

When I got back to the car, Reggie said, "Did Mitzi hear about the murder?"

"She didn't say anything."

"There's stuff like that in the news every day," Reggie said.

On Wednesday Dad and I had finished closing and were ready to head home.

"Sit down, Donny," my dad said, pointing at a stack of tires. He had a look on his face and I knew this would be serious. I perched on the tires and watched him. He had his hands on his hips and he looked into my eyes.

"Donny, I want to tell you how sorry I am, how terribly sorry that I've blamed you, held it against you for four terrible years. I think I've been punishing—"

"But I disobeyed you, you told me not to—"

"It was a terrible, terrible *accident.* You never meant to hurt anyone, you never meant to do anything wrong. Now I know how it feels, now I *know.*"

He limped around the garage.

"By God, I know. I killed Uncle Ellie-Ellie as surely as if I pulled the trigger. *Who* can forgive *me* for my drinking and gambling? He's dead, and I can't tell him I'm sorry. I'm so ashamed of how I've been acting, so damn ashamed. The woman I love is ashamed of me, ashamed of how I've neglected her darlings. Helen looks down from heaven and she's *ashamed of me!*"

He spun around, looked me in the eye, and pounded his fist into his crippled hand.

"I'm done with the drink. I'll never drink another drop of that poison as long as my heart beats! I swear it on my love for your mother. I will never drink another drop!"

Somehow, sitting on a stack of Atlas tires in our Standard Station, I believed him for the first time in a long time. We didn't speak for a minute. Dad stood looking out at the traffic on Marshall.

"It all happened because I'm short," I said.

"No . . . no, Donny, you're not cursed because you're short."

He turned and his eyes were wet.

"No, no, don't you see!" I said, "I don't mean that way, cursed or jinxed. *I was too short!* I put the clutch in and shift-ed into reverse. Then I turned to look out the back window the way you taught me. I let the clutch out slowly, but I was too short and my foot came off the pedal. The car jumped backward. I panicked. I jammed my foot for the brake but I hit the gas pedal instead. I'm so sorry . . . so sorry."

I was bawling like a baby, I couldn't stop it anymore. It was a flooding river roaring out of the mountains, the Onion River pouring into Splendid's pool, my weeping heart remembering my mother's laughing face.

My dad came over and put a hand on my shoulder.

"Don't do that, don't cry, Donny, here, here, don't cry."

My dad squatted next to me and we cried, out loud, with our hands covering our faces. Two small boys who had been forbidden to cry, who didn't know how, two small boys with horror in their memories.

I didn't tell Dad what I planned on doing. I got out of fifth period study hall and I caught a ride hitching down Lexington Boulevard. The guy dropped me at Grand and I hustled the four blocks to Victoria and Fitzsimmons' Chevrolet on the corner. Two guys in rumpled suits stood beside a new Chevy in the showroom. One look at me and they figured I wasn't a prospective buyer. They'd been eating too many doughnuts.

I found a snazzy-dressed woman at a desk in the middle of the showroom.

"Pardon me, but is Mr. Fitzsimmons here?"

She had a nice smile and talked to me as if I were twelve.

"Why, yes, Mr. Fitzsimmons is here. Is there something I can help you with?"

"No, thanks. I gotta talk to Mr. Fitzsimmons."

"What is it about, maybe I can—"

"Donald," John Fitzsimmons said as he came through a door behind the receptionist. "Nice to see you. Isn't school still in session?"

"Yes, I got out of study hall."

"Are you here to buy a car?" We both laughed.

"I'd like to talk to you for a minute if I could."

"Sure, sure, come on back."

He led me to an office with a huge desk and all kinds of automotive stuff on the walls: trophies, pennants, awards, Chevy advertising. He motioned for me to sit in a leather chair and he settled behind his desk.

"There, now, Donald, what can I do for you?"

"You're the only one I could come to. My family's in a lot of trouble, big trouble, and I don't know what to do."

His eyes narrowed. "What kind of trouble are you talking about?"

I told him about Dad drinking and then getting mixed up with the gamblers, how he got further and further in debt, how they killed Uncle Ellie-Ellie, and how they were going to break Dad's legs if he didn't pay soon. I told him about the smashed finger and toe and that we owed them over three thousand dollars.

"I want to borrow it from you, Mr. Fitzsimmons. I don't want anyone to know about it, just you and me. I'll pay you back, I'll have a full-time job this summer and I'll get a second job. I'll pay you the same interest the bank pays. It might take a year or two, but I'll—"

"Whoa, whoa, Donald. Why don't you go to the police? Let them deal with these crooks."

"We can't. They warned Dad that if he went to the police, they'd hurt his family. My brothers and sister."

"Can't they nab them when the money is delivered? The police can set a trap. Catch the rats."

"Dad says they call him and tell him where to leave the money. Sometimes it's a bar. The guy at the bar doesn't know anything about it or even what's in the envelope or who will pick it up. They do this until it's lost in the shuffle."

"Did anyone see the thugs who killed your neighbor?"

"Yeah, I did."

The moment I said it I felt a shiver of cold run down my back. I caught my breath as if I were trying to suck the words back before John Fitzsimmons could hear them. Would this be the test? No one knew about an eye witness except the police.

"That must have been a horrible thing for you to witness, Donald."

"Yes, sir, it was. Uncle Ellie-Ellie was our family."

We talked for another half hour. John Fitzsimmons tried to think of a way to catch the criminals, as if he hated giving them any money.

"All right, Donald, I'll have someone drive you back to school. You call your father at the station and tell him to contact the gangsters. Tell them the money will be there after five this afternoon."

"Gosh, Mr. Fitzsimmons, I don't know how to thank you. I'll pay back every dime no matter how long it takes. I'm a good—"

"You call your father. I just wish we could catch these rats. I'd like to take a sledgehammer to a few of them."

The whole time I talked to Mr. Fitzsimmons I could tell he was really steamed about those gangsters and how much he wanted to nail them. And Fitzsimmons proved to be a man of his word. The money, in a manila envelope, was delivered to our station that afternoon. In shock, my dad counted it three times. Shortly afterwards, a taxi pulled in, asked for the package, and drove away.

That night we all let out a big sigh of relief. The legbreakers had been paid off. Nana Riley had us over for supper, as if the woman needed something to do to keep her busy, to keep her mind occupied, to keep her heart from dying. I knew about keeping busy.

While we ate pot roast, Irene asked Nana, "Were you and Uncle Ellie-Ellie sweethearts in school?"

"Land sakes, no. I turned that man down three times when he wanted to marry me."

"Then how come you got married?" Reenie said.

We all watched Nana. She thought for a moment, going back in her memory.

"When he came back from basic training and I saw him in his Army uniform, my heart just melted. I could see the *man* in him."

"Did you get married before he went to France?" I said.

"No, he wouldn't hear of it, said he might never come back. I worried over him for better than a year. We got married out at Fort Snelling a few weeks after he came home."

I remember thinking how lucky we were to have the Rileys living across the alley from us. And I remember thinking how we take people for granted until they're gone.

When the kids were in bed, I explained to Dad the deal I'd made with John Fitzsimmons, but I never let on I'd overheard Sgt. Riley name him as the top suspect of the gambling ring. That night, I figured neither of us could decide if John Fitzsimmons was a decent man who had bailed us out of a terrible spot, or if under his fancy clothes, he was a brutal man to fear.

Chapter 35

Just before the bell in wood shop, some of the football players grabbed me and stuck me upside down in an upper locker. They did it quickly because they knew Mr. Wabley always stepped into the room right at the bell. They didn't do it to be mean, they liked me, and I was laughing when they shut the locker door, leaving me standing on my head. I had my hands against the bottom of the locker for support and my legs were bent at the knees so I'd fit. The narrow locker held me in place. I felt like toothpaste in the tube.

I could hear them laughing and talking. The only problem, the locker could pop open and I'd hit the concrete floor like a wounded duck. So the boys wedged a piece of wood between the locker door and the nearest work bench.

The bell rang, and I figured Mr. Wabley walked in because everyone started pounding on their bench with some kind of tool. They made more racket than a jackhammer. I heard Mr. Wabley shouting.

"Knock it off! Stop the racket! Pipe down!"

Finally, the banging stopped. So I figured I'd start banging. My head felt like a sponge full of water. With my fist, I banged on the locker, hard, loud, Rocky Marciano sparring. The shop went perfectly silent. I could imagine Mr. Wabley looking at the lockers with a puzzled expression. All that racket from lockers that no one was touching. I kept pounding away like a drummer in Mr. Hambull's marching band and I hoped the kids were getting their money's worth.

I couldn't help but think how much my life was like this, upside down. I'd been upside down much of my senior year, trying to get back on my feet, trying to make some sense out of it all. Every time I seemed to be getting to my feet, something else would knock me for a loop. Now we were having fun with Mr. Wabley with little Donny Cunningham stuck upside down in a locker. I kept banging.

All of a sudden, Mr. Wabley yanked the wood brace away from the locker and out I came, trick-or-treat, right into Mr. Wabley's arms. Only I hung upside down with my face in the teacher's crotch. The class roared. Mr. Wabley held on to keep me from dropping onto the concrete floor head first. Off balance, he danced a few steps until Roger Lundbeck and Chuck Brown grabbed me and turned me right side up.

Mr. Wabley stomped to the front of the shop and straightened his tie and glasses. Then he glared at the class.

"All right, wise guys, I want to know who put Mr. Cunningham in the locker."

Nobody blinked. Mr. Wabley was smart enough to know that I wouldn't rat on them, as small as I was. The teacher didn't even look at me. I was smiling as the blood flowed back down into my body.

"Those responsible step forward right now or the whole class will have seventh period for the entire week. The whole class except for Mr. Cunningham."

That didn't seem fair. I was having as much fun as anyone. The class stood there beside their work benches. Nobody moved. Then Bill Beardsley raised his hand and I wondered what he'd come up with. He wasn't one of the guys who stuck me in the locker.

"I confess, Mr. Wabley," Bill said, "Sandy did it."

The class howled. Sandy laughed. The teacher fought off a smile. He gave them seventh period for two days. I felt like volunteering to go with them so I could sit next to Sandy. As I worked on my oak bookends, I wondered if this had been a sign. Dad had quit drinking. Stewy was at home, and hopefully no longer a ward of the county, and the gangsters had been paid off. Somehow if felt like my life was no longer upside down, like I'd landed on both feet.

Wednesday evening low overcast clouds made it dark early. I'd been careless, walking out to the alley with the garbage. I'd started believing the killer didn't know there was an eyewitness, that he wouldn't risk coming back. Luckily, I caught a glimpse. Something blurred in his hand. A gun? With only a second to spare, I darted through the back door and down the basement steps. He came seconds behind me. I crawled headfirst into the old furnace, pulled my legs through, and slowly closed the oval door. Inside it was pitch black. I huddled, afraid to move, afraid I'd bump something that would give me away.

I heard him on the creaking stairs. He must have been desperate to come into the house like that, or he'd been watching and knew I was the only one home. He had come to kill me, the only one who could put him in the electric chair. I heard him ransacking the basement, things hitting the floor, glass breaking, furniture dragged, uncovering every nook and corner that could hide me. It sounded like a tornado had touched down in our basement.

Darn! I should've gone through the kitchen and out the front door. There is only one way in or out of the basement. The stairs. The basement windows are too small to crawl through even if I got the chance. I prayed Irene wouldn't come home, or Clark and Dad. He'd kill them. No witnesses this time. I had the crazy thought to crawl out and run for the stairs, get it over with before any of them came home. I wondered what it felt like to be shot, to die. I hated that face, that man, and I wanted to kill him for what he'd done. But he had me.

Then I realized I couldn't hear him. The basement turned deathly quiet. He hadn't climbed the stairs, I'd recognize their wooden creak. He was very close, sniffing like a rabid dog. I couldn't tell if I heard my breathing or his. My thumping heart echoed against the cast-iron sides of the furnace until I was sure he could hear me. I tried not to move a finger, an eyelash. I expected him to try the furnace door any second. Did he know I was in there? Would a bullet go through the cast-iron side?

Then I heard him on the stairs. Could he be confused? When you come in our back door, you can step up to the right and you're in the kitchen. Straight ahead you're on the basement stairs. Was he doubting himself now, wondering if he'd guessed wrong? Was he convinced I wasn't in the basement? He climbed the stairs.

Then I jumped from a booming gunshot! The sound of it bounced around inside the furnace. I held my breath. Someone on the stairs came crashing down. Then silence. I couldn't move! Who did he shoot? Oh God, not Irene, please God, no more. I'd go out and face the monster. I opened the door. Then voices. Someone came down the stairs.

"Donny! Donny! Are you down here, are you all right?"

Irene. I gulped for air. She came to the furnace. I crawled out, I could see again. I hugged her.

"I thought he shot you," I said, holding her close.

"We thought he killed *you*. Oh, Donny, I'm so glad you're alive."

My eyes adjusted to the light. One basement light bulb hung over a body at the bottom of the stairs. I recognized him. His eyes were wide open in surprise, the man with only one nostril. One neat hole in his chest oozed blood.

I pushed Irene up the stairs. We'd seen too many dead people.

"Who shot him? Did Sergeant Riley get here?" I said.

We went into the kitchen. Nana Riley sat there with Stewy. "There wasn't time," Irene said. "Nana shot him!"

"*Nana!* How . . . with what?" I said.

They told me the story while we waited for the police. Stewy had been in the oak when the legbreaker came after me behind the house. He slid down the swing rope and ran to Nana's. She knew there wasn't time to call for help, that I'd be dead before the police could make it. She got Uncle Ellie-Ellie's rifle and the one bullet that was left from France. The bullet in his plaque on the living room wall. She broke the glass, took the bullet, and loaded the rifle. Uncle Ellie-Ellie had shown her how years ago.

She hurried across the alley and into the house, just as the killer started up the steps. She held the rifle at her hip and pointed it at his chest. They were only fifteen feet apart. He raised his pistol too late. She pulled the trigger and blew him backwards onto the concrete floor. She killed him with the Springfield 1903 bolt-operated, magazine-fed .30-caliber rifle! The gun powder in that one bullet, loaded for combat in 1917, thirty-three years ago, had stayed the course.

I identified the killer as the man who shot Uncle Ellie-Ellie. Nana Riley had ended his murdering life. She was a hero alongside her husband. The two of them had saved Dad and me. Sergeant Riley was proud of his mom, beating him to the punch with the killer.

Sunday we took Nana Riley out to Roselawn Cemetery to visit Uncle Ellie-Ellie's grave. We brought flowers and I left three newspaper articles about his brave fight. One headline was "GOOD NEIGHBOR IS TIMELY HERO."

"We got the guy who shot you, Uncle Ellie-Ellie," I said out loud. "He won't ever kill anyone again."

"I know you would've hidden the Jews," Irene said. "Thank you for saving my daddy."

A few days later Nana was over helping with supper like Uncle Ellie-Ellie used to. She ate with us a lot now. Irene and I were setting the table and doing what we could.

"Nana," Irene said. "I thought you said we shouldn't hate bad people when they hurt us, that we should forgive them."

"That's right, girl," Nana said. "We *must* forgive them."

"Well, how about that man you killed?"

"I forgave him," she said, "and *then* I shot him."

Chapter 36

"Donald, Donald, I'm here."

I'm walking through familiar woods and I can hear my mother's voice but I can't find her.

"I'm here, Mother, I'm here," I call, bushwhacking through the underbrush. Then I realize, it's the woods along the Onion River. I'm on the North Shore.

"Donald, Donald!" she calls.

I hurry, pushing through the willows, frantic that I'll miss her.

Then I see her, standing on the other side of Splendid's pool. She is radiant, beautiful, wearing her favorite blue dress, and it's ruffling in a breeze. Her blonde hair, tied with a blue ribbon, is long to her shoulders and it shines in the sunlight. She has no scars! She's holding Patches in her arms and he's all right. I can see Splendid, circling in his pool.

"Can you see how happy I am, Donald? We're all here, Splendid and I and Patches. Why didn't you tell me about Patches?"

"I was afraid, I didn't think—"

"I would have understood. You were so young then. I want you to be happy, and I know you're not. We forgive you, and God forgives you. You must forgive yourself."

"I know, but—"

"You made choices, and in that world bad things happen. It was an accident, Donald, you knew how much I hated backing out of the garage. You wanted to practice, but you were also being helpful. You had no malice in your heart, you couldn't help it, it was an accident."

I want to hurry around the pool to hug her but I can't move. I hear scuffling in the woods behind her but I can't see anything. Then, rolling into a clearing, I see Uncle Ellie-Ellie wrestling with the Coca-Cola bear. They're playing like

Reggie and I. The bear has a beautiful black coat and Uncle Ellie-Ellie is a young man.

"Remember Runt, the hobo?" she says.

"Yeah, Mom, I remember him."

"He was an angel, sent to you."

"An *angel!*"

"Yes, to show you what your life will be like if you don't forgive yourself. You'll be burdened with sadness and regret, forever rootless and lost in a desert of despair. Forgive yourself and go on with your life. Don't let it kill you, too, for then it will have killed both of us."

She turns to go.

"Are you leaving?" I say.

"Yes, but see how peaceful and happy we are. Remember that, always, Donald."

"Don't go, please don't go yet. There's so much I want to ask you, to tell you."

"Be happy, my darling boy. Be happy, my precious son. Remember, none of it was your fault. *None of it* was your fault. I want you to live your life with joy, the best years of your life. Good-bye, Donald. I love you deeply and I will always walk beside you."

"Wait, Mother, don't go!"

Stewy shook my arm and suddenly I awoke. I was sitting in my bed and calling out loud, "Don't go, Mother!"

I felt a breeze on my face but the window was shut. I could smell my mother's perfume, as if she were standing next to me. I felt overwhelmingly happy. Not like when your team wins or you've got a date with a swell girl or you get what you want at Christmas. It was a happiness that you know is in every cell of your body, a part of you, and it can't wash away.

"Did Mother come back?" Stewy said.

"Yes . . . no, I was dreaming. She was in my dream."

"I wish she'd be in my dream."

"She will, Stewy, some night she'll be in your dream. But she's happy, she's all healed up, and she's *all right.*"

The last two months of my senior year flew quickly away. June had arrived, and our last week of school. In Mr. Thorton's math class the big windows along the south side of the room were open to the summer weather. Mr. Thorton took attendance, as usual, and then wrote problems on the blackboard on the side of the room. With the teacher's back to the class, Jerry crept up to Mr. Thorton's desk and squeezed into the space meant for your legs and feet when you sit at the desk. The class, used to Jerry's pranks, acted normally. The teacher turned from the blackboard and started going over the problems with us. He went on for several minutes before he noticed that Jerry was missing.

He hurried over to the windows and stuck his head out. Then he dashed out of the room, on his way to room 119 to catch Jerry. The minute Mr. Thorton was out of the room, Jerry crawled out from under the desk, sat at his own desk and started working on the day's problems. In a minute, Mr. Thorton came through the door, saw Jerry working at his desk, and stopped in his tracks. He stood there, looking at Jerry and shaking his head. Then he went to the blackboard and wrote UNCLE in big letters. He walked over to Jerry, took a hold of his wrist, and held Jerry's arm in the air, the winner.

We all cheered and clapped and whistled. When the class calmed down, Thorton said, "I'm going to flunk you, Jerry. I'm going to flunk you so you can come back and spark up my classes next year."

We all cheered again and I thought I might like that, having another year at Central.

That next day, when Reggie and I were hitchhiking home, he told me who his true love was, the heartthrob he said he'd love the rest of his life. Lola Muldoon! Cripes, I could've guessed that. Half the boys at Central were in love with Lola Muldoon. She and Tom Bradford went steady and I knew Reggie didn't have a chance. But Lola couldn't have done

better than with my great friend, Reggie. I think he liked
Virginia more than he knew. I jumped him and got him in a
hammerlock.

The day came, June sixteenth, that night we'd graduate. We
only had school during our homeroom periods to turn in
books and athletic uniforms and combination locks. Kids left
quickly as if they were glad to be done. The building was
nearly deserted when I walked through the halls. I felt a deep
sadness, like I didn't want it to end, like I'd missed so much. I
had even thought about flunking my finals to see if they'd let
me come back next fall.

I wandered, stepping into my math class where Mr. Thorton thought he was cracking up; the auditorium, where Miss
Whalman danced with the marbles; my homeroom where I'd
talk with Mitzi; down to the lunchroom, where I'd eat with
the boys and watch Sandy; the wood shop where they stuck
me in the locker upside down. Only a few kids and teachers
echoed through the building.

Mitzi and I were doubling with Reggie and Virginia to the
commencement dance after our graduation exercises at the
Saint Paul Auditorium. Mitzi and I had gone out a lot the past
two months, but I didn't stand on my tiptoes anymore.

I figured everybody stands on his tiptoes sometime. Everybody tries to become what another person wants them to be,
so they'll be loved. Standing on my toes so Mitzi would like
me was only a shadow of what everybody does. I stood on
my tiptoes with those teenage boys to be the tough kid they
wanted me to be when they drowned Patches. I stood on my
tiptoes to be what Sarah wanted me to be when I killed
Splendid. We were all standing on tiptoes to be accepted, to
be loved, trying to be someone we weren't. Everyone must
have the equivalent of bulging calves. Everyone, at times, is
on tiptoes. Maybe I stood on my toes with God so He'd take
it all back and make things right again.

My life had returned to something more like normal. Dad hadn't touched a drop since Uncle Ellie-Ellie was killed. Stewy was no longer a temporary ward of Ramsey County and he was back in two kindergartens. At noon he'd catch himself starting to put on his Shirley Temple outfit to walk to Gordon. I was going to confession again. Nana Riley took Uncle Ellie-Ellie's place in our house and family. Her boy, Sergeant Riley, got stabbed by some madman he tried to arrest, but he's going to be all right. Irene claimed she was still in love with Brandon, confident she could entice him to fall in love with her over the summer.

Clark had had his fourteenth birthday and he'd be going to Central in the fall. He had Snow White eating out of his hand. I had turned eighteen on April 22nd and I got my driver's license a week later. Evenings, Dad took me out in the old Hudson with the kids in the back seat, yelling and warning me about traffic. Dad thought the pressure made for good practice. One Sunday he'd let me drive all the way to Afton and back.

I walked through front hall and glanced in Nurse Armstrong's office. She was shuffling paperwork on her desk.

"Donny! Good to see you." She pushed the files aside and gave me a big smile.

"Hi." I was glad to see her.

"What are you doing?"

"Saying good-bye to Central. I'm in no hurry to walk out the door for the last time. Prolonging it, you know."

"I know. What are you going to do now?"

"I'm going to raise my brothers and sister and save money for college." I didn't mention paying off our debt to John Fitzsimmons.

"Sounds like a good plan. Are you going to the dance tonight?"

"Yeah, with Mitzi Fitzsimmons."

"Ah . . . I don't think I know her. Say, while you're here, let's give it one more try." She nodded at the scale.

"Naw, it'll just waste your time."

"C'mon." She stood up.

I kicked off my shoes and stepped on the scale. She brought the metal rod down on the top of my head and read the scale.

"Donny! Sixty inches! *Sixty inches!*"

"Shoot! you're pulling my leg, trying to make me feel good my last day at school."

"No, I'm not. Watch."

She had me turn around so I could see the numbers on the metal shaft. She lowered the arm on top of my head and pushed it tight. I read it. Sixty inches, even a hair over!

"Holy cow, I'm five feet tall! I've started growing again."

"That's right, and there's no telling where you'll stop."

I pulled on my shoes and I wanted to shout.

"Golly, Miss Armstrong, I can't thank you enough. *Five feet.*"

"Now Donny, you come back and say hello sometime, I mean it. I'll miss you."

"I will, I will. Good-bye."

Doggone it, tears blurred my vision and I ducked out into front hall. It was completely empty. I wandered toward the side doors, stopping a few times and listening. I could hear all the kids, jamming the halls between class, jabbering, calling, laughing, slamming lockers.

I still didn't know what to think of John Fitzsimmons. I think I was falling in love with Mitzi, but afraid to love anyone the way Dad loved Mom. If Mitzi's dad was the lousy rat behind the gambling and leg breaking and murder, I wanted to help her when she found out. It would be a crushing blow if he ended up in the penitentiary at Stillwater for the rest of his life. She thought he was a great dad. He always acted stern but kind with me. We'd made two small payments in the past months and he told me that the loan would be interest free. He'd given up waiting at the door when I brought Mitzi home.

Sauntering through the halls, I ended up at the side door that opened onto the parking lot. I paused. I turned around. I felt scared. My life would never be the same as it was here. I took a deep breath, whispered good-bye, and pushed the door open. Reggie was waiting in the Hudson. My dad had given me the keys that morning and told me that a guy ought to drive to school once in his lifetime. I got in and started the engine. As I pulled around, I spotted Cal Gant and Sandy talking out on the lawn. They'd both been through a hard time the past two months and I felt close to them. I honked and shouted, "Sandy, Cal!"

"Hey, Donny, see you tonight!" Sandy yelled. "Where have you been?"

"Growing an inch!"

I waved. Then I turned out onto Marshall and drove away from my life at Central. I felt taller. I hoped my pants wouldn't be too short at the dance. I had hope that the best years of my life were ahead.

∾ THE END

Author's Note

Although the main plot and characters are fictitious, I have incidentally used the names of actual students who were present at Saint Paul Central in 1949. Footprints in the concrete so to speak. "They were there."

The story of the cat at Wood Lake in Wisconsin is a slip into nonfiction, into autobiography. The skinny kid in the photo, next to the big fish he caught, is the author with his father and little brother. The photo was taken in 1939 at Wood Lake. As I study that face, I try to discern if the photo was taken before or after that tragic experience.

Like Donny's family, mine spent time on the North Shore every August in the late thirties and early forties. I fished the Onion River many times each of those summers and never saw another fisherman. The story of Splendid is fictitious. The last time I crossed the Onion River on Highway 61 many years ago, there was a small sign pointing out that the river was there. The secret was out.

All public events, dates, scores, news items, and locations are historically accurate.

–Stanley G. West, May 2003

Saint Paul Central as it appeared in 1949.

Saint Paul Central no longer exists as it did in 1949. The building was demolished in the 1980s and a new school building erected. All that remains of the past is the name . . . and the memories.